THE RIDERS MADE A
HALF CIRCLE
AROUND JEFF.

One of them, a huge fellow with a cruel grin on his heavy face, said, "You've come to the end of yore crooked trail, Mr. Holdup. We don't aim to let you ever kill another man or rob another stage."

Jeff's glance shuttled over the group and rested on a middle-aged man in a wrinkled corduroy suit. He looked like a responsible cattleman. His frank face gave the impression of force.

"You've found the wrong man," Jeff said quietly.

"Get his gun, Jack," the wearer of the corduroys said curtly.

"We've got you covered," a little man with a scar on his chin told Jeff. "Lift a finger and we'll blow you to hell and breakfast."

*   *   *

**JUSTICE COMES
TO TOMAHAWK**

Also by William MacLeod Raine

The Black Tolts*
The Fighting Edge
Gunsight Pass*
Run of the Brush*
West of the Law

Published by
POPULAR LIBRARY

* forthcoming

WILLIAM MacLEOD RAINE

JUSTICE COMES TO TOMAHAWK

POPULAR LIBRARY

An Imprint of Warner Books, Inc.

A Warner Communications Company

I

Jeff Carr was lost, trapped in the high country among a vast tumble of huge rocks flung up by some tremendous upheaval when the world was young. At Sarasota a cowboy had drawn for him in the sand a sketchy map of the short cut to Tomahawk, but somewhere in the hills he had taken a wrong turn and followed blind leads for hours. With darkness near he knew he would have to sleep outdoors. This did not disturb him, but he was pleased when one of his tries to escape the maze brought him by way of a gulch into a small mountain park with a stream gurgling through it to a defile beyond.

He had no food but there was grass for his tired horse. After picketing the animal he lit a fire of dead branches. Night closed in on him, bringing with it the weird loneliness of solitude. The shadowy peaks shut him off from a faraway world, and the mournful sough of the wind in the pine tops stressed an eerie wildness. But stars were out by thousands and a sliver of a wafer moon rode the sky. He endured his predicament cheerfully, though he slept badly on account of the cold. Several times he rose to renew the fire and warm his chilled bones.

As soon as it was light enough he saddled and followed the creek into the trough, through which it noisily leaped to other gorges below. The going was rough and rocky but he stayed with the brook. Eventually it would bring him down to the desert floor. The sun was high when he reached a grassy valley nestling in the hills. He was moving down the

1

slope of the saucer when there came to him the sound of something stirring in the willows to his right. His guess was that it might be a deer. A moment later a horse and rider emerged from the thicket.

The man's swift furtive glance swept the valley and lighted on Carr. The rifle he carried jumped up instantly.

Carr lifted an arm in the peace sign. "I'm lost," he said. "Been out all night."

"Git yore hands on the horn quick," the fellow ordered. He was tall and lean as a scrub steer. Fear was written in the milk-blue eyes set deep in a small mean face.

Carr put his hands on the pommel of the saddle. "I tried to take the hill short cut from Sarasota to Tomahawk and got lost," he explained. "If you'll set me on the road I'll be obliged."

"Don't lie to me," the stranger snarled. "You're with a posse. Where are the rest of them at?"

The situation did not need any elucidation. The man was fugitive, the terror of possible capture riding him. Because his nerves were shaken Jeff was in imminent danger.

"No friend, you've got me wrong," Carr answered, his voice cool and easy. "I'm from San Francisco. Never been in this country before."

Again the man's jerky glance searched the valley. He was trying to make up his mind. If there was a posse in the neighborhood the sound of a shot would bring it here on the gallop. On the other hand the story of the man he covered might be true. In which case it would be safer to destroy him. He was not carrying a rifle. That fact backed the reason he had given for being here. A posseman would probably have a Winchester. Yet he might be trying to hold the hunted man until his companions arrived.

Carr read the doubt in the mind of the fugitive. He smiled derisively. "If you could be sure," he suggested. "Am I one of the men over the hill hunting you or am I not? You would like to put a slug in me but you can't afford to make a mistake—or to wait too long."

The last words tilted the scale to an immediate decision.

"Reach for the sky and slide down to the ground. No monkeyin' if you want to live," the outlaw growled.

Carr lifted a leg over the saddle horn and slid down. He knew that he was about to fake an involuntary trade of his fresh horse for the sweat-stained exhausted one of the fugitive, but it was a good deal better to lose his horse than his life. There was still a chance he might lose both, if at the last moment the fellow's itching fingers obeyed an impulse to send a bullet crashing into him.

The lank outlaw, not lifting his gaze for an instant from Carr, swung out of the saddle and came forward warily.

"I ought to gun you, fellow," he ground out. "I've a mind to do it."

"Quit wasting time, you lunkhead, and pull your freight," Carr told him contemptuously. "When you get through with my horse, send it to Tomahawk."

"Back away from the bridle and don't get any notions."

"I haven't any." Carr took a few steps backward and watched the man mount. He waved a hand casually. "Be seeing you at your trial."

The outlaw ripped out an oath, swung the horse, and put it to a gallop. A minute later he vanished over the lip of the valley.

As Carr walked toward the drooping horse he had acquired, he felt a little shaky. It was his opinion that he had escaped death by a narrow margin. Fortunately for him the hunted man had not believed fully the story that he was lost. Later Jeff had helped to correct that first mistake by increasing the man's doubt.

Jeff looked the sorrel cow pony over without pleasure. It had been ridden far and hard. Not many miles of travel were left in it, but perhaps enough to get him down to some ranch house where he could pick up another. He swung into the hull and started down the creek. Before he had gone fifty yards a shot rang out. He turned his head, to see five men clattering down a rocky slope toward him. A puff of smoke billowed from a second gun.

Carr drew a handkerchief from his pocket and waved it. The riders came on at a gallop. The first of them pulled up his mount, leaped from the saddle, and flung a Winchester up to be ready for action.

"Hold it," the man cried.

"Sure," Carr answered. "Take it easy. Why all the smoke?" He knew the answer to his question. They had mistaken him for the man they were hunting.

The riders made a half-circle around him. One of them, a huge fellow with a cruel grin on his heavy face, said, "You've come to the end of yore crooked trail, Mr. Holdup. We don't aim to let you ever kill another man or rob another stage."

Jeff's glance shuttled over the group and rested on a middle-aged man in a wrinkled corduroy suit and big pinched-in hat. He looked like a responsible cattleman. Criss-crossed wrinkles made a pattern on the back of his tanned neck. His frank face gave the impression of force.

"You have found the wrong man," Carr said quietly.

"Get his gun, Jack," the wearer of the corduroys said curtly.

"Y'betcha!" A slim lad in chaps swung from a saddle and bowlegged forward.

"We've got you covered," a little man with a scar on his chin told Carr. "Lift a finger and we'll blow you to hell and breakfast."

"Don't rush this, Foley," Corduroy ordered. "This man has a lot to tell us that we want to know."

"That's right, Mr. Dunham," a black-haired graceful posseman, broad-shouldered and good-looking, contributed pleasantly. "Before we start him kicking in air this bird has got to sing."

"That's no way to talk, Linc," Dunham corrected sharply. "We represent the law."

Linc Jackman's lip curled derisively. "Hell, we are the law," he drawled. "Better law than any we'd get if a slick lawyer got a chance to talk him out of this."

"It's our say-so," the huge ruffian agreed. "We caught him. I aim to pull on the rope that jerks him up to that live-oak branch over there."

"I'll have a word to say about that, Rudabaugh," Dunham

told him sternly, and to the dismounted man said, "Make sure that's the only gun he has, Jack."

"Just the one," the cowboy replied. "Unless he's toting it beneath his skin."

"Perhaps you'll listen while I explain this, Mr. Dunham," Carr interrupted. "I didn't even know there had been a holdup till you got here."

Dunham dismounted and examined the front left hoof of the tired horse the prisoner was riding. "The hoof is broken like one of the tracks showed where the bandits picketed their mounts and it's a sorrel with a white splash on its face as Hank Mains described it. The same horse, I would say." As he straightened, the accused man noticed a star on his vest.

"I think you are right," Carr said. "Not fifteen minutes ago a man rode out of those willows, covered me with a rifle, and made me swap horses with him. He thought I was one of your posse. The only reason he did not kill me was he feared you might be near and would hear the shot."

Jackman laughed, but with no kindness in his mirth. "I been wonderin' what kind of fairy tale this guy was going to tell. I reckon the innocent-bystander one is as good as any. But it ain't good enough."

"He went through the live oaks. You could probably catch him if you hurry." Carr did not raise his voice. There was no flutter of fear in his manner or face. He realized he had to speak reasonably to convince Dunham of the truth of his story, or at least of the possibility of its truth.

"We ain't aimin' to hurry," Rudabaugh said, his grin showing a mouthful of tobacco-stained teeth. "We already done our hurryin' for today. Fellow, yore goose is cooked."

"At what time and where was this stage robbed?" Carr asked.

"Ain't that interesting?" Foley mocked. "Wants to know from us when and where at he held up the stage."

"What's your name?" Dunham demanded.

"Jefferson Carr."

The captured man chanced to be looking at Linc Jackman and he caught an expression on that young man's face that

puzzled him. He thought, *This fellow knew my name before
I gave it.*

"Where are you from?" the sheriff asked. "I don't recollect
ever seeing you before."

"I blew in from Frisco. Colorado is my home state. Born
in Pueblo."

"What are you doing here?"

Jackman interrupted with a sarcastic grin. "That's an easy
one. He is robbing stages and killing the guards."

"Fact is," Carr continued, disregarding the intervention of
Jackman, "I'm a kinda fiddlefooted fellow and the grass always looks greener to me somewhere that I ain't."

"Come clean," Dunham ordered. "You belong to the Crows'
Nest gang."

"Never heard of them. We'd get at the truth quicker, Mr.
Dunham, if you would give me a chance to prove I was at
some other spot when this holdup took place."

"Sure," Foley fleered. "He was probably in Phoenix having dinner with the governor."

The sheriff ignored the man. "You'll get that chance," he
told the prisoner. "The Sandy Wash Stage was robbed yesterday about ten in the morning at or near the Four Crossings,
halfway station between Tomahawk and El Molino."

"Then I'm in the clear. About that time I was saddling at
Sarasota to start for Tomahawk. The keeper of the Lone Star
corral will testify to that. A cowboy squatting in the corral
made a map in the sand to guide me over the short cut. I got
lost and spent the night in the hills!"

"What are we waiting for?" Foley asked. "We've caught
the guy. If he didn't shoot Jim Haley one of his pals did.
There's a rope and a tree handy. I say stop his clock right
damn now."

Carr looked at the little man with the scarred chin and the
shifty hooded eyes. He was a person of no importance. A
glance told him that. But the world is full of insignificant
people who foment trouble.

"Regardless of whether I am innocent or guilty?" the captured man asked coldly.

"After you and the rest of the gang split up the dough,

what did you do with your share?" Jackman demanded. "Cached it somewhere, I reckon. Funny you didn't ride to the Crows' Nest with the others."

"You're barking up the wrong tree. I was forty miles away from the stage when it was robbed. That I can prove."

"By one of yore gang," Foley sneered. "If you got a chance."

Dunham cut in sharply. "Enough of that talk, Foley. This man is my prisoner and I'm going to take him in to Tomahawk. Be sure of that. It is possible he is telling the truth." In his saddlebags he found a pair of handcuffs and passed them to the lad who had searched Carr. "Snap them on, Jack," he said.

"Y'betcha!" Jack fastened the cuffs on the wrists of Carr. "None of my put-in maybe, but this galoot don't look to me like any dirty killer. I'm sap enough to believe his story."

The sheriff had some doubt himself, though in his long experience he had known many bad men who wore a front of convincing innocence. In the face of Jefferson Carr—if that was his real name—he read the toughness of a spirit that would go through an undertaking to a fighting finish. The chill steady eyes mirrored a cynical audacity. They were vigilant and wary but they showed no fear. His long lean body backed this promise of strength. It sat the saddle easily, relaxed and almost slack, and with none of the tightness that might have been expected in one upon whom life-or-death judgment was being discussed.

"And the guilty gent is burning the wind for a getaway less than half a mile from here while you sit around chatting," Carr said softly with a thin smile.

"He's right here with us and he's not making any getaway," Rudabaugh differed. "No use being too damned legal about this, Sheriff. Jim Haley was a nice boy. We all liked him. They didn't give him a chance for his white alley. We'll make this fellow tell who was with him on this job and then string him up nice."

"He's going to town with me alive," Dunham said firmly.

"No use us having a fuss about it," Foley urged. "Let's take a vote. Majority rules."

"You're a fool and always will be, Foley," the sheriff told him impatiently. "No brains and so crazy to hang a man that you can't see a majority of the people in this county elected me to represent them. I'm the majority present."

"Being elected to an office can swell a guy's head up sure," Jackman jeered. "All right, boys. Mr. Big Mogul Sheriff wins this time. We'll postpone the necktie party. Where do we go from here?"

Dunham ignored the insulting words. "We go up through the live oaks and see if we can cut sign on a bandit riding in a hurry to make himself an absentee from here."

"Fine," Jackman agreed with a scornful laugh. "Might as well swallow this smooth guy's alibi hook, line, and sinker by looking for a ghost he cooked up to save his hide. I'll bet he can even give us a description of him."

"I can," Carr answered quietly. "He is tall and lean as a rake, with heavy-lidded pale blue eyes in a pinched, mean face. Short on nerve but dangerous if he is crowded. He is wearing levis and an old white hat that has a rattlesnake skin for a band."

"Like I said, slick as a greased shoat," Jackman scoffed. "Saw this ghost guy only once for two-three minutes but knows him as he does his brother. Probably can tell us whether he has a mole on his right hip."

Carr caught the swift hidden look of warning Jackman flashed at Rudabaugh. In this situation there was something under cover, an understanding which neither the sheriff nor the young fellow they had called Jack shared.

They rode through the scatter of live oaks to the rock rim fencing the mountain park. The sheriff and Jackman dismounted and quartered the ground for recent tracks of a horse. In a sandy arroyo back of the rim they found what they were seeking, marks of hoofs in the soft earth made so lately that the sun had not yet cooked the crumbling edges. The tracks, far apart and deep, told the story of a man riding in a desperate hurry with fear in his heart.

"Probably a partner of this guy we caught," Jackman suggested. "Going hell-for-leather to reach the Crows' Nest."

"He'll soon be safe in the gorges of these badlands," Dunham said. "But we'll follow the tracks on a chance."

Hours later he gave up and headed for Tomahawk.

II

Ranse Jackman came out of the Gilson House after a noon breakfast and stopped on the porch to light a cigar. As usual several old-timers were holding the chairs there and absorbing the pleasant sunshine. They had reached an age when it was good to sit against a wall and let warmth soak into their ancient bones while they wrangled mildly over memories of long-past days and current gossip.

Their faded eyes shifted to take in Jackman's superb figure. The man was an eye-filling spectacle, six feet two in height, with shoulders deep and broad. His dark bony face was well modeled. Its keen eyes and hawk nose, set above a strong mouth adorned by a long drooping mustache, advertised him as both arrogant and forceful. In the coal-black eyebrows, hair, and goatee a strain of Indian blood showed and also in the high cheekbones. His expensive clothes were chosen with care—a low-crowned black hat, polished custom-made boots, a fine frilled lawn shirt beneath a flowered silk vest and a broadcloth coat known then as a Prince Albert, a style affected in the West only by professional gamblers.

"Heard the news, Mr. Jackman?" piped up Hank Todd in the high-pitched falsetto of an octogenarian. "They done caught one of the vinegaroons that robbed the stage and killed Jim Haley."

Jackman held the lighted match poised for an instant before throwing it away. He was a deputy United States marshal as well as a gambler and this interested him both personally and officially.

"Is this rumor or fact?" he asked.

"They passed here not ten minutes ago while you was eating," Todd replied. "Yore brother Linc was with them. The whole bunch went into the Palace, I reckon to wet their whistles after a dusty ride."

"Who was the prisoner?" the marshal inquired, his voice carefully casual.

"Never saw him before. Belongs to the Crows' Nest Gang. I shouldn't wonder."

"Fast work," Jackman commented. "Linc is a go-getter."

"Bet yore boots," Todd assented. He noted that the officer gave his brother the credit of the capture. That was like him. Ranse Jackman and Walter Dunham were leaders of opposing factions in Tomahawk and a bitter quarrel between them was in the making. The sheriff's office was worth nearly twenty thousand dollars a year. At the approaching election Jackman intended to run for the position and expected to win.

The old men watched him as his reaching stride took him down the street, the muscles rippling beneath his coat like those under the skin of a prowling tiger. At this time of day, when the miners were either underground or sleeping until their next shift, the town usually lay in a coma of drowsiness, practically in a siesta until the activity of late afternoon began to foreshadow the noisy night life. But now excitement was running high. Not much more than twenty-four hours earlier the Sandy Wash stage had been held up. That in itself was not unusual. There had been three stages robbed in as many months. But in this case murder had been added, and as it chanced, the victim was a gay happy-go-lucky young man expecting to be married next September. The simmering anger of the town was ready to boil over.

Old Fort Street, the business thoroughfare of the town, was wide and arrow-straight. A thousand hoofs had pounded the road bed into fine dust and ore wagons stirred the dry particles to choking clouds when they rolled past. Plank sidewalks lined both sides back of which were the false-front wooden buildings that housed the stores and saloons. Here and there cards littered the walks. The pattern of the town was like a dozen others on the frontier familiar to Jackman, with the exception that it was rawer and more uninhibited. For this was a new mining camp where many of the floating riffraff had flocked to prey on the workers. Back of Old Fort Street the town had grown in haphazard fashion. Some of the houses were neat and well-cared for with flowers in the yards struggling to survive the heat and drought, others were ramshackle cabins of adobe, the walls already crumbling.

Before Jackman came to the Palace, men began to pour out of it like pips from a squeezed orange. Among them was his brother Lincoln.

There was a thin satiric smile on the face of Ranse. "Hear you captured one of the holdups," he said.

"In the hills above the cutoff," Linc answered. His narrowed eyes sent a message to Ranse. "Fellow gave his name as Jefferson Carr."

"So what we heard is true and he is here already." The voice of the older Jackman rasped like a file.

"Johnny-on-the-spot. Dunham has taken him to the courthouse to be identified by the passengers on the stage. He went out of the Palace the back way to miss the crowd. I aim to be there when he pulls off his show."

Rudabaugh and Foley had joined them. The big man cut in with information. "Me, I thought it would be a good idea to wind up the fellow's ball of yarn right there, but Dunham got hell in the neck and handed us law talk. You know what a sanctimonious son of a gun he is. I was ready to start smokin' but Linc backed down."

"The fellow is still here," Linc said with a grin. "Thought I'd let you play the hand, Ranse. Seeing you'll be sheriff next month."

"Linc was right, Karl. You were one of the sheriff's posse. That is not the time to get on the prod." Ranse turned to his brother. "How come you to arrest him as one of the bandits?"

"He was riding a bronc one of the holdups rode. No doubt about its being Shep Bascom's sorrel. His story is that it was wished on him by a guy at the point of a rifle a few minutes before we caught up with him."

Foley tittered. "It suited me fine for him to be one of the stage robbers. Still does."

The cold warning eyes of Ranse Jackman rubbed out the titter. A man on the sidewalk was brushing past them.

They turned in at the courthouse square and found Dunham in his office with the captured man. The sheriff nodded stiffly to Ranse without rising from the chair back of a desk where he was seated. The prisoner was still handcuffed. At the door a deputy was stationed.

"I've sent for the witnesses, Hank Mains and the three passengers." Dunham looked out of the window at the gathering crowd. "A lot of travel headed this way. No room for them here. Tim will keep out those not needed. You are entitled to be present, Ranse, and the boys on the posse."

"We'll be the jury," Rudabaugh announced. "See the guy gets what is coming to him."

The sheriff's steady eyes met his. "This isn't a trial, Karl. You are a courtesy visitor and have nothing to say unless called as a witness."

"That's what you think," Rudabaugh retorted. His next jeering words were addressed to the younger Jackman but pointed at the sheriff. "We made a mistake, certain, in not finishing this job up in the hills but we can fix that yet."

"Don't get on the prod, Karl!" Ranse Jackman said curtly. "Justice will be done. I'm here to see to that."

Dunham flushed angrily. "I'm still sheriff of this county," he reminded the Jackmans.

The prisoner was in a tight place but he gave no sign of disturbance. On his face was a thin smile, as if he found some inner amusement at the cross currents of anger in the room. For a handcuffed man to appear at ease is difficult, but he succeeded in doing so. He leaned back relaxed in the chair, more like an interested spectator than an unfortunate principal whose fate was about to be decided.

Ranse Jackman was surprised at his assurance. Carr was

young, hard-bitten, bronzed, entirely master of his nerves. The well-packed muscles of his legs and shoulders were smooth rather than bulky. The gambler read in his face a hint of devil-may-care recklessness. His feet might have carried him on wild and crooked trails but not from weakness. He did not look a man who would crumple up under the pressure of danger and let the wind of fear unnerve him.

The deputy at the door admitted into the room a group of five, then turned the key on others clamoring to enter. One of those let in was a young lady. Ranse Jackman rose and gave her his chair.

"Sorry I'm a little late, Walt," a fat short man in jeans and a seersucker coat told the sheriff. "Took me longer than I expected to round up all of them." He mopped his perspiring face with a bandanna handkerchief.

"You're just in time, Art," Dunham replied. "We'll get going now. It won't take long. A man has been arrested. I want to know if any of you who were present at the holdup can identify this handcuffed man as one of the bandits. You first, Hank. Take a good look at him."

The stage driver, Hank Mains, squinted sun-narrowed eyes at the prisoner. Mains was an old-timer in the West. This was written on every inch of his garb and appearance. He chewed his cud of tobacco for several seconds before he answered.

"The guys were all masked," he mentioned.

"We know that. But how about his clothes—the general look of him?"

Before entering the room Hank had made up his mind not to recognize the arrested man. He had to ride the stage every day. There would be other holdups. If he testified against one of the robbers the companions of the man would remember it and consider him a danger. This was a risk he did not intend to take. He had talked too much already.

Mains shook his head. "I wouldn't know, Walt. The horses were right restless and I had trouble keeping them under control. I didn't pay no mind to the road agents."

"You described accurately the horse we found this man riding," the sheriff said.

"Well, horses are my speciality, you might say. No, Walt, I cain't honestly say this is or isn't one of the gents."

One of the passengers on the stage was a St. Louis drummer for a patent medicine. He was dapper and very confident. "Yes, sir. This is one of the outlaws. You bet. He is the spittin' image of the fellow who searched the passengers."

Carr slid in a question. "You remember the clothes I wore?"

"That's right, young fellow," the drummer said importantly. "I'm peculiar that way. Once I see a thing I don't forget it."

"Interesting if true," the prisoner commented. "By the way, can you describe my hat?"

The accused man was bareheaded and his hat was not in sight. His smiling confidence discomfited the witness, who floundered, his face reddening. "I don't have to discuss it with you," he answered.

"Perhaps you would rather tell me then," the sheriff suggested.

The drummer hesitated. "A big hat—cowboy style," he guessed.

"Color, please?" Carr murmured.

Dunham nodded assent. "Tell him, Mr. Godfrey."

Godfrey's questing eyes swept the room for hats and chose the prevailing color. "White," he hazarded.

Carr drew a black hat from back of him. "I must have dyed it since," he said gently, as if to himself.

Linc Jackman cut in with an explanation. "He may have swapped hats with one of his pals."

"Not unless I swapped names too. An envelope in my pocket has on it my name, Jefferson Carr. Stamped in the band of my hat are the initials J.C."

Dunham examined the envelope and the hat band. "That is true," he said, and passed them both to Ranse Jackman.

"All right," Rudabaugh called out impatiently. "Godfrey made a mistake about the hat. That doesn't clear this Carr, if that's his name."

"It only discredits Mr. Godfrey's testimony," replied Carr. "He was wrong about the hat. Probably he is about the clothes."

The prisoner was pleased. With some difficulty, since he

was handcuffed, he had slipped the hat back of him. He had played a long shot and it had come off. If Godfrey had guessed right it would have counted heavily against the arrested man.

An argument between the doorkeeper and a man trying to enter attracted the attention of the sheriff. "Let Mr. Haddon in, Tim," Dunham ordered.

The newcomer was a clean-scrubbed pink-cheeked Englishman wearing custom-made riding breeches and boots. He walked across the room to the young woman and said, "I just heard about this hearing, Bob."

She nodded, smiling at him, "Nice of you to come, Harold." Her name was Margaret Atherton, but as a small girl she had wanted to be a boy and all her friends called her Bob.

Ranse Jackman raised a point with a surface smile of apology to Dunham for interrupting. "Aren't we overlooking an important fact, Sheriff? This man claims he was held up by one of the outlaws and his mount taken. Yet you found a gun on him. Wouldn't a bandit have disarmed him and not left a revolver on this innocent traveler with the opportunity to shoot him in the back as he rode away?"

"I think so," Dunham agreed. He turned to the shackled man. "Any explanation?"

"The fellow was afraid that at any moment the posse might ride into sight. He knew it was close on his heels. I could see he was jittery, his whole mind occupied with the hope of getting away safely. At no time was he nearer than thirty or forty feet from me. My guess is that the reason he did not make me drop my weapon was his fear that when I drew it from the holster I would start smoking. He had not the nerve to risk it."

"He gave you too much credit, didn't he?" Linc Jackman jeered. "For though you had a gun, you let him ride away with your horse scot-free."

Carr answered pleasantly, "Quite true. I was glad to escape with my life. A six-gun is no match for a rifle except at close quarters." He added, his cool sarcasm addressed to the younger Jackman, "I'm a timid guy, no hero like you manhunting gents."

A young cowboy named Vail Booth had been the second

passenger on the stage. His evidence was noncommittal. "Might be one of the galoots who held us up. Kinda favors the fellow who lifted our dough from us. But, holy smoke, I can say that of twenty other men in this town. You can't hang 'em all."

The sheriff called on Margaret Atherton. She had just arrived from England to visit her brother Maxwell Atherton who had recently bought a cattle ranch in the vicinity. From the moment she had entered the room every man present had been keenly aware of her. She was a lovely young girl with the warm coloring of her race, tall and slenderly full, dressed in well-cut tweeds that did not conceal her light and supple grace.

Her brother had written home about the freedom and lawlessness of this fascinating West where he had come to live. She had been a passive witness before she reached Tomahawk of a scene of murderous violence that had greatly shocked her. Already she knew that existence here was very different from what it was in the combed and gentle Surrey where she had spent her early years. But surely the code of ethics at bottom must be fundamentally the same. As she looked into the lean sun-tanned face of Jefferson Carr, sensitive and mobile, she felt it was not possible that he could be a ruthless killer. Her eyes had met his twice in the past few minutes and each time she had felt a queer little tug at her heart. She was on his side. He was an innocent man trapped by circumstances.

"Do you recognize this man as one of the bandits who robbed the stage, Miss Atherton?" asked Dunham.

The eyes of the prisoner were no longer either mocking or hard. They seemed to make a claim on her that stirred a disturbing flutter of the blood. Later she was annoyed at that, but for the moment she brushed thoughts of it aside. There were men in the room determined to convict him.

"No," she said with quiet assurance, "I don't think he was one. He doesn't look at all like any of them."

Ranse Jackman offered a deferential suggestion. "You were greatly frightened were you not, Miss Atherton?"

She saw where this was leading. "Yes, so much so that I was afraid to lift my eyes from them. I couldn't be mistaken."

Ranse said, with a short incredulous laugh, "I hope you are right." His information warned him of danger in this young man.

The sheriff was impressed by her testimony. The evidence against Carr was inconclusive, though it was a damning point that he had been caught on a horse ridden by one of the outlaws. Dunham decided to play safe on account of the Jackman hostility and hold him for the present.

Carr recalled to the memory of the sheriff, almost casually, the tracks of a second horse found above the rim of the park where he had been arrested.

"For what it is worth in bearing out his story, that is true," Dunham said. "We did find hoofprints so new the sun had not yet dried them."

"Doesn't mean a thing," Rudabaugh burst out. "The bronc that made them was ridden by one of the fellow's pals making a getaway."

"Might be," agreed the sheriff. "I'm going to keep this man under detention till we hear from his witnesses at Sarasota."

"If he has any," Linc Jackman scoffed.

"Correct. If he has any."

Ranse Jackman moved toward the door. His fleering voice reached everybody in the room. "A Daniel come to judgment! Yea, a Daniel!" he quoted.

In the hallway Harold Haddon and the girl met Ranse Jackman waiting for them.

"You needn't have been afraid of the fellow, Miss Atherton," he said. "There would have been no danger in recognizing him."

She said, color sweeping into her cheeks, "You don't want him proved innocent, do you?"

"Not if he is guilty—and he is."

"I don't think so." She slipped a hand under Haddon's arm and walked down the corridor to the courthouse door.

Eyes focused on the English couple as they moved along the sidewalk to the hotel. Remittance men from across the water were numerous enough to stir up no interest, but a girl like this one, with Cherokee roses that came and went in her soft cheeks, one who carried herself with such light grace, was new in their experience.

Haddon said, "Carr can thank you if he gets out of this."

"You think I helped him?"

"A great deal. This town believes him guilty, but you were so sure, it is bound to raise a doubt."

"Do you think he did it?" she asked. "A man who looks as he does."

He shrugged his shoulders. "How can I tell? I'm sorry you got mixed in this, Bob, though of course you could not help it. The cattle country has a lot of bad characters in it. Quite a few nice-looking young cowboys are tied up with bandits. This Carr may be one of them."

Now that the accused man, so fearless and debonair, was not present to sway her opinion she was less certain of his innocence. Her face reflected a troubled spirit. "I'm not so sure as I pretended to be, Harold. How could I be when all of them had their faces covered? But I can't believe he is one of those dreadful men. He does not look or act like a villain. I had to help him if I could. Could you not feel the hatred beating on him? Before I went to the sheriff's office I overheard men at the hotel say he ought to be lynched. They talked as if they did not mean to give him a chance to prove he was not one of the outlaws."

"I think you have taken some of the heat off him," Haddon replied. "The hotheads will wait to see what his witnesses say. If he is bluffing and hasn't any I wouldn't give sixpence for his chance." He glanced at his watch. "You look fagged out. I don't wonder, after your long trip and shocking experience. Lie down and rest for a few hours. By dinnertime Max ought to be here. As soon as the messenger with the news that you have arrived reaches him he'll leave the cattle drive in charge of the foreman and hurry back."

"I wrote him when I was coming," she mentioned.

"We get mail once a week. Probably your letter is lying in the post office. Max has been counting the days. He wants you to like this country as much as he does. I think you will."

"Shall I?" she asked wearily, doubt in her voice.

III

The sheriff sat on the cot in Carr's cell and watched him devour the dinner he had brought from the hotel. Steak, potatoes, corn bread, and coffee disappeared rapidly.

"You eat like you are hungry," Dunham said.

"First food I've had since yesterday morning," Carr replied. "My stomach was flat as an empty mail sack. I'll recommend your calaboose when I get out."

"If you do. I'll have to hear what the boss of the Lone Star corral at Sarasota and the cowboy you claimed drew a map for you have to say before I let you out. Did you get the name of the cowboy?"

"No. We were strangers who did not expect ever to see each other again. Maybe the corral man knew him."

"I hope so. A range rider who has vanished into thin air won't do you much good."

Carr frowned, his eyes narrowing in thought. "I don't quite get this setup. The town is sore about the killing of the shotgun messenger. That I can understand. But there is something more back of this situation. The whole Jackman outfit wants to get rid of me *muy pronto* and I don't think they give a damn whether I am innocent or guilty. Perhaps you can tell me why."

The sheriff slanted a long look of appraisal at his prisoner. He liked the manner and appearance of this young fellow, but he had not made up his mind about him yet. Back of his cool composure, at times close to insolence, the officer was not sure what kind of man lived. He was hard and tough, but his character might be good or bad.

"Maybe you've got something there," Dunham said cautiously. "But I wouldn't know for sure. Fact is, I'm not friendly with the Jackman's. They don't like me and I don't like them. It could be that they want through you to discredit me."

"I could see they were trying to push you around. They made no bones about that."

"The election is in three weeks and Ranse is running for sheriff against me. It's the best-paying job in the county and it will give him a good deal more power, though he already is a political boss here. The crowd that want a wide-open town are for him. He and his brother Clem own the Capitol, the biggest gambling house in town."

"Can he beat you?"

"I don't know. He claims I'm a do-nothing sheriff because I have not arrested any of the Crows' Nest gang for robbing the stages. Since Jim Haley was killed a good many citizens feel I ought to have found the guilty men. But how can I without any proof? It's an open-and-shut case according to Ranse that the outlaws at the Nest did it. I need more than suspicion to go on."

"I gather that the Jackmans are ruthless, unscrupulous fighters."

"Better ask somebody else than me," Dunham answered with some bitterness. "I don't like a hair of the head of any of them. Let it ride at that."

"Do they stay inside the law?"

"Depends on what you mean by that. Ranse is ambitious as the devil. He talks big about upholding law, but one of his right-hand men is Karl Rudabaugh, a gunslinger known to have killed seven men."

The sheriff picked up the tray, walked out of the cell, and turned the key behind him.

Carr lay on the cot with his fingers locked back of his head. He had come to make trouble for others and had run into a pack of it himself. This was unfortunate, even though he expected to free himself shortly of the robbery charge. He had wanted to pass as a cowboy on the chuck line, a drifter looking for a ranch job, the run-of-the-brush type that was a dime a dozen in this country. But by sheer bad luck the limelight had been turned on him. He would be about as inconspicuous as John L. Sullivan at a Tammany Hall picnic.

The reason the sheriff offered for the Jackman urge to rub him out might be a factor, but it did not seem to Carr strong enough to account for the vindictiveness with which they pressed the case against him. There was, too, the fact that Linc Jackman had seemed to know his name. He wondered if there could have been a leak at headquarters, a warning to the Jackmans that he was coming. This pointed to the assumption that they were connected with the crimes he had come to investigate, and he had no evidence to support this.

His thoughts drifted to the girl who had testified for him. In the drab office her vital beauty had bloomed like a rose rising proudly from a dust heap. He could not get her out of his mind. The men in the room had been rough frontiersmen, men used to the hard tough realities of a parched desert, but all of them had been impressed by her alien fineness, her unconscious loveliness. He had noticed how Ranse Jackman's eyes had returned to watch her again and again. Her evidence had put a spoke in the man's wheel. It would be broadcast through the town and build up for Carr a sentiment based on doubt as to his guilt. In fancy he saw again the soft planes of her oval face, the violet eyes, the mouth sweet and tremulous. In the long hours that followed he thought of her often. It was a mistake, he felt, to bring a girl like this one, brought up so daintily and no doubt with loving care, into such a lawless and turbulent region.

It was in the late afternoon of the next day that Dunham brought up a man to see him, the owner of the Lone Star corral at Sarasota.

"This is Mr. Houston," the sheriff said. "Do you recollect ever having met him before?"

"At Sarasota, two days ago," the prisoner answered promptly. He added with a grin, "I don't remember ever being more glad to see a man again."

"He's the guy all right who stabled his horse with me Monday night and left next morning," Houston said.

"Sure?" the officer asked.

"Dead certain."

"Do you know who the cowboy is that was loafing in the corral when I left, the one who drew a map of the cutoff for me in the sand?"

"Never met him till that day. Probably a floater drifting through."

"But there was such a man," Dunham insisted. "You actually saw him draw a map of the cutoff."

"That's right."

Houston was a well-known citizen whose word Dunham thought good. The sheriff took his story in the form of an affidavit and within the hour released the prisoner. Dunham gave him a word of advice.

"If I were you I would leave town before word of this gets out. There are some here who might make you trouble."

"In a nice quiet town like this?" Carr drawled.

"I don't mind telling you that I've been uneasy ever since I have had you in this cell for fear an attack might be made on the jail. Certain parties have been busy inflaming the minds of the riffraff."

"When they find out I have been cleared of the stage holdup they won't bother me, I reckon. Maybe I'll stick around a while. Tomahawk looks like a live town. By the way, if you are through borrowing my cutter I'd like it back."

Dunham returned his weapon reluctantly. "Take it easy," he advised. "A lot of wild coots have hit this burg since the gold strike. Take Rudabaugh, for instance. He's a bad *hombre*, ready to fight at the drop of a hat."

"I've noticed that he is on the prod," Carr replied carelessly. "I'll certainly sidestep the gent. He's too tough for me." As he was leaving he turned, as if by an afterthought. "Oh, whereabouts is the Atherton ranch?"

"The L Lazy C? Six or seven miles north of here. Someone from the ranch is in here 'most every day if you want to get in touch with it."

"I might want to do that. The young lady went all the way for me. I suppose the Athertons have plenty of money."

"They must have. The ranch is quite a big one and they have been making a lot of improvements."

"This young fellow Haddon. Is he part owner?"

"He lives out there. Maybe he is just a remittance man. I wouldn't know about that. The Englishmen in the cattle country sort of hang together."

Jeff Carr strolled down Fort Street. The stir of evening activity was beginning to ripple over the business district. Horses were tied at the racks in front of most of the saloons, and miners not on the current shift were moving in and out of the amusement spots. Nobody paid any attention to Carr. He reached the edge of the town and walked to the top of a small incline known as Bald Knob. Tomahawk seemed to sit on the top of the world. In the clear untempered light of Arizona the mining camp looked down on a roll of hills and valleys that fell away to the jagged horizon line of gaunt stark mountains—the Dragoons and the Huachucas, the Mules and the Whetstones, the fastnesses of the Apaches when they broke away in sporadic raids from the reservations where approaching civilization had corralled them. It was an odd paradox, he thought, that this raw huddle of humanity should be set in a scene so peaceful and magnificent.

The sun was sliding down to a crotch in the porphyry range, its rays streaming over the silvery sheen of the mesquite. A golden blur of distance softened the garish desert details. The joyous note of a meadow lark lifted. In a few minutes the purple lakes in the pockets of the mountains, the fire that lit the crags and flung ribbons of the rainbow colors streaming across the sky, would dull into the blue of approaching night.

He turned to descend the slope and saw that a man and a

woman were just topping the crown of the rise. The woman was Margaret Atherton.

At sight of him she was surprised and a little startled.

"They have let you out," she said impulsively.

"I had good witnesses to help me."

Perhaps his smile took too much for granted. She turned to the young man with her and said stiffly. "This is the man arrested for robbing the stage, Max." A deeper color was beating into her cheeks.

The family resemblance of the two could be seen at a glance. Beneath the tan, Maxwell Atherton had the same warmth of coloring as his sister and his fine blue eyes were of the same shade as hers. But the controlled reserve of his lean face was as masculine as the hard-packed muscles of his broad shoulders. His level gaze took in the stranger silently. That Carr was no ignorant ruffian was clear, but Atherton had met within the month a gay and charming youth who was without doubt a killer and an outlaw. This man might be of the same breed.

"I am right glad to get a chance to thank Miss Atherton for her supporting testimony," Carr said. "Without it I'm afraid I would have been in a bad spot."

"My sister feels now she was a little too sure," Atherton said coldly. "What she said was entirely impersonal. I hope she was right. In any case you owe her nothing." The Englishman turned toward the painted mountain tops and sky. "In a minute the colors will fade," he told the girl. "We are just in time, Bob."

Carr had been brushed off the map, but Margaret was not quite happy at her brother's cool dismissal of the man. If he was innocent—and her feeling clamored that he was—a slap in the face like this was insulting. She understood Maxwell's viewpoint, that he would not allow any doubtful character under suspicion of crime to become acquainted with his sister. But this was begging the question, since they did not know whether he came in that category.

As Carr passed back of them to go down the hill she turned quickly. "I think you ought to leave here at once, sir. Perhaps you have not heard it, but there is talk of violence directed against you."

He answered, a cynical smile twitching at his lips, "The wicked flee when no man pursueth: but the righteous are bold as a lion." He backed his biblical quotation with a bit of information. "A witness for me reached town this afternoon, the keeper of the corral at Sarasota, and he confirmed my story that I was in his wagon yard an hour before the stage was robbed forty miles away. He also described the horse I was riding. It was a dark bay, not the sorrel I was riding when the posse arrested me."

Carr made this explanation to Miss Atherton and not to her brother. Very likely he would never see her again, but he did not want to go out of her life leaving the impression that he was a miscreant.

The situation embarrassed Atherton. He still did not know whether this man was guilty, but he did not want to kick when he was down one who might be innocent.

"We are glad to know this and hope the criminals will be caught to exonerate you completely," he said.

Carr said dryly, "I share that hope."

He left them on the hill and walked through the straggling suburb of the town to Fort Street, turning in at the Gilson House. In the lobby he registered for a room. Supper was being served and he strolled into the dining room. After he had sat down at a side table he made a discovery. Linc Jackman was one of two men seated so near him that he could have reached out and almost touched him.

Young Jackman did not trouble to lower his voice. "We're honored, Clem," he said. "The gent who has just arrived is the stage robber Dunham turned loose an hour ago."

Clem Jackman swung around in his chair and let his gaze travel up and down the stranger insolently. Like his brothers, he was a dark rangy six-footer.

"Fixed it up nice with Dunham, I reckon," he gibed. "The lives of shotgun messengers come cheap these days."

Three other customers were in the restaurant. All of them stopped eating to stare at the accused man. Carr's cool scornful eyes shuttled from the gamblers to the others present.

"Some of you probably know Alec Houston, who runs the Line Star corral at Sarasota," he said quietly. "Today he signed an affidavit that I was in his wagon yard a few minutes before the stage was robbed fifty miles from there."

"A fine witness," Clem said with a mocking smile. "When the rustlers of the Crows' Nest gang go to Sarasota to hurrah the town they put their horses up at the Lone Star corral."

Through the swing door leading to the kitchen a young woman came to Carr's table. "Beefsteak, pork chop, sausage, ham and eggs," she parroted.

The waitress was still in her teens and very pretty, but her eyes were swollen from weeping. She was Ella Gilson and she had been engaged to marry the stage shotgun messenger Jim Haley.

"Beefsteak," Carr decided. "Not too well done."

"Maybe you would like to be introduced to the customer, Ella," Linc Jackman suggested. "He's one of the fellows who killed poor Jim and our good sheriff has just turned him loose. A gent from the Crows' Nest country."

The girl drew back from Carr in horror. She was a passionate, undisciplined young creature filled with anger and resentment at the murderer of her lover. With youth's shortsighted vision she saw all the happiness of her life shattered. This ruffian who had killed Jim was free to ride away without punishment. Her eyes fell on the revolver in the holster hanging from Linc Jackman's belt. A surge of madness swept over her and she dragged the weapon from its case.

Jeff Carr's hand, resting on the table, moved swiftly to the vinegar cruet. As the girl's arm lifted, the cruet struck down the barrel of the .45 and a bullet crashed into the floor. Carr dived for her and tore the weapon from her fingers.

Ella stared at him, her face ashen, all her passion gone. She had almost killed a man and panic flooded her being. A wail lifted from her throat and she covered her face with her hands, the slim body torn with sobs. She turned and ran into the kitchen.

Rising from the chair, Linc Jackman said, "I'll take my gun."

Carr handed it back. "You're hardly experienced enough to carry a six-shooter," he said. "Not when a girl can come along and take it from you as easily as a kid can take candy from a baby."

Linc flushed angrily. "Maybe you would like to try taking it."

"No thanks." Carr rose and took his hat from the rack. He laid twenty-five cents on the table to pay for the meal he had decided not to eat. Under the circumstances he would not be a welcome paying guest at the Gilson House and there was no use in forcing an unpleasant situation.

Young Jackman moved to bar the way between the two tables. "Fellow, I don't like you," he said hotly. "Didn't from the first minute I saw you."

There was a slurring drawl in Carr's voice, a satiric indifference almost disdainful. "That distresses me," he said. "Afraid there's nothing I can do about it."

"You can get out of this town, and by God! you had better—damn quick, if you don't want to go to sleep for keeps in smoke."

"Are you advising or threatening me, Mr. Jackman?" asked Carr blandly, his unwinking eyes fastened on the furious man.

"Take it any way you like, but light a shuck sudden."

Clem Jackman spoke. He had a mouth tight as a steel trap and when he talked his lips scarcely moved. "Get my brother right. The citizens in this town don't believe your alibi. They think you are guilty as hell. Better go while the road is still open."

"I'll give that thought," Carr replied, his face inscrutable. "Of course I'm deeply grateful for your interest in my welfare."

Since the younger Jackman still barred the way, he circled the table and sauntered to the door. Standing in the entrance with his back to the Jackmans he rolled and lit a cigarette, then without looking back stepped to the sidewalk and moved down it.

Linc glared at the disappearing man. "I gave him a chance to draw. He wouldn't take it."

The older brother slid a warning look at him. His words were for the onlookers. "You were a fool, Linc. We've got nothing against him personally."

IV

Carr ate at Wun Lung's Chinese restaurant. Nobody in town knew the owner's real name, but he had come to cure a touch of tuberculosis and a wag had once fitted an appropriate label to him that the Oriental accepted without protest. After Carr had eaten he found a room at a lodginghouse on a side street. When he returned to Fort Street the place was already roaring with life. Men jostled one another going in and out of the gambling houses and the honky-tonks. Dusty freighters, sallow miners, and tanned cowboys crowded the dance halls and surrounded the tables presided over by impressive housemen. The whir of the wheels, the rattle of chips, the sawing of fiddles, and the thumping boots of those engaged in a quadrille beat out from the buildings to the road. Gaudily dressed women in the variety halls drank with customers and plied them with liquor and blandishments. Rich man and poor man, beggar and thief, flung their money away at roulette, faro, poker, and Mexican monte.

From the Legal Tender to the Silver Dollar, into Jack's Grand Theater and out of it to the Occidental Saloon, Carr wandered unnoticed. Until he reached the Capitol nobody paid the least attention to him.

He was watching a faro game when a voice behind him said, "Just eyeballing, Mr. Carr?"

He turned, to see Ranse Jackman.

"Getting acquainted with the town," he answered.

"Is it worth while for so short a stay?" the gambler inquired.

"I'm beginning to like the place. There are opportunities here for a young man."

"Not your type, unless you like to live dangerously."

"Can't say I do. I'm the timid sort." Carr added pleasantly: "What is my type? Explain me to myself."

"You are what is called a buttinsky, one who doesn't mind his own business. In this town we don't like that."

"Wrong guess. I am going to attend to my own business strictly. It would please me if your friends would do the same."

"We might talk this over in my office over a drink," the gambler suggested.

"If you wish," agreed Carr. It would be a chance to learn more about this man.

He followed Jackman to a small room on a balcony at the back of the room. "If you will excuse me I'll pass up the drink just now," he said. "It is so soon after my dinner. Another day, if your offer still stands."

Jackman pushed away the bottle he had started to uncork. He leaned back in the chair, his narrowed eyes raking the man opposite him.

"You say you are looking for a town that holds a good chance for an enterprising man to make money. I recommend Tombstone, the livest camp in the territory."

"What has Tombstone got that Tomahawk hasn't?" Carr asked.

"It has safety."

Carr did not need the point stressed. He had now no doubt that the Jackmans had been sent a tip as to the reason he had come here. The urgency of these men to get rid of him in one way or another was an indication of their vulnerability. They were in a position so far outside the law that an investigation might prove dangerous to them. The fear of it was so great that they were laying it on the line to him He was to leave or be rubbed out. It was an option he did not like, but he had come to do a job and he meant to see it through

"This looks like a nice quiet town," he said "A man not looking for trouble ought to get along all right "

"You are sitting on a powder keg I advise you not to wait until somebody sets it off "

"Who would do that?" Carr asked innocently.

"Only a fool whistles over his own grave," Ranse told him abruptly: "I'm a deputy United States marshal. I don't want an unnecessary killing here. This town's anger at you may explode any hour. I'm telling you to get out."

"That sounds like an order," Carr replied mildly.

"Call it what you like, but go."

"My business ought not to take long. When it's finished—"

"It will be too late then."

"One can't always tell. I'm an obstinate bird. I think I'll stay a while and look around."

Jackman rose, his face set to harsh lines. "Suit yourself," he snapped and flung open the door. "While you are looking take a tour of Boot Hill and count on the headstones the names of those who stayed too long."

Jeff stood on the sidewalk outside of the Capitol trying to make up his mind whether to go to his room. It was a breathless night and the heat of the day still radiated from the sunbaked earth. His small hall bedroom would for hours be an oven, since no breeze was stirring. He lit a cigarette, dropping the match into one of the barrels of water placed at intervals along the street for use in case of fire, then crossed the road and strolled down a narrow lane into the Mexican quarter.

As he disappeared into it two men standing in the alcove of a store entrance watched him. One of them, a huge muscle-bound fellow, murmured to his companion, "It's that guy Carr." His right hand moved to the butt of a revolver.

"Not right now, Karl," the small man beside him warned. "Too light here. You can get him in an alley on his way back."

Rudabaugh nodded. "Mr. Carr is a dead man but doesn't know it yet," he replied with a cruel grin.

The ruffian followed Carr into the lane keeping thirty or forty yards back of him. He did not intend to give his victim any warning. At an *acequia*, beyond which lay virgin desert, the road came to a dead end, but a path ran to the right behind a group of adobe houses.

Carr took the trail along the canal. It brought him to another street up which he turned. A Mexican passed him with a cheerful *"Buenas noches, Senor."*

It was a minute or two later that a faint rumor of sound behind him drew Carr's attention. He stopped and looked back. The night was moonless and starless, and in this narrow canyon of houses little light penetrated. To him there came the soft shuffling of feet that died away into stillness. Whoever it was had stopped in the pit of darkness beyond his vision.

His imagination might be playing him tricks, but if this was an assassin at his heels he did not want to be the surprised party. He kept on his way, noiselessly as he could, until he reached an alley crossing the road. At the intersection was a water barrel. He crouched behind it.

Presently he heard again a stirring in the night. A heavy-bodied man flatfooted with extreme caution out of the deep shadow. He stopped at the crossing, not sure which of the three ways to follow. The man was Rudabaugh, and in his hand was a revolver.

Jeff helped him make up his mind. "Keep going," he advised. The distance between them was not more than two yards.

"Goddlemighty!" Rudabaugh ripped out, and for a big man moved incredibly fast.

He lurched down the alley and dodged back of an adobe Mexican oven. As he vanished his .45 blazed. The bullet crashed into the water barrel. From his position back of it Carr could hear water pouring as if a faucet had been turned on. The gurgle of the small stream running down the barrel staves was the only sound except the distant noise of the town's night life.

Carr listened, his nerves keyed up, for any movement of

his attacker. Concealed by the barrel, Jeff might have crept up the alley until out of range and raced for safety. But that solution Carr rejected. Unless he was willing to give up and leave the town it would be a mistake to run away at the first attack. He could not afford to let his enemies think he was the frightened-rabbit type. It would be better to hold his ground and see if Rudabaugh's nerve would not crack. Assassins from ambush were not usually game men.

From back of the oven a streak of fire flamed. Carr did not answer the shot. His foe was too well protected. He waited, pistol held close to his side. The seconds ticked away— became minutes. Rudabaugh's weapon roared again. A third bullet tore into the barrel. The long silence was getting to the killer. It carried to him unknown threats of danger in the darkness. The stillness filled him with alarm. What was Carr doing? Was he sneaking up on him in the blackness of the night? The suspense became intolerable. Rudabaugh bolted down the alley.

Instantly Carr gave chase. The lumbering giant had no chance to outrun his pursuer. He whirled and fired. Jeff's .45 boomed down the alley setting echoes flying, the bullet plowing into the big man's shoulder. An instant later the smoking barrel of Carr's pistol landed on his forehead and staggered him. He closed with his wiry opponent, clinging tightly to him. The fellow was strong and awkward as a bear, but he was shaken by his wounds. Blood covered his face and dripped down his chest. Even now for sheer power Carr was no match for him. Jeff realized that as he struggled to keep his feet. Too close to use his weapon, he dropped it to seize the hairy wrist of the other man and keep the barrel of his revolver directed from him.

They went down and their legs thrashed wildly as each tried to pin his adversary to the ground. Neither had time to get set. They rolled over, first one on top and then the other. Rudabaugh's thumb searched for Carr's eye socket to gouge the ball. To protect himself Jeff pushed his head into his foe's shoulder. Both hands circled the ruffian's wrist and hammered the barrel of the revolver against his mouth and nose.

Rudabaugh bellowed with pain and rage. He dropped the

.45 to have the use of both hands and with a tremendous effort flung the lighter man from him and against the oven. He scrambled to his feet and broke into a run to get away. He had had enough, his face beaten to a pulp, a hammer pounding in his head, and pain throbbing from the shoulder wound.

Carr was in no condition to pursue. His head had struck the adobe wall of the oven and he was faint from the shock of the blow. He rose dizzily and leaned against the oven until the swimming in his head passed. He was lucky to be alive. It had been a foolish idea to tackle this huge fellow in a rough-and-tumble fight. There had been a few moments at the end when he was completely at Rudabaugh's mercy. Only the fellow's panicky wish to escape had kept him from seeing that his enemy was helpless.

Quartering over the battle ground, Carr found not only his own pistol but Rudabaugh's weapon and hat. He took them with him when he walked back to Fort Street.

A man was standing in front of the Legal Tender Saloon. He stared at Carr open-mouthed. The man was Foley. His astonishment was not only at Carr's battered face, but at the fact he was there at all. It had not been ten minutes since Karl Rudabaugh had soft-footed after this stranger into the Mexican quarter to murder him. Foley was filled with curiosity to know what had occurred. Evidently Karl had mauled the man. But why had he not left him dead? Foley had heard the hammering of guns.

"Had a little trouble, Mr. Carr?" he asked with a malicious smirk.

Carr's glance swept the man but he did not give him the satisfaction of an answer.

V

Since the chances were that none of his enemies knew where he was staying Carr did not expect any immediate repercussion from his battle with Rudabaugh, but he took no unnecessary risk. Long ago the keys to the rooms at his lodginghouse had been lost. The best he could do was to prop a chair under the doorknob and cover the floor with crumpled pages of a newspaper. He was a light sleeper and if somebody succeeded in getting in during the night the rustling of the paper would awaken him.

After bathing his bruised face and body he lay down on the bed and thought over the situation. Two points stood out plainly: that the Jackmans knew he had been sent by the Pacific & Southern Express Company to investigate the stage robberies and that they were implicated in the holdups. Their determination to get rid of him one way or another left no doubt of this. They had struck before he could gather any evidence of their guilt. In their haste was a suggestion of panic, which implied that they had left loose ends not too well covered.

That Rudabaugh had been acting under a direct order from the United States deputy marshal to kill him Carr doubted. Unless it had been arranged beforehand the big ruffian must have been playing his own hand. There had been no time for Ranse Jackman to get in touch with him after the talk in his office, and if Carr's death had been decided on there was no need to urge him to leave town.

Carr's intention of working under cover was gone. The

men he had come to convict had him spotted. It would be well, he thought, to take the sheriff into his confidence.

After breakfast next morning he dropped into the office of the *Tomahawk Blade* and ordered fifty posters set with display type. The editor was a thin little nearsighted man named Joshua Pike. He read the copy, took in the customer's battered face, and drew his own conclusions, helped to them by a talk he had had with his friend Doctor Lindsay in which the physician had told him of a visit from Rudabaugh to have a wounded shoulder treated.

Pike said, peering over his spectacles, "Young man, I hope you know what you are doing."

"I think so," Jeff answered cheerfully.

"Plain suicide, I would say." Pike rubbed a bristly chin with the palm of his hand. "None of my business of course, but you are new in this town. Perhaps you don't know Karl Rudabaugh's reputation. This copy is pointed straight at him. I wouldn't like to be printing your obituary in the next issue of the *Blade*."

It hurt Carr's bruised face to smile, but he did. "I wouldn't like that either. We can forget that. I feel reasonably healthy."

The editor's eyes swept over the paper again. It read:

FOUND

In the alley crossing San Felipe Street
One Colt's .45 with seven notches on it
And one white hat
Initialed K.R. in the sweatband.
Owner can obtain same by claiming and proving title.
Apply to Jefferson Carr
At the office of the P. & S. stage company.

"If you don't know you are asking for trouble, young fellow, you are either crazy or a plumb fool," Pike snapped. "You 'most wrecked this K.R. last night. He is sore as a boiled owl. Do you have to devil him publicly? Smart thing to do is to get away from here on a fast horse like the heel flies were after you."

"I have business here," Jeff told him mildly.

"Hell's fire!" Pike exploded. "I'd say your first business was to stay alive."

"This K.R. gent left last night in a kind of hurry. I've got to get his property back to him. How soon can you run off the posters?"

"All right. I'll print them for you. If I don't somebody else will. But don't say I didn't warn you that there will be another notch on this bad man's gun." Pike added in a sudden heat of irritation, "Just because you had luck with him last night doesn't mean a thing. He'll lay for you. Want to know, I think you're a brash young fool."

Carr thought he might be right. But his experience was that the best way to meet danger was to show no fear. There was no doubt that Rudabaugh would never rest without trying to kill him. He was a bully proud of his bad record. The one thing he could not stand was to lose face with the men who were his familiars. Given this extra prod, he might be furious enough to strike in the open next time. Jeff knew he walked in hourly peril. Since it had to be, he had better do it with his head up.

When Carr stepped into the office of the sheriff, Dunham looked at him in quick surprise. A rumor had reached him that Rudabaugh had been wounded and beaten by some mysterious assailant. At sight of this young man's bruised and swollen face his mind jumped to a guess.

"Have you been tangling with Karl Rudabaugh?" he demanded.

"How did you guess it?" Jeff asked. "We did have a little rookus." He sat down and rolled a cigarette.

"Tell it to me," Dunham said.

Carr told the story of the evening, beginning with the talk in Ranse Jackman's office and ending with the fight in the alley.

"I don't get it," the sheriff said. "There's something back of this you haven't told me. Did you know the Jackmans when they were in Dodge or any other place before they came here?"

"Never saw any of them until this week. I'll come clean,

sheriff. My uncle is the vice-president of the P. & S. Express Company. I have been a rolling stone, but the family finally euchred me into the office of the company at San Francisco. I couldn't stand desk work, and when it was decided to send a man to investigate the stage robberies I persuaded the top men to let me come. There must have been a leak somewhere, for the Jackmans put the finger on me at once."

"You are suggesting that the Jackmans are in on the hold-ups?"

Jeff blew a fat smoke wreath and watched it thin down. "Doesn't it look as if *they* have been suggesting it pretty loudly?" he inquired.

"It has been thought the Crows' Nest gang are the guilty parties," the sheriff replied. "But maybe you are right. A cousin of the Jackmans, Norm Roberts, is the P. & S. agent here. He could have tipped them off when there was a gold shipment. I don't say he did."

Carr's eyes narrowed in thought. It occurred to him that here was the explanation of the reason that the Jackmans recognized him when he gave his name to them. One of the company officials had written Roberts that he was coming, asking him to turn over to Carr all the information about the robberies he had. The man had probably relayed the news of the arriving investigator to his cousins.

"That explains a point that was puzzling me," Carr said. "From the first the Jackmans have been set to get rid of me. They are a hard, tough bunch of fighting men, not the kind that scare easily. This hurry to rub me out convinces me not only of their guilt but also that they feel their position is vulnerable and that they are afraid of an investigation."

Dunham could not quite fall in with this view. "Might be," he admitted, "but I don't think so." He paced the office floor as he explained why. "I wouldn't put any deviltry past Ranse. If he wasn't a bad lot he wouldn't keep Rudabaugh for a hanger-on, a fellow known to be a killer. But it is important to him to keep his skirts clean, or at least not to be caught in crime."

"Someone tried to murder me in ambush," Carr mentioned. "Don't you think the Jackmans were back of Rudabaugh?"

"Probably. But highway robbery is different. Ranse wants to go a long way. Sheriff first, and afterward governor. A killing can be condoned in this country, especially if it is in the open. But a stage holdup is too far outside the law."

"If it is proved on him, but he didn't expect it to be found out. Since he is ambitious he could use the loot he has been getting. More than fifty thousand dollars has been taken from the stages in the last three holdups. My size-up of him is that he is both bold and crafty. He would not hesitate to take a risk, figuring his tracks were covered."

"Maybe—maybe. No scruples would stop him if he thought it would pay off." The sheriff turned abruptly on his visitor. "Assuming you are right, what in thunder are you doing here? You have been warned and your life attempted. Nobody but a foolhardy kid would stick around."

"I'm in a peculiar position," Carr explained. "I come of an old family, very respectable. Even as a kid I was wild. Later I got kicked out of college and drifted around for a while. I was a cowboy with the Hashknife outfit, did a lot of gambling, soldiered as a private under General Miles when he was hunting Geronimo. In fact I was the black sheep of the family. My father wrote me a letter asking me to come home because my mother was so unhappy about me. So I went to work for our company in the office and hated it. Inside of three months I had proved myself a misfit. When this job of investigation came up I wouldn't rest till my uncle gave it to me. I've got to stick it out or admit I am a complete flop. I am not going back to explain that I got frightened and ran out on it."

Dunham did not argue the point. Carr had made up his mind. His opinion was that this young fellow with the strong well-boned face and the lean whipcord body was quite a man. When he started on a trail he would follow it to the end. He was also of the opinion that for him the end would be violent and sudden.

"They will be watching every move you make. How do you expect to find out anything?"

"That I don't know. For one thing I would like to meet again the fellow who swapped horses with me in the hills. I think I could soften him up. And I would appreciate any information you could give me about the Jackmans or their followers. Or the names of anybody else who might have a line on them."

The sheriff told him all he knew about the Jackmans and their intimates. He offered as a guess the suggestion that the horse trader might be Shep Bascom, a ne'er-do-well reputed to be a rustler, thought also to be one of the Crows' Nest gang. It might pay him to talk with Luke Kasford, a cattleman on whose range two of the holdups had occurred.

Before Carr left he put a question to the officer. "How did you happen to have three of the Jackman crowd on your posse, since you do not like them?"

"Some townsmen would be no good on a posse and most of those who would be useful don't want to serve," Dunham replied. "I had sent out one bunch with my deputy Harris. Linc Jackman and his pals had volunteered. There was no reason for me to turn them down, but I took them with me to keep an eye on them rather than letting them go with Harris. For a man-hunting job you have to take what you can get."

Dunham followed his visitor to the door. "For heaven's sake, be careful," he warned.

Carr grinned at him. "Careful is my middle name," he said.

The sheriff watched him move down the street with a light-stepping gait that was almost jaunty. There was an anxious frown on the face of the officer. Maybe he had not put it strongly enough to this young fellow that the black mark of death had been pinned on him.

VI

Since Ranse Jackman rarely left the Capitol until two in the morning he was always a late riser. His brother Clem joined him at the breakfast table with the news of Rudabaugh's unlucky misadventure. Karl was not making a public appearance and would not until the marks of battle had healed. Clem had got his information from Foley, who kept bachelor quarters with Rudabaugh in a cabin near the *acequia*.

"Might know the fool would go ahead without orders and blunder it," Ranse said irritably. "I'd better drop around and get the story from him."

Clem drew a folded paper from his pocket. "Show him this," he said dryly. "It will please him."

Ranse read the poster Carr had ordered printed. "Where did you get this?" he asked grimly. An angry color had beaten into his face.

"Found it tacked on the front door of the Capitol. There are dozens of them nailed on trees and walls and inside stores all over town. A Mexican boy put them up. I saw him later. Carr paid him a dollar to do the job."

"It's a declaration of war against us. The fellow has signed his death warrant. But we've got to move carefully—and in the dark. What we do must not come home to roost."

"Carr has nerve. I'll say that for him."

"He is a fool." Ranse rose from the table and walked out of the Gilson House with his brother. At the sidewalk they separated, Ranse to take a path leading to the *acequia*.

He found both Rudabaugh and Foley at home. Karl was

lying on a cot in a vile humor. His shoulder pained him and he had a headache from the pistol whipping he had received.

Jackman looked down at the battered face. "This Carr must be some bearcat," he said with malice. "Next time you had better tackle somebody your own size."

Rudabaugh poured out a string of oaths followed by a boast. "I can whop the tar outa him with one hand tied behind me," he growled.

"Too bad you didn't have it tied up then," Ranse jeered. "Let's have the story."

The wounded man edited the facts to salve his pride. Carr had lain in wait for him and shot from ambush. Before he had recovered from the shock of the wound the man had attacked him savagely with a pistol and beat him over the head.

"Not the way I heard it," Jackman differed bluntly. "You started after him to get him and he outfoxed and outfought you."

"Anyone who told you that is a liar," Rudabaugh roared with more profanity.

"We'll have to send out a nursemaid with you when you go for a walk, Karl. We can't allow a big bully to jump you and beat you up. But try not to worry about it if people snicker when they see you. They have got to have their fun, you know."

The killer was so furious he could only sputter threats. Dark blood poured angrily into his beefy face.

Jackman gave him a curt order to let Carr alone until he had instructions to go after him. "I'll give it to you plainly in short words so you'll get it through your thick skull. This fellow has big backing behind him. When he is bumped off there must be no trail leading to us."

"You'll sit around till he gets something on us," Rudabaugh complained.

"When the trap is set I'll let you spring it," Jackman promised. "But you won't lift a finger till I give the word." He took the poster from his pocket and handed it to the wounded man. "You seem to have been in a hurry when you left him last night. He's reminding you he has some of your property. I reckon it will be a pleasure for you to take up unfinished business and wind up his ball of yarn."

The big ruffian exploded again. He had a low boiling point, and the chief pride on which his vanity fed was that he was a killer so dangerous men went out of their way not to cross him. The contemptuous challenge back of the printed words made him wild with fury.

"I'll pour lead into him first time we meet," he ripped out.

"Take it easy, Karl," Jackman warned. "You'll have your chance to make a rag doll of him, but not just yet. He has asked for it, and he'll get it." Having stirred his tool to a frenzy of hate, Ranse soothed him with flattery. Rudabaugh was the greatest gunfighter in the country, he declared, and compared to him Carr was only a strutting tenderfoot. At the showdown Karl would make him look like a plugged nickel.

VII

Carr wanted to buy a horse and at the suggestion of Dunham went to the Maverick corral to look at a chestnut gelding that was for sale. The sheriff knew the horse. It had both stamina and speed, he said. After looking the animal over carefully Carr swung to the saddle for a try-out. He found the chestnut had both plenty of spirit and an easy gait. The price was right and he bought it.

Within five minutes of the purchase he was headed northward for the L Lazy C. The day was pleasantly warm and he had a feeling of relief at getting into the country where nobody was likely to be lying in wait to send a slug into him.

The spring rains had helped the alfilaria and the few cattle he saw were fat.

He came to a road sign bearing the legend L Lazy C Ranch. It pointed to a trail leading up an arroyo shaded by live oaks bearded with hanging mistletoe. It brought him to the small holding of a nester. The windmill in the corral was working and he swung down to get a drink. A woman came to the door of the house. She was tall, lank, and sun-dried, with clothes that looked as if they had been made hurriedly from a sack.

Carr deflected from the corral toward her. "Good morning, ma'am," he said. "I stopped for a drink if you don't mind."

"You are welcome, stranger," she replied. "I'll get you a glass of cool milk."

She went into the house and got a glass and led the way to a shallow brook where under the shade of cottonwoods pans of sweet milk were sitting in the water. As they walked back a bandy-legged young fellow in chaps showed up at the corner of the house. He had a bridle in one hand:

"Great jumpin' horn toads!" he whooped. "If it ain't the stage robber. Howcome you're loose? They was fixin' to put a rope round yore neck last time I saw you."

He was one of the possemen who had arrested Carr, the young fellow the sheriff had called Jack. Jeff grinned. There was no animosity in this lad.

"They changed their minds, Jack. It turned out I was innocent."

"Dog nab it, I'm sure glad. Some of the guys on that posse were plumb ornery." He turned to the woman. "Mother, this is Mr. Carr, the man I was tellin' you about. He never did look like a stage robber to me."

The woman shook hands with Carr. "Our name is Adams," she said. "Pleased to meet you. If anybody needs hanging it is that murderous brute Karl Rudabaugh."

"What you been doing to that face?" Jack inquired. "Looks like you been chawed up by a cougar."

"Some love taps from Mr. Rudabaugh. He wasn't quite satisfied when the sheriff freed me."

"He beat you up?"

"That's right."

"Lucky you aren't hurt worse. He's a bad *hombre*."

"Yes. His intention was to put me out of business, but his shooting wasn't quite good enough. He's carrying one of my bullets as a souvenir."

"You shot him?"

"In the shoulder. Not a serious wound. I am afraid."

"Then why ain't you high-tailin' it for parts far away? He'll never rest till he's got you."

"Soon as I have finished a little business I'll be leaving." He thanked Mrs. Adams for the milk and asked if he was on the right road for the L Lazy C.

"Right over the hill about three miles ahead. You can't miss it," the woman said.

"They're nice folks," her son added, "but so doggoned English they can't say hell with their hands tied behind them."

Jeff topped the hill and rose across a mesa. He heard the far, faint bawling of cattle. They were being either worked or driven. From the edge of the mesa he caught sight of them as he dropped down into the valley at the far end of which was a cluster of buildings. Half a dozen riders fenced a bunch of stock. Another was in the herd cutting out the calves. Still others were grouped around a fire heating irons or busy with a blatting yearling. Evidently the L Lazy C had ridden circle that morning and rounded up young stuff for branding. To Carr it was an old story of which he had been a part a good many times. But it stirred memories of the days when he had been a cowpoke with never a care in his thoughts. Youth had been in the saddle riding a world that belonged to the man on horseback. Sometime, if he lived, he would go back to it.

He rode closer. A woman in a buggy was watching the branding. She got out of the rig to pick some desert wild flowers. As soon as she was in motion he recognized her. She moved with the light free grace of one who loved life, the mere living. He started his mount toward her, a little disturbed. They ought to have told her that a rider is fairly safe among the wildest hill cattle, but a man on foot is likely to be attacked when a herd is excited, as it always is when massed after a gather.

As if his fear for her had been a cue, a big longhorned steer tore out of the herd and made for the branders. There was a wild scurry for safety. Iron and ropes were dropped in the flight to the saddles. A *vaquero* cut in and beat the animal over the head with a rope. It turned to escape, caught sight of the girl, and charged at her. A cowboy let out a yell of warning. Margaret Atherton looked up, realized her danger, and ran for the buggy.

Carr had already lifted the chestnut to a gallop. He saw the girl could not reach the buggy in time and that the *vaquero* pursuing the animal would be too late. Pounding over the ground at full speed, he knew it was a race between him and the infuriated steer for her life. By a fraction of a second he won, guiding the horse so as to bring it between her and the lowered horns. He dropped the reins, leaning far to the side and stooping, his eyes fastened on her to time the lift. Without slackening the pace, his hands caught the girl beneath the armpits and swept her to the saddle in front of him. So near a thing was it that a horn of the steer grazed the rump of the chestnut.

The girl lay in Jeff's arms, breathless and shaken, her face buried in his shoulder, her heart beating against his. She was hardly yet conscious that she had shaved death by a hair's breadth. Not until he handed her into the arms of her brother did she open her eyes.

Maxwell Atherton's face was a map of tortured emotion. He had watched the wild race and been helpless to do anything for her. It seemed to him that a miracle had intervened to save her. He held his sister tightly in his arms.

"God! What a fool I was not to warn you," he cried.

"It's all right, Max," she murmured, trembling like an aspen leaf.

Maxwell looked up at Carr. If this man had not been on just that spot at the right time, if he had not acted instantly and efficiently, his sister would probably have been torn to death or left a helpless invalid. No words could express his thanks. They did not mean enough. But he tried.

Carr said lightly, "Glad I was near enough to help." He grinned at the other riders who had ridden up. "I'll bet your boys are sore they didn't get the chance."

But though he spoke casually, the warmth inside of him told him that his coolness was a lie. She had lain in his arms and clung to him as if she would never let him go. The beat of her heart still strummed through his blood. This was an important hour in his life.

Atherton decided to take his sister home in the buggy. He asked Carr to ride with them to the ranch house. Jeff explained that he had been headed for it when he turned aside to see the branding.

VIII

The L Lazy C Ranch House was a one-story, rambling building with a clapboard roof and wide porches on three sides. Though not a pretentious dwelling, it had been well built and furnished with a view to comfort. A worn Brussels carpet covered the floor of the living room and in one corner was an upright piano. On the wall was a reproduction in color of a picture of Sir Garnet Wolseley in uniform and another of Queen Victoria taken when she was a girl of eighteen. There was also an original, a portrait of an officer of the Black Watch, the father of Maxwell and Margaret. In a home-made bookcase were shelves of well-selected books.

Carr found himself drinking tea with the brother and sister. The cups were china and the spoons silver. On the cozy a motto had been stitched, "Unless the Kettle boiling be, Filling the teapot spoils the tea." As he sipped from the cup and ate the pound cake he thought it was all very British.

Jeff was surprised to find that neither of them were at all stuffy. Maxwell liked America and in his liking there was no patronage. He asked Carr how to set about applying for citizenship. He had come to stay and was already in the process of becoming what he called a Yankee.

"I have been told that you have to catch an Englishman young to make a good American of him," he said smilingly. "With a Scot it is different. He takes to your way of life more readily. Since my father is from Perthshire maybe I can fit in easily."

The girl had changed from tweeds to a sprigged muslin, in which she looked charmingly cool and dainty. Her fingers touched the fragile china lightly and deftly. She did not talk much but he had an impression that she was pleased he had come, even not counting the factor that he had saved her life. Perhaps she too shared the undercurrent of emotion too deep for words.

He explained his presence in Arizona and asked her if she could describe any of the men who had robbed the stage. Considering the fright in which she had been in, she did pretty well. The one who had shot the guard was a great shambling profane man. Another was tall and thin with a big floppy white hat. That would be Shep Bascom, thought Jeff, and the first she had mentioned, Karl Rudabaugh. The leader had handed her purse back to her with a bow and the comment in a pleasant voice that they did not annoy ladies. He had shown a quick flash of anger at the big man for shooting Jim Haley needlessly. Carr made a third guess, that this one was a Jackman, probably Lincoln. He realized that suspicion went for nothing unless it could be backed by evidence.

In answer to a question, Atherton told him that the Crow's Nest Gang were a bunch of outlaws living near the headwaters of the Mesquite River. Their chief business was rustling stock and trailing it through the mountains into northern Arizona and New Mexico, but it was fairly certain that they operated also as highwaymen robbing stages and banks. It was his opinion that all of the Sandy Wash stage robberies had been pulled off by this band.

"Are the Jackmans associated with these outlaws, either for or against?" Carr asked.

"Their leader is a fellow called Alec Black. The town they frequent most is Sarasota, but they come to Tomahawk occasionally. They ride in quite openly, tie at a rack, and go into a saloon or gambling place. I have seen Black talking with Ranse Jackman, but that doesn't mean anything. He is a genial villain and talks with anybody."

After tea Harold Haddon dropped in wearing riding breeches and carrying a crop. Carr felt a slight resentment at his obvious good looks and somewhat possessive manner toward the girl. He had a free-and-easy way with her. If he was in love, and Jeff supposed he was, he took for granted quite casually her interest in him and adroitly excluded the American by carrying the talk back to old memories. He maneuvered Margaret to the piano and by request she sang "Auld Lang Syne," the men joining in the chorus.

Though both Margaret and her brother urged Carr to come again soon, he was carrying away with him a disappointed sense of frustration. The arrival of Haddon had changed the atmosphere and made him an outsider. After Margaret had shaken hands with him in farewell he was surprised and pleased that she went with him to the porch.

She said shyly, in a low voice, "I'll never forget."

Their eyes met for an instant before she turned and went swiftly back into the house. It was strange, he thought as he rode away, that three words could lift a man's heart from cold depression to warm hope.

IX

Before Jeff Carr had ridden down the trail as far as the Adams place the sun was disappearing in a burst of splendor back of a crotch in the range. He found Jack shoeing a horse at an outdoor primitive blacksmith shop and stopped apparently to watch him at work. His real reason was that he wanted information.

Jack said with a grin, "So you're headin' back to Tomahawk where Karl Rudabaugh can get another crack at you."

"Wrong guess," Carr corrected. "My present destination is the Crows' Nest country."

"What you lost up there?" Adams queried.

"One dark bay horse named Nugget. A guy called Shep Bascom may be able to tell me where it is."

After a moment's thought Adams agreed. "Might be you are right."

"Know him?" Carr asked.

"Yeah, I know him. Bad egg. If I was you I'd figure that Nugget hoss a total loss and forget it."

"You think him dangerous?"

"Mean as they come. Shoot you in the back if he gets a chance."

"I'll remember that when I meet him again. How do I get up into this Crows' Nest district?"

Jack lifted his shoulders in a shrug. "If you're set on going I'll show you the way. It's quite some distance. Light and spend the night with us and we'll get an early start."

"Your mother—"

Adams cut in on his visitor's protest. "Mother will like to have you stay. She gets lonesome to see people."

The house was clean and neat. Most of the furniture had been brought by covered wagon from Tennessee. The small guest room assigned to Carr had a rag carpet and chintz curtains for the window. Its duplicate could have been found in a thousand homes of the Middle West States.

During supper Jeff drifted the talk to the Crows' Nest country and its inhabitants. Did they run cattle? If not, how did they live?

Jack skirted the subject rather cautiously. They owned quite a bit of stock and they traded around some. The ranches farther north offered a market for any cattle they sold.

His mother put the facts bluntly. "They are a bunch of outlaws. Every head that passes through their hands is stolen in Mexico or rustled stock taken from the ranches in the valleys. On top of that they rob stages. Strangers aren't welcome up there, Mr. Carr, unless they are fugitives from justice."

"I don't understand how if they are known as bandits they can ride down to Sarasota and even to Tomahawk without being arrested," Carr said.

"It has never been proved in court that they are outlaws," Jack explained. "A lot of cattle have been stolen and headed up that way. But there is no one man or group of men absolutely known to be guilty of taking them. There's another point. They are tough and they hang together. When a bunch of them go down to Sarasota to raise hell the marshal looks the other way. After all they don't do more harm in town than any wild bunch of cowboys and they spend a lot of money."

"Are they friends of the Jackmans?"

"That's hard to answer. They used to be thick as thieves, but the story going around now is that Alec Black and Ranse Jackman have fallen out. I don't rightly know why. They are both high-steppin' arbitrary guys who want to rule the roost." The eyes of young Adams lit with boyish enthusiasm. "Alec is sure enough a case. First off, he is tall, well built, and handsome, and most of the time he dresses up fit to kill. He comes to town in a gold-embroidered buckskin Mexican short jacket and a fancy sombrero wearing the most expensive silverspurred boots he can buy. He is friendly and laughs a lot, but if he's riled he'll fight at the drop of a hat. Several times he has stopped and eaten with us. Mother likes him and reads the riot act to him for being what he is. He teases her to go on and cuss him out more."

"I don't like him," Mrs. Adams differed. "I like the good in him and hate the evil. But I've known worse men."

They ate breakfast by the light of a coal-oil lamp and were in the saddle before darkness was out of the sky. Mrs. Adams watched them go with misgivings in her heart. She had strongly advised Carr to give up this trip into enemy country but she could not get him to change his mind. For her son she was not much worried. He was going only as far as the pass that looked down into the forbidden land.

The two men rode through a country rising gradually toward the distant mountain range. As they traveled forward the character of the vegetation changed. The prickly pear and cholla grew thin and stunted. Mesquite and huisache gave place to live oaks and ocotillo. Spanish bayonets and saguaros studded the hillsides. Arroyos were supplanted by steep rocky gulches. They were moving into the mountain defiles that led to the summits far above.

Narrow gorges ran between the ridges piled here, huddled close together, some carrying scant vegetation and others with pine forests reaching up the slopes. It was a country so rough and torn, so filled with ravines and hidden pockets, that few ventured into it except those night riders who traveled on nefarious business.

By way of a deep cut in a rock rim they came to a precipice which looked down on a basin watered by a stream fed from snow-filled canyons far above. From this height its floor looked flat enough, but Carr guessed its surface was broken by washes, hills, dips, and boulders.

Adams pointed to a scatter of timber near the far end of the valley, back of which a thin skein of smoke lifted.

"Jugtown," he said. "Nothing there but a saloon, a store,

and a few shacks, I'm told. I ain't ever been closer than this.
Most of the galoots roostin' up here come in from their hide-
outs to meet up with their pals in Jugtown." He glanced at
his companion. "Still time to change yore mind."

Carr shook his head. "I'm a kinda stubborn pilgrim. Much
obliged for everything. Be seeing you." He set his horse in
motion along a rock scarp, to follow a narrow trail descending
to the valley far below. Rubble started by the feet of his horse
rolled over the edge and dropped a hundred feet before striking earth. Eroded gullies, too steep to follow, fell away from
the trail to the shoulders below. There must be another way
in, he realized. Cattle could not be driven along this knife-
sharp edge.

As he came closer to the floor of the large mountain park,
details grew clearer. He could see that the surface was chopped
by scores of alleys angling in every direction. It was an ideal
country for men on the dodge. They could take refuge in
pockets safe from any posse. No sign of any inhabitants
appeared, but it was possible that already eyes were watching
him.

At the foot of the trail he hesitated, uncertain which way
to go in this tangle of broken country. He decided to head in
the direction of Jugtown. Now that he had reached the Crows'
Nest it seemed to him that he had come on a fool's errand.
What chance had he of finding Shep Bascom? And if he
found him the fellow would very likely be with others of the
same breed. Unless Bascom was alone he could not be made
to talk.

He rode across a slope sprinkled with yucca and dropped
into an arroyo leading to a walled canyon. The lower end of
this opened into a grassy park fed by a small creek. There
was a cabin set against a background of scrub mesquite. As
his glance swept the terrain a sparkle of light held his eyes.
Carr's stomach muscles tightened. The sun was shining on
the barrel of a rifle pointed at him over the top of a boulder.

"Make a move and I'll cut loose," a voice threatened.

From back of the rock a man stepped, a huge bullnecked
fellow, bowlegged and barrel-chested.

Carr raised his hands. "Don't rush it," he said. "I'm harm-less."

Protruding eyes light as skim milk scanned him. "Hit the ground on this side of yore hoss, arms still reaching for the sky."

Jeff Carr did as he was told.

"Make medicine fast," his captor ordered. "What you doing here?"

"A fellow borrowed my horse. I came to get it."

Splenetic laughter spilled out of the man. There were forty borrowed horses in the Crows' Nest but this was the first owner who had come to reclaim one. "Maybe he ain't through borrowing it yet," the bullnecked one said. "Who is this guy you lent it to?"

"I didn't exactly lend it," Carr explained mildly. "He took it from a hitch rack in front of a saloon. The gent didn't leave his name."

"So you come here lookin' for him. You made a mistake certain."

Bullneck relieved Carr of his six-shooter.

The disarmed man mentally agreed that he had made a mistake but he did not intend to make another by naming Bascom. If he was taken to that scoundrel he would be rubbed out promptly. His best chance was to get to the top man.

"I have a message for Alec Black," he mentioned. "From Ranse Jackman."

"From that double-crossing rat," the big fellow yelped. "What is it?"

"I'm to give it only to Black."

"Cough it up. If it is to Alec it's for all of us."

"I've got my instructions. Black can tell you if he likes."

The outlaw rapped him over the head with the barrel of the rifle. "Talk," he snarled.

Carr swayed. The earth tilted up to meet the sky. He went down dizzily. Bullneck's heavy boot drove into his ribs. The ruffian caught his shirt below the neck and dragged him to his feet. "Spill it," he commanded harshly.

"Listen," Carr began. "Ranse told me not to—"

He got no farther. A hairy fist crashed against his cheek.

He went down weak and groggy. Strong fingers jerked him from the ground again. "Ready to talk?" his assailant barked.

Carr said, "I'll talk to Black."

Heavy knuckles battered his face again and again. His knees buckled beneath him. When he came back to consciousness the world was swaying crazily. It steadied enough for him to see a gargoyle face glaring down at him.

"Get on your bronc," the owner of it ordered.

Carr gathered himself together and got up slowly and staggered to his horse. He leaned against it, clinging to the saddle horn. At his third attempt to mount he succeeded in getting a leg across the back of the animal.

"Turn left," the big fellow snapped. "Make a break and I'll pour lead into you."

Back of a cluster of rocks a saddled horse was waiting. Its master swung into the hull. He rode behind his captive. They took a well-worn trail that led over the rim of the valley saucer into the hills beyond.

With the bandanna that was around his throat Carr mopped the blood from his face and head. A sickness ran through him, but he fought it down and strength flowed back into him. He asked no questions, but the direction in which they moved pointed to Jugtown, he thought. For nearly an hour they traveled over rough country fast enough to jar Carr's aching body.

Swinging around a hogback, they rode plump into a scatter of buildings, perhaps half a dozen in all.

Several men lounged in front of the largest one, a combination saloon and store. They stared in surprise at Carr. "Where did you pick that up, Crawley?" one of them wanted to know.

"Got it under a rock. Where's Alec at?"

"He's inside."

A man appeared in the doorway and leaned against the jamb. Carr knew at once that this must be Alec Black. He was of medium height, lithe and graceful as a panther, with light curly hair above a well-modeled face that showed a boyish charm.

"Looking for me, Crawley?" he asked.

"This bird says he is looking for you," Rufe Crawley answered sourly "He wouldn't sing, so I beat hell outa him and brought him here."

Black took note of the hair matted with dried blood and the bruised bleeding face. "I see you welcomed him nice, Rufe," he drawled.

"Fellow says he's got a message for you from Ranse Jackman," growled Crawley. "Wouldn't tell me what it is."

"Oh, from Mr. Jackman." Black pronounced the name with obvious sarcasm. "Are you one of his heelers?" he asked Carr.

"No. He intends to kill me."

"Interesting. So he sends me a message by you. Who are you anyhow?"

"My name is Jeff Carr. I had a little trouble with the Jackmans." The captured man swung from the saddle. His head and body hurt at every motion he made, but there was a touch of jauntiness in the tilt of his hat and in his smiling eyes. "It's a long story, Mr. Black. I'd like to wash away the evidence of Bullneck's welcome first if you don't mind."

Crawley lit on the ground, his fists doubled for action. "I'll tear him apart," he threatened as he moved forward.

The leader of the group barred the way. "Not just yet, Rufe. Our uninvited guest gets a chance to talk. When I was at Tomahawk yesterday I heard a lot about a Jeff Carr. We'll hear his story—after he has made repairs."

There was a pump and a horse trough in the middle of the street. Black sent a man for a towel and Carr pumped water on one end of it to bathe his head and face. The cold water stung but drew the heat out of the wounds.

Black took him into the building and ordered a drink for him. "You look like you need it. But don't get the idea you're out of the tight spot you've butted yourself into. Law men aren't welcome here."

"You are right," Carr said lightly. "I do need it. Your friend Bullneck worked me over considerably." He lifted the glass toward Black before drinking. "Without prejudice."

The big ruffian slammed a fist on the bar. "My name's

Crawley," he growled. "Call me that again and I'll bust you wide open."

"Again?" Carr asked. "I wouldn't enjoy that. I must remember your name isn't Bullneck." He knew he was treading on thin ice but he felt it to be important that he show no anxiety about the outcome.

"What are we jawing about?" Crawley demanded of Black. "Let him spit out that message."

"Rufe is in a hurry and we must not keep him waiting," Black said in ironic apology to the prisoner. "The message, Mr. Carr."

"Oh, the message!" Carr laid the empty glass on the bar. "Afraid there isn't any. Mr. B-Crawley was showing violent impulses, and I thought it a good idea to have a talk with you."

"What about?" The eyes of the outlaw leader were cold and hard as ice balls.

"About the Jackmans mainly."

In spite of Carr's easy manner he was aware of tensity in the room. There were now eight men present counting the bartender. He caught shifting eyes that asked questions one of another. What was this stranger doing here? Had he, hidden in the hills somewhere, a posse with him? If not, how could he maintain, with peril hanging heavily over his head, that air of almost casual indifference? Black had called him a law man. Had he inside information about this fellow?

"We're listening," Black said. "Tell us about the Jackmans."

Carr turned his back to the bar, elbows resting on it and a heel hitched to the rail below. "I reckon I'd better tell you about myself first. I was headed for Tomahawk and at Sarasota a cowboy drew in the sand for me a map of the short cut across the mountains. I took it and got lost. That was the morning of the holdup of the Sandy Wash stage. A fellow bumped into me after I had spent the night in the open, covered me with a Winchester, and made me give him my fresh horse in exchange for his weary one. Soon after that, Sheriff Dunham's posse arrested me. Linc Jackman was on the posse and two other men who trail with him. A witness proved I couldn't have been at the holdup, but Ranse Jackman ordered me out of town. He got an idea I intended to make trouble for his outfit. Half an hour later one of his men, Karl Rudabaugh, tried to kill me from ambush. We had a gun-and-fist fight. I was lucky and had the best of it."

"So I heard. You took Rudabaugh's gun and hat from him, then advertised that he could get them back by coming to you for them. You had your nerve, young fellow, to pump a bullet into that wolf, beat him up, and then openly jeer at him. But what's all this got to do with us?" Black snapped the question at Carr sharply, steady eyes fixed on him.

"The Jackmans have got the wind up about the Sandy Wash holdups. I am confident Ranse engineered them and that his brother Linc, Rudabaugh, and a little chap named Foley were three of the four who pulled the last one off. To divert suspicion he is spreading the word that men from up here did it."

Alec Black had discovered from friends in Tomahawk that Ranse Jackman had told several people the Crows' Nest Gang had done the Sandy Wash stage robberies. It was a story that most people in Tomahawk and Sarasota were ready to believe. The Crows' Nest had had transactions with the Jackmans and felt this was a double cross. The only surprising angle in Carr's information was that he suspected the Jackmans of the gold thefts.

"Got any evidence implicating them?" the outlaw asked.

"No evidence, but a well-grounded suspicion."

"Come clean. You rode up here because you thought some of us were in it too. If you did you are barking up the wrong tree. None of us have had anything to do with any one of the three Sandy Wash holdups."

"I came to get my horse back. The fellow who took it was seen riding in this direction."

"Do you see him in this room?"

"No."

"Do you know who he is?"

"I think it was a man called Shep Bascom. He may not be one of the stage robbers at all. All I want is my horse. Nothing more up here."

'Bascom lives fifteen miles away from the Crows' Nest on a small ranch. He isn't one of us. He may have drifted in if the chase after him got hot. Prove to me that he is tied up with the Jackmans and I'll kick him out. I won't have a spy around, law man or crook."

A man walked into the room and up to the bar. "Gimme a snort," he told the bartender. He was a lean lank customer and his heavy-lidded pale eyes set deep in a pinched face swept the room. They came to rest on Carr. The whisky spilled out of the glass as he put it down and moved his hand fast to the six-shooter in his belt.

"Hold it, Bascom," ordered Black sharply. He waited till the man dropped his hand, then laughed. "Talk of angels and you hear the flutter of their wings."

"What's *he* doing here?" Bascom asked, worry already in his eyes.

"That's what we are trying to find out," the outlaw chief said with a grin. "Can you help us?"

Bascom's gaze slid around the room to pick up in hangdog fashion those present. "Never saw him before," he muttered.

"Think again. You've given yourself away. Did you see him last when you were borrowing his horse?"

"Borrowed horses ain't so scarce around here," Bascom replied sulkily.

Carr glanced out of the window to the hitch rack. "My horse is out there now. It as a B Bar Y branded on the hip."

"We don't give a damn about the horse," Black said. "Bascom means no more to us than you do. We don't like the Jackmans or their friends, not since we have found out they are trying to fix those stage holdups on us. And we like spies even less. I heard at Tomahawk you are a detective. We're going to get the truth."

Carr felt himself the focus of hostile eyes glittering with menace. Any law officer was anathema to them. He knew he was in a tight spot and he had to make an instant decision. To tell the truth would be dangerous but perhaps no more so than to lie.

"I'm not a detective but a clerk in the San Francisco office of the P. & S. Express Company. We think the Sandy Wash

stage robberies are an inside job, that the bandits are tipped
off when there will be gold shipments I was sent to check
up on it In the home office there must have been a leak, for
from the moment I was arrested in the hills the Jackman
crowd never knew who I was They overplayed their hand
By their determination to get rid of me I was fairly sure they
were the guilty men Bascom was one of the robbers I hoped
to get him alone and make him talk " Carr made his explanation coolly, his voice even and steady, to a circle watching
him intently in silence

"He admits he is a spy," Crawley cried triumphantly. "I
knew it all the time."

A bearded man beside him nodded agreement. "Sure. We
got to play this safe and get rid of him."

"That's right," agreed another. "Rub him out."

Alec Black spoke. He had been watching the prisoner
closely, his gaze not shifting from him. Without turning his
head his words slapped at Bascom who was sliding along the
wall unobtrusively toward the door. "Stay where you're at,
fellow. We'll let you know when to go."

Bascom pulled up, alarm in his shifty eyes. "I thought—"

"We'll do the thinking," Black told him curtly.

The bearded man moved to the door and stayed there.

"About this fellow Carr, I'm not so sure as you guys,"
Black said. "We don't want to push on the reins. Maybe he
has laid all his cards on the table. I'm not satisfied that he
has. But some points stick out that back his story. He tangled
with the Jackmans. That's a fact. And he beat up Rudabaugh
and slammed a bullet into his shoulder. Afterward he had the
guts to print a poster calling for a showdown with the whole
Jackman clanjamfry. I hate a quitter. He's my kind of a fighter.
If he is telling the truth—and I kind of think he is—we
would be numskulls to keep him from digging up evidence
to prove the Jackmans did the Sandy Wash stage holdups.
Ranse is laying them on us. We've already got a bad enough
rep without taking the credit for his deviltry. It would be nice
if this Jackman claim that we are guilty came home to roost
on their own shoulders."

"How do we know the whole thing ain't a frame-up—I

mean this story of his trouble with the Jackmans?" inquired
a bald tubby little man.

"And even if it's straight, what's to prevent him going
after us too?" Crawley demanded.

"Taking Fatty's question," Black answered. "Carr's rookus
with the Jackmans is no fix. They were keen to hang him
in the hills without bringing him to town. Sheriff Dunham
told me that. He had trouble at the hotel with Linc who
offered him a gunplay he avoided. I talked with Doc Lindsay. He dug a bullet from Rudabaugh's shoulder and washed
up the fellow's face which was beaten up bad. Lindsay
would not lie. On top of that I saw myself that the riffraff
hangers-on of the Jackmans were talking up a lynching
because they claimed Carr had helped kill the stage shotgun
messenger. But when you come to Rufe's point you've got
me. Carr may be trying to make a roundup that will include
us too."

"So we turn him loose and wait to find out," Crawley
jeered.

"No, Rufe, we keep him a close prisoner till we make
sure."

"Damned if I like it," exploded Crawley. He turned to the
others. "How about it, boys? I vote we stop his clock right
now."

Carr felt the chill silence run through him as the seconds
raced into the past. The eyes stabbing into him were like a
pressing weight. It seemed to him they were impatient to get
this over with.

The prisoner's gaze traveled the circle slowly. A tight cold
grip twisted his stomach, but he kept his fear inside him. The
quiet voice in which he spoke was even and not ragged.

"If you've got to kill a man innocent of any harm to you
I'll be just as dead if you do it tomorrow instead of today,"
he said, rolling and lighting a cigarette with steady fingers.
"You might change your minds if you wait. A wire from my
boss in San Francisco would clear things up."

There sounded the clip-clop of a cantering horse's hoofs. It stopped at the hitch rack in front of the store. A young woman came into the room, stopped in the doorway, and swept the scene with inquiring eyes.

X

She was tall, finely built, and startlingly good-looking. She wore high-heeled boots into the tops of which jeans were folded. Her flannel shirt was a large-checked black and red. Around the throat lay loosely knotted a silk bandanna. A Mexican sombrero crowned her black hair.

"What's going on here?" she asked.

Carr answered, slightly drawling the words. "They are deciding when to hang a man—or shoot him, I'm not sure which."

"What man—you?" she demanded.

"Right first guess, miss." He added, "Jeff Carr, the name is."

Her dark eyes rested on him and then swept to Black. "What has he done?"

The curly-haired young man grinned. "Fact is, Mollie, we're not sure whether he is friend or foe. There is a difference of opinion about that."

The bearded man moved forward from the door. "This is man-business, Mollie. We don't want you here," he said impatiently. He was her brother.

Mollie said bluntly, "I'm going to stay, Jim Kenton."

"Get yore shopping done and beat it. This is no place for a woman. If you had a lick of sense you would know it."

She stepped to the bar and leaned against it.

"Don't you hear me?" Kenton stormed. "I'd ought to skin yore back with a quirt."

Her black eyes sparkled. "Before you start, better send for Doc Smith to fix you up afterward," she warned.

Kenton flung up his hands. "What can a fellow do with a sister like this?"

"About a dozen young fellows in the Crows' Nest country could give you an answer to that," Black replied lightly. "Let her stay, Jim. We need a woman to keep us from going too fast."

The young Amazon rested her eyes on Carr again. "Nobody has told me yet what it's all about," she complained.

"We're not sure ourselves," Black replied, and told her all he knew.

"His answers to our questions don't satisfy us," growled Crawley. "We think he came here spying."

"By the look of him you must have been asking your questions with a club," Mollie said dryly. To the prisoner she said bitterly. "Do you have to come here to do your spying? Didn't anybody tell you this is the home of wild savages?"

She whipped the leg of her boot sharply with the quirt dangling from her wrist. Carr thought, *She is a stormy young savage herself, imperious and wilful*.

"I heard plenty about the Crows' Nest at Tomahawk," he told her. "According to the Jackmans your friends here robbed the Sandy Wash stage three times. I didn't believe it. They pulled off the holdups themselves. Because I'm in this country to prove that, I'm marked for death by them. I came up here to find the man who tried to slink out of the room five minutes ago." His finger pointed straight at Bascom. "Why don't you put pressure on him and clear yourselves of the gold robberies?"

The battery of eyes shifted from Carr to Bascom. The man cringed.

"So help me I hadn't a thing to do with the holdups," he pleaded.

"You were riding a horse identified as a mount of one of the robbers," Carr charged.

"That's yore story. It ain't true."

"It's true," Black cut in swiftly. "Dunham looked up your brand and the sorrel carries it." He added, an edge in the soft-spoken words. "I think you're going to begin talking turkey, Mr. Bascom."

"I got nothing to say." The color had drained from Bascom's face.

Black looked up at the rafters. "Get a rope, Fatty," he ordered.

Fatty left the room to get a rope from his saddle.

Mollie's eyes met those of Black. He said to her: "This isn't going to be pretty. You'd better take a walk."

Her gaze shifted to Bascom. He was babbling pleas for mercy and his rubbery legs looked ready to collapse. With a rope around his neck he would talk plenty. There was no stiff will to resist in him.

"I'll stick around," she answered.

"Some things a woman had better not see," Black murmured. "If you would go home—"

"And sit in the kitchen wringing my hands while you and Jim play judge, jury, and hangman," she flung at him scornfully.

Laughter touched his eyes. He spoke so low that only the girl could hear him. "I'll ring one of your hands for you, Mollie. And as for this bird Bascom, you don't need to worry about him. He's no man. Can't you see he's ready to bust out crying?"

"I'm thinking of the other one—Carr."

"I like that guy. He's game. If some of the boys have got notions about him they are not going to pay off. I'll see to that."

Fatty walked in and dropped the looped end of a rope around the neck of Bascom. He flung the other end over a rafter. "All set," he said.

"Don't!" the victim begged. "For God's sake, don't. I'll tell anything you want to know." He fell on his knees.

The story came out brokenly bit by bit. He had known the

Jackmans at Ellsworth when it was a trail-end town and so he had run with them some after they came to Tomahawk. He had not had a thing to do with the first two Sandy Wash stage holdups, but Ranse had talked him into the last one. The other three with him in it were Rudabaugh, Foley, and Linc Jackman. It was Rudabaugh who had shot the gold guard Jim Haley. He, Bascom, had not got a nickel of the treasure taken from the box. It had gone to Tomahawk with the others.

Crawley laughed harshly. "Think up another one, fellow. That won't wash about you not getting yore share. Where is it? We want it."

"He didn't have it with him when we met in the hills," Carr said. "My guess is that he is telling the truth. It is waiting for him at Tomahawk, maybe in the safe at the office of the P. & S."

"In the company's safe?" Mollie cried incredulously.

"That's a shot in the dark," Carr admitted. "Norman Roberts is the company agent at Tomahawk. He is a cousin of the Jackmans. If this is an inside job the finger points at him."

"Is Roberts in cahoots with the gang?" Black inquired of Bascom.

The frightened man said he did not know. His companions had been close-mouthed except when they had been drinking. Rudabaugh had dropped just enough references to the other holdups to let him know they had been implicated.

"One thing I don't get," Black said. "Unless the Jackmans were crowded, why did they jump on us for the guilty parties? It doesn't make sense. We hadn't done them any harm."

Carr mentioned a possible explanation. Ranse Jackman was anxious to supplant Dunham as sheriff. He wanted to make face with the voters. If he put the blame on the Crows' Nest group and Dunham made no move about it he would get the reputation of a do-nothing officer.

A young man with a dark saturnine face spoke for the first time. "All right. We know Bascom is a road agent and a horse thief. Where do we go from here? Me, I'm not so lily-white I'm shocked at what he's done, and I reckon you fellows aren't either. But if we turn him loose he'll run right down to the Jackmans and blab. Maybe that won't hurt us. I don't know."

A glimmer of a plan to use Bascom against the Jackmans had come to Black's mind. "We'll keep Mr. Bascom with us for a while and think this over. And until we're more sure about him we'll hold Mr. Carr too as our guest. Any objections?"

There were no spoken ones and the meeting adjourned on that note.

XI

An open gallery roofed over ran between the two rooms of the log cabin in which Carr was confined. It had been built for a storehouse and had no windows but beneath the eaves were small openings admitting air. The doors were built of heavy whipsawed timber and were padlocked on the outside. Occasionally he could hear Bascom threshing around in the other end of the building.

Jeff's sense of hearing was acute and he made out sounds of activity in the neighborhood. The soft jingle of riders' spurs or the creak of saddle leather reached him at times. Once the bawling of cattle that had been driven hard woke him during the night. He guessed there had been a raid on some ranch. In the darkness coyotes barked from a hilltop.

Except at mealtime he was left alone. Jim Kenton was his jailer and the food he brought was well cooked. Carr guessed that Mollie had prepared it. Probably she was an efficient and capable young woman. Kenton treated him gruffly but not harshly.

On the third day Alec Black substituted for Kenton at dinnertime. Mollie was with him. She carried a small coffee pot and a tin cup.

"An unexpected pleasure," Carr said.

The girl paid no attention to the compliment. "I brought you some coffee," she mentioned.

"Thank you, Miss Kenton," he answered. "You run a fine hotel. The food is so good I can't leave you."

To Black she said, "I don't like smart-alecks."

"Sent to your address, Carr," the young outlaw said with a grin. "I don't agree with Miss Kenton. A guy has to hold his head up and not get down on his marrowbones like Bascom. If you are losing, you still play out your string."

Despite the young woman's hostility Carr was persuaded she had come because she was still worried about the situation. Since she was troubled she was irritable.

"You act like everything is a game," she reproached Black. "He ought never to have come here. Nobody but a fool would have. You know what Rufe Crawley and his crowd want to do to him. If you are chief here why don't you insist on freeing him?"

"I'm no czar, Mollie," he explained. "You know that. I can't ramrod my way through against their wishes."

"You're just top man among a bunch of ruffians," she flung at him hotly. "You must be proud of the honor."

"There are good and bad men here in the Crows' Nest, Mollie. Rufe Crawley is one of the worst."

"And you are one of the good ones." She leered.

Carr guessed that there was a strong attraction between these two and that Mollie fought against it. She resented much of what the community stood for, its lawlessness and turbulence, and she was unhappy that Alec Black was involved in its nefarious riding, as she was that her brother was a part of it.

Black's smile was cynical. "You might call me a good bad man," he suggested. "The influence of a good woman—"

She flung up her hand in an angry gesture and stamped her foot.

The prisoner, in search of information, put out a feeler. "Crawley is still on the prod, I gather."

"He is a crazy *toro* always ready for trouble," Black answered. "We don't want him here."

"Then why don't you have him kicked out?" Mollie cried impatiently. "You know he is a killer wanted for murder. Folks think all of us are like him."

The outlaw ran a hand through his curly hair. It was not easy to explain. "The Crows' Nest is a sort of sanctuary. A hunted man is supposed to be safe here. I can't draw a hard-and-fast line." He turned to Carr. "The fellow suspects everybody. He is afraid some one of us will betray him. His anger against you is largely fear, the thought that you may have come to drag him back to justice. Since a dozen others here are wanted by the law, he gets considerable backing."

Mollie changed the subject abruptly. "I suppose time drags with you," she said to Carr. "Would you like a book to read?"

Jeff was surprised at the offer. Though the room was dark for reading he accepted the suggestion gratefully.

"I'll send it by Jim when he brings your supper," she promised. Her dark eyes held his for a moment. "I don't want to bother unless you mean to read it."

"I'd read even a dictionary if I had one."

Apparently bored by the whole affair, Mollie said shortly, "Let's go, Alec."

Carr's eyes followed them as they left, not without admiration. To back their striking physiques, they were mentally strong, independent, and self-willed. If they married each other, it was unlikely they would find happiness, for both were trapped by evil circumstance. Black had taken the wrong fork of the road and the chances were that he would not turn back. There would be bitter quarrels and eager reconciliations—and in the passing years no peace.

When Kenton brought supper he tossed a book on the cot. "Mollie said she promised you this," he said gruffly.

Carr picked up the book and read the title, *Pilgrim's Progress*. He laid it down unopened. "Please thank her for me," he replied.

"Father used to read it aloud to her when she was a little

girl," Kenton mentioned. "It's a religious book. If you don't like it, let it alone."

"I have read bits of it," Carr replied. "I like it."

After he had eaten, Kenton chained him to the cot as usual.

As soon as his jailer was gone Carr riffled the pages of the book and was not surprised to find a loose slip of paper inside. He struck a match and read what was written on it. The words were:

Late tonight I'll be back.

His heart lifted. There could be only one reason for her to return—to free him. Her brother had the keys both to the door padlock and the one that bound him to the cot. She must mean to wait until Kenton was asleep and get the keys. With luck, if he could lay hold of a horse and find the way through a tangle of gorges, he might escape from the Crows' Nest country.

He had never spent hours that dragged more. On most nights the lights of Jugtown went out before nine o'clock, but this was one of the exceptions when men hung around the bar of the store-saloon and drank. Carr was afraid they were not going home at all, but about half past eleven they trooped out noisily to the hitch rack and galloped in diverse directions from the village.

Unless Mollie had been prevented from coming—and he imagined many reasons why she might have been—it could not be long now. He struck a match and looked at his watch. He would give her fifteen minutes. That surely would be long enough. At the end of what he judged must be a quarter of an hour he checked the time again and found that only five minutes had passed.

At last he heard light footsteps outside. A big key grated in the heavy padlock. The door opened and closed. A dark figure had come into the room. The flare of a match lit Mollie's face as she put the flame to a candle.

She knelt beside the cot and started to unlock the handcuffs around his wrists.

"Won't they guess you freed me?" he asked.

"I'll have to tell them or Jim would be blamed. . . . This key sticks."

"But you'll be in trouble for doing this."

"That's my grief. I can take it. . . . There. I've got it at last."

A tendril of her hair had brushed his cheek. The sweet scent of her young body filled his nostrils. She was risking much for him. He had to crush down the impulse to take her in his arms.

"Can you find your way out of the Crows' Nest?" she asked.

"I don't know. I can try." He quoted her with a grin. "That's my grief. First I have to find a horse."

"I got your horse out of the corral and saddled it. The horse that was stolen. It's tied back of the store."

"You think of everything."

"I want to get you out of the park." She shook her head. "You'd never make it. You would get lost. I'll have to guide you."

He protested that she had done enough. He could not let her do more. Already he was forever in her debt.

"I'm not doing this for you," she told him, almost savagely. "I don't want my brother involved in a murder."

Two horses were tied behind the store. They mounted and she led the way. It was a starless night with clouds hanging heavily in the sky. The darkness closed on them as they rode into the gashed terrain of ravines, pockets, and huddled hills. The girl guided her horse in the black night with a confidence that surprised him. Only once she stopped to make sure which of two branches of a fork to take. They traveled in silence except for the small sounds of wild life occasionally stirring about them.

Her straight flat back in front of him was his guide. He could see from her seat in the saddle that from childhood she had lived much of her life on a horse. He wondered about this girl. She was heady and passionate, but beneath her wildness was a fundamental integrity. Trapped as she was, it was difficult to see how she could escape being mauled by life.

They were following a trail of sorts, probably the one by which stock was driven in to this rustlers' haven. It threaded gulches, crossed steep shoulders, and climbed ridges that he knew must be leading to the rim of the saucer that bounded the Crows' Nest. Mollie drew up at last on a shale ledge that looked down on a gulf of blackness below.

She broke the silence to say, "You're out of our country now and on your own."

"Thanks to you." He was not content to pass out of her orbit with only perfunctory words. Swinging his horse around, he drew alongside of her face to face, their knees touching. "I'll likely never see you again. But you can't make me a stranger to you, not after what you have done for me. You're a grand person, Mollie Kenton. If I were God I would see you had a happy life."

"I am sure I shall have," she said bitterly.

He knew he was on ground where angels fear to tread, but if it was folly he had to risk it. "You hate it here." His arm swept toward the shadowed darkness into which he was about to ride. "Why don't you go down with me into that other world where there is hope and peace—make a clean break tonight?"

For the past two days Carr had been a great deal in her thoughts and inevitably she had compared him with Alec Black. They were much alike, she felt—strong and reckless, with a vein of indomitable gaiety in their make-up. But there was a difference. This man would take through life a straight trail and Alec a crooked one.

She said with a sardonic smile, "There is peace for you in Tomahawk then?"

That she was refusing to consider his question he knew. But there had been no anger in her voice, no sense of outrage at his intrusion into her private life.

"What is it holds you here?" he insisted. "You can do nothing for your brother. He has chosen his way."

"I can do nothing for anybody," she replied wearily.

He guessed of whom she was thinking. "Are you in love with Alec Black?" he asked gently.

"Do I make it plain to everybody?" she cried with a flare of angry pride, "that I want to be the wife of an outlaw?"

"You make it plain that you don't want to be that," he answered.

"I am glad you see it." She flung up a despairing hand. "Yet I shall probably be one. It frightens me."

He had broken through her stiff reserve as nobody had ever done before. She caught him by the lapels of his coat. "You can't do anything for me. Nobody can. But I am glad you tried. You are right. Never again will you be a stranger to me." There was an eager breathlessness in her passionate abandon, the sudden loosing of the distress she had kept locked up in her heart.

Jeff put his arms around her and drew the girl's warm young body to him. Their lips met in a long kiss.

Mollie released herself and looked at him with startled eyes.

"Be careful," she said, so low the words were almost a murmur. "Don't let them kill you."

She wheeled her horse and went clattering down the back trail at a gallop.

XII

Jeff let his mount pick a way down the shale descent through the dark night to the broken country below. In a hill pocket he dismounted and picketed the horse. Until day broke he could not possibly find his bearing in this tricky country of gullies, cliffs, and blind ends.

After he had lit a fire he lay close to it with his saddle for a pillow. It was a long time before sleep came to him. The scudding clouds were disappearing and stars were coming out. He stared up at them, his mind full of the experiences the past few days had brought him.

Women had played a small part of his life, though some of them had taken his fancy lightly. Now in a space of days he had met two who attracted him, women totally unlike in character and background; one gentle, dainty, sheltered all her years by watchful care, the other wild and undisciplined but generous and fine. Both of them were alien to his way of life. He was a lone wolf who traveled alone. Better put them out of his thoughts. He had a job to do that demanded all his attention.

His visit to the Crows' Nest had turned out better than he had a right to hope. He had come out alive after learning to his own satisfaction that the Jackmans were responsible for robbing the P. & S. stage. It was a pity he could not have brought Bascom with him. As yet, he had no evidence that would stand up in court to implicate the gamblers.

Whenever he relaxed his thoughts Mollie Kenton drifted back into them. She kept knocking at the door of his memory. He ought not to have left her with that bunch of ruffians. But what else could he have done? To turn his back on her and ride away after she had done so much for him seemed to him a desertion. She had been in his arms, for that moment at least, and the nearness of her had set his pulses throbbing. Yet that swift excitement was an end and not a beginning.

As soon as light was sifting into the sky he paddled. There was no trail for him to follow, but he knew he must bear to the left and keep heading downhill. His zigzag course brought him at last to a plateau from which he could see the smoke of Tomahawk.

His watch told him it was eight o'clock when he rode down Fort Street and tied in front of Wun Lung's restaurant. As he stepped to the sidewalk he almost ran into Karl Rudabaugh heading for the same place.

The big man stopped, straddling the planks, his beefy face darkening almost to purple.

Jeff said lightly, "Good morning, Mr. Rudabaugh, I hope you are entirely recovered."

Rudabaugh's throat choked. It took him a few seconds to find words, a jumble of threats and oaths.

"You mustn't get excited," Carr warned him. "Full-blooded men like you go off with apoplexy if they aren't careful."

He stepped around the man and into the restaurant, not looking behind him. But when he took a seat it was one facing the door.

Rudabaugh was still there, trying to make up his slow mind what to do. Presently he lumbered away, still fuming and cursing.

Wun Lung came to the table. "Mlistah Ludabaugh mad?" he asked.

"I gather that he is annoyed," the customer answered. "Ham, eggs, sunny side up, flapjacks, and coffee."

For a peaceful guy who likes a quiet life, Jeff thought, *I certainly meet with a lot of tough luck.*

After breakfast he sauntered to his room, intent on a few hours of sleep. Before noon he was awakened by a knock on his door. He reached for the .45 on the small table beside the bed and before he removed the chair propped against the door asked, "Who's there?"

A small voice answered, "Ella Gilson."

He slipped the weapon under his waistband and opened the door. The girl was flushed with embarrassment and her shy eyes fell before his.

"Will you come in?" he asked.

She shook her head. "I—I heard something, while I was waiting on table. I thought you ought to know."

"So you're on my side now," he said, smiling at her.

Color flooded her face. She twisted a handkerchief in her hands. "I must have been crazy when I tried to—to—" the sentence died away.

"You don't think now that I was one of those who killed Jim Haley?"

"I'm sure you weren't. I talked with the corral keeper from Sarasato. You couldn't have been." She continued: "Karl Rudabaugh came in while Ranse Jackman was eating. He was excited and though Mr. Jackman kept telling him to keep his voice down he couldn't. He was threatening to kill you."

"What did Ranse Jackman say to that?"

"He told Karl not to be a fool, that he was making trouble for himself."

"It's nice of you to come and tell me, Miss Gilson. I'm obliged to you. I'll be watching."

He would have been watching anyhow, but he did not tell the girl so. He was grateful for her kindness in coming.

"Better not tell anybody you warned me," he advised. "If it reached Linc Jackman he wouldn't like it."

Again her pretty face flew a color flag. "He pesters me," she said. "I'm afraid of him. He's so—so bossy, like he owned me."

"Keep in mind that he doesn't. Face him down with the truth that you are mistress of your own life and he can't do a thing about it. Just be brave and don't let him bully you."

After she had gone Jeff sat down and wrote out the story of his experiences at the Crows' Nest, omitting the part that Mollie had played in his rescue and stressing the confession of Bascom. This he took to Sheriff Dunham to put in his safe.

"In case I should have an accident," he explained. "Don't forget that nearly a dozen people heard Bascom's confession implicating the Jackman crowd."

"I don't doubt its truth but it would not have much weight in court," the sheriff said. "For two reasons. The witnesses all belong to the Crows' Nest gang and Bascom made the confession with a rope around his neck."

Jeff agreed with him that a jury would give little consideration to such a confession. But he still felt that Bascom was the weak link in the Jackman chain and that through him it might be broken.

"We'll have to move fast," Dunham urged. "If proof of the Jackman guilt isn't found inside of two weeks Ranse will probably be sheriff and in a position to stamp out any evidence of their complicity in the holdups. We're racing against time."

Carr admitted this was true. "Ranse is probably banking on that. Do you think the election will go against you?"

"I'm sunk unless we can tie up Ranse with the stage robberies before election day."

Jeff had been feeling out voters. His guess was that Dunham had sized the situation up correctly.

XIII

On a wooded ridge far above Tomahawk from which they could look down on its toy-sized houses seven horsemen drew up to breathe their mounts. Alec Black gave his men last minute instructions.

"Kenton, you stay here with Bascom and the rest of us will ride into town. In about two hours bring him down. Come in over the hill and down the gulch so as not to be seen. Soon as you reach the gateway of the gulch, slip back up it. Nick will be posted back of the rocks there where he can cover Bascom with a Winchester." Black turned to the prisoner. "You know what you are to do. Go straight to the Capitol and see Ranse Jackman alone. Ask him for your share of the stick-up loot. I don't think he will stall, but if he does, act sore. He'll dig it up. After you have it you will go down to the Maverick corral. I'll be waiting there. Get it?"

"Yeah, sure I get it," Bascom replied sullenly. "If I play your game the Jackmans bump me off and if I stick with them you do."

"Don't try to double-cross us. You'll be watched all the way. If you breathe a word to Ranse you're a dead man. You wouldn't live an hour. Salt that down as certain. Play it right and we'll protect you from the Jackmans. You can throw in with us and ride back to the Crows' Nest guarded."

"And have a rope thrown around my gullet any time one of you gets sore at me," Bascom growled.

"Not if you go through for us today."

Kenton stayed with Bascom on the ridge and the other five filed down a draw to strike a road below. They rode into town in a body and tied at the Nugget opposite the Capitol.

Ranse Jackman, his brother Clem, and Karl Rudabaugh were standing on the sidewalk in front of the gambling house owned by the Jackmans. From across the wide street the two groups glared at each other.

To his brother Ranse said in a low voice from the corner of his mouth. "What in the devil are they doing here? Does this mean trouble?"

Black was dressed in the flash finery of his Mexican costume—silver-spurred custom-made boots, richly decorated sombrero, the finest linen shirt obtainable, over which was a short gold-embroidered jacket of buckskin. He looked like a dashing young Spanish *caballero*. The man was in his most reckless mood, excitement churning in him.

"You're an officer, Ranse," he called out. "And you claim we're stage robbers. You'll never have a better chance to take us—if you have the sand in your craw to do it."

Ranse said coldly, "You're talking nonsense, Alex. I never said you robbed stages. You're free to come and go in this town as you please."

"Nice of you to let us do that after giving it out that we are bandits," Black jeered. "Don't try to rue back from what you said. I might think you a liar."

"Be careful," Ranse warned. "That kind of talk spells trouble."

Black laughed scornfully. "I'm trying to find out if it does. For a guy with the rep of being tough you're taking a good deal. Listen to some more. You're a double-crossing crook tied in with the Sandy Wash stage robberies and trying to shift the blame."

A dozen men from windows, doorways, and behind wagons were listening to this blunt challenge. That Ranse Jackman held back from drawing his .45 surprised them. He was considered a fighting man, steel-cold and hard.

"You must be drunk, Alec," the deputy United States marshal said curtly. "Go away and sleep it off, then if you feel like it come back when you are sober and talk."

"I'm cold sober, Ranse." The intrepid outlaw sauntered from the sidewalk and halfway across the street. "You've asked for trouble. Here it is waiting for you. This thing could run into a lot of killings. But why should it? You and I alone can settle it right now. One of us will go to hell in a wooden box and that will end the difficulty."

"Don't be a fool, Black," Jackman retorted angrily. "I'm a law officer. I don't fight duels on the street. I've put up today with more from you than I ever have from anybody in my life. Take your friends with you and get out of town while there is still time."

"You would like that, wouldn't you? Apparently fighting isn't your game, Ranse. How about that shadow of yours, Rudabaugh? He claims to be a bad man with a string of killings to his credit. Take a chance, Karl. Maybe I'm easier than that tenderfoot who whopped the stuffing out of you and took yore gun from you."

Rudabaugh's face took on a purple hue. His urgent impulse was to drag a revolver out and start blazing, but there was something about the audacity of this young fighting fool that daunted him.

Curbing his fury, Ranse spoke with studied patience. He knew he was losing face, but he was an ambitious man and a street battle with a suspected outlaw could do him no possible good even if he survived it.

"Why go off the deep end and go crazy, Alec," he said reasonably. "There need be no trouble between you and us. When you are in a more peaceful mood we'll talk it over."

"I reckon you know now we're not sitting ducks waiting for you to knock us off, Jackman." Black turned his back contemptuously on his enemies and said to his men, "They are tougher than billy-be-damn but they left their fighting clothes at home today."

From the sidewalk in front of the Capitol came a sound of scuffling. A thick voice cried, "Dammit, lemme go."

Black whirled swiftly, dragging out his revolver. Rudabaugh had his weapon half out of the holster and was trying to wrench free from Ranse Jackman, both of whose hands were fastened to the fellow's thick wrist.

"Not now, Karl," Ranse ordered. "You're playing his game, you lunkhead."

The eyes of Black were bright and shining. "Turn him loose," he snapped. "He was aiming to shoot me in the back. Let's see if he has the nerve to try it when I'm looking."

"Put up your gun, Black," the deputy marshal said severely. "There isn't going to be any fireworks. It was your own fault. You deviled him till he couldn't stand it."

Rudabaugh's rage had spent itself, to the extent at least that his native caution was whispering wisdom to him. If he had killed Black after the outlaw had turned his back not even the influence of the Jackmans could have protected him from the public indignation. With a show of reluctance he let himself be led into the Capitol.

"Why didn't you let me gun him when I had the chance?" he demanded.

Clem Jackman answered him scornfully. "How long would you have lived if you had got Black? His friends would have riddled you at once. You had your chance at him earlier but you didn't take it."

"You had yores too, but I notice you didn't start smoking," Rudabaugh grumbled.

"No use explaining anything to you," Ranse said. "No brains."

The Crows' Nest faction disappeared into the Nugget to celebrate with a drink.

"You sure made 'em climb a tree, Alec," Fatty said jubilantly. "That Ranse Jackman ain't so much. He let you tell him off and took it like he was a kid up before his teacher with a hickory limb."

"Don't get the idea Ranse was scared of me," Black warned. "That guy don't scare. He's got his eyes set on big things and he can't afford to have a difficulty on the street with an outfit like us. Different with Rudabaugh. I thought he had a yellow streak, now I know it certain."

An hour later Black looked at his watch. It was time they got ready for Bascom's arrival. He gave orders where his men were to be posted. They were dispersed in such positions that Bascom would be in sight of one or another of them every minute except when he was in the Capitol with Jackman.

As Black sauntered down the street he met Jeff Carr coming out of the office of the sheriff. The two men grinned at each other.

"You must have a way with the ladies, fellow, to get one to go all out for you when she had never spoken four sentences to you," the outlaw said.

"She was careful to explain to me that she was doing it to keep her friends from becoming guilty of murder," Carr replied. "I hope she didn't get into trouble over helping me."

"The boys were some sore, but what could they do? Mollie doesn't kowtow to any of them." Black chuckled. "Fact is, she laid into them proper for getting notions about terminating your interesting career. There's only one Mollie. I reckon the Lord broke the mold after making her."

Jeff could see that this young scamp was pleased at his escape from the Crows' Nest and proud of Mollie's courage and self-reliance.

"Of course I'm deeply grateful to her," Carr said. "I wish there was something I could do for her in return."

"I'll bet you do." Black looked at him shrewdly from slanted eyes. "But there's not a thing. Closed incident, you might say." He tucked an arm under the elbow of Carr and led him back into the office of the sheriff.

Dunham said casually, "Paying Tomahawk a visit, Alec?"

"That's right," Black answered, a twinkle in his eyes. "A law-abiding citizen helping this country's officers put an end to crime."

He outlined his plan for getting evidence against the Jackmans. If the sheriff would drop down to the Maverick corral he could arrest Bascom with his share of the stage-robbery gold on him. On the spot he could take down the man's confession. After word of this reached the Jackmans the man betraying them would not be safe in the Tomahawk jail. Black proposed to take him back to the Crows' Nest and hold him there until he was needed as a witness at the trial.

The sheriff did not entirely like to release an arrested man to the custody of a bunch of rustlers, but he did not see what else he could do. To put Bascom in jail would be a warning to the Jackmans and they would get busy at once either to free the man or to destroy him.

"There's a lot of question about whether your plan will work," Dunham demurred. "Bascom may blow the whole thing to Ranse. Or maybe the gold will not be handy to give the man. And if he gets it we can't prove it is the same as that stolen from the stage."

"We've got him covered every minute while he is in the open. He won't dare throw in with the Jackmans. Bascom came to town without a nickel. We saw to that. Ranse is sure to give him a roll of bills even if he doesn't give the full amount. Since the only time he is out of our sight is while he is in the Capitol that is the only place he could have got whatever money he has." Black shrugged his shoulders. "Sure, it's no certainty, but we have a better than fifty-fifty chance for it to work."

Dunham closed his desk. "Carr and I will be down at the corral in a few minutes. We had not better go there at the same time as you, Alec. Somebody would go running to the Capitol with the word that we were hobnobbing together and that might upset the applecart."

"Right." Black's face lit to a smile. "Seeing that I am so helpful you will probably want to hire me for a deputy to help run down bad characters."

With that parting shot he left them, walking down the sidewalk as jauntily as if there were springs in the balls of his feet. The sheriff's gaze followed him, a half-smile on the lips of his weather-beaten face.

"Have you heard that half an hour ago Black stood out in the open street and challenged both Ranse Jackman and Karl Rudabaugh to a showdown gun battle? He sure is a wampus cat, a fighter from where they laid the chunk. Too bad he is following a crooked trail. There's a lot of good in him."

"I think so," Carr agreed.

He wondered if there had not been a time in his life when he too, faced with the option of taking the straight or crooked path, had chosen the right one only by the grace of God.

XIV

Shep Bascom tied his mount at the hitch rack in front of the Capitol. His furtive gaze swept around and lit on Fatty leaning against an adobe wall across the street thirty yards farther down. The plump man was rolling a cigarette but his eyes were fixed on the dismounted horseman at the rack. Bascom was so nervous that his hands shook as he made the tie. Whatever he did today would make him enemies. If he got through safely he would light out of the country as soon as he could. The immediate danger came from the Crows' Nest gang. He had to play this out their way or he would be buried tomorrow in Boot Hill. But he did not like any part of it.

He pushed through the swing doors, walked to the bar, and took two swift drinks. They made him feel less jittery and he downed a third. On his way to the small room used as an office he brushed shoulders with Rufe Crawley apparently eyeballing a faro game. The big ruffian showed his teeth in a grin, but one carrying a threat rather than friendliness.

Ranse Jackman looked up as the lank man entered. "I've been expecting you," he said bleakly.

"Thought I'd better lie low for a spell before I came," Bascom said. "How's everything?"

"Rotten," the gambler answered. He was in a vile humor,

still surging with anger at the encounter in front of the building and disturbed because the outlaw had openly charged him with participation in the stage robberies. Black must have been making a shot in the dark, but even though he probably knew nothing it showed there was beginning to be talk involving the Jackmans. Ranse blamed himself for ever having planned the holdups, but at the time it had looked quite safe.

Bascom mopped his perspiring face with a dirty handkerchief. "Dunham's posse mighty near got me," he said plaintively. "Just in time I grabbed a stranger's horse from him."

"I heard about that."

"They got me spotted. Looks like I'd better light outta this neck of the woods sudden."

The dark hard eyes of Jackman rested on the man and appraised his weakness. If he was picked up by Dunham the fellow would probably break down and confess.

"All right. Get out today. Go back to Kansas if that is where you came from. This is no country for men without guts." Jackman opened the safe and took from it a roll of greenbacks. He counted twenty-five hundred dollars in a separate pile and pushed it across the table to Bascom.

"That's your share of the take. What you mean by saying they have you spotted?"

"Two-three fellows saw me with the horse I swapped mine for. I reckon they blabbed to others." He added petulantly, "I dunno why I'm picked on and nobody jumps the others."

Jackman's frowning gaze clamped fast to the man. "Has anybody claimed you were in the holdup? If so, who?"

The nester's shifty eyes slid away. He was talking too much. Panic began to stir in him. He smiled weakly.

"They don't say anything but look kinda funny at the horse. Mebbe I'm just goosy."

"Why didn't you get rid of the horse? Where is it?"

In the eyes of the gambler was a diamond-hard glitter. He looked ready to pounce. Bascom's heart died under his ribs. Carr had ridden the horse to town. Maybe Ranse knew that.

"I dunno where it is," the man pleaded. "I turned it loose on the range."

"After several men had seen you with it. Only a dumb

buzzard head would have kept it that long. I'm through with you. Take the first stage that goes out and keep traveling. Understand—the first."

"Sure, Y'betcha!"

"Go to Karl's cabin and stay hidden till you go," Ranse ordered.

Bascom turned away, greatly relieved. He had taken the first hurdle safely.

As he passed through the big room he saw that Crawley had shifted to the roulette table. The big man's gaze covered him from the moment when he came down from the office until he pushed aside the swing doors in front. Fatty was still lounging against the adobe wall. Only his eyes moved as Bascom walked down the street. Nick took over before the harried man reached the hotel. The rifle had been left somewhere and its owner sat on one of the steps smoking a cigar placidly. None of these men assigned to watch Bascom betrayed any interest in him, but he knew it would be fatal not to walk the straight line set him.

Nick got up, stretched, and at a distance of a dozen yards sauntered down to the Maverick corral after the nester. He was a slim lad with a lean whipcord body who had by some evil wind of chance been driven into outlawry.

In the small corral office Black, Carr, and Sheriff Dunham were waiting. Nick followed Bascom into the room.

"One slabsided guy long as a rail who drags the ground when he walks delivered as per contract," he said cheerfully.

"How did it go, Shep?" Black asked.

Bascom's startled eyes shifted to the sheriff and Carr. The pit of his stomach turned icy. He was going to be turned over to the law and Ranse Jackman would break into the jail and get rid of him inside of twenty-four hours. That must be what these men planned.

"Don't worry, I'm taking care of you," Black said. "You're only a two-spot in this game. We'll keep you safe up at the Crows' Nest. I asked a question. Did you get the *dinero*?"

The trapped man drew the roll of bills out of his pocket and gave them to Black, who flipped them over to see the domination of them before passing the contribution over to the sheriff.

"To live up to my name I ought to hold you up and take them back again," Alec told Dunham with a laugh.

"Ranse gave you this money as your share of the last stage holdup?" the sheriff asked.

Bascom's heavy-lidded pale eyes shifted from one to another. "You-all want me to play yore game, but what do I get out of it but a kick in the face?" he snarled.

Dunham said, "You get a light sentence if you turn state's evidence and help clean up this business. Might be you will get off entirely. Better talk."

"The boys will bump me off certain when they know," Bascom moaned despondently.

But he admitted the money had been given him by Ranse Jackman as his share of the stage robbery. Dunham led him through the whole story, setting down the confession on paper. The prisoner put his name to it and the others present signed as witnesses.

The rest of the Crows' Nest group drifted one by one to the corral. An hour later they took the home trail, Bascom riding with them.

Black turned in the saddle at the corral gate. "Get busy and fasten the stick-ups on the Jackman bunch," he called to Dunham. An imp of mischief danced in his eyes. "It's been a pleasure to serve the country as a deputy sheriff. I hate to give up the job." He finished with a tag of bronco Spanish. *"Tengo mucho dolor. Adios, senores."*

Dunham watched him follow his companions at a canter. Black had an engaging sang-froid. "You can't help liking the scamp," he said. "But I reckon it doesn't give him much grief to start being a rustler again."

"No," Carr agreed. "I'm afraid he will be a miscreant to the end of his trail. I'm sorry. He saved my life when I made that fool trip to the Crows' Nest."

The sheriff looked at the paper in his hand. "This gives

us a start. But that is all. I think we had better keep this confession under our hats for the present. No use warning the Jackmans."

On that point Carr was at one with him.

XV

Norman Roberts was checking waybills when he glanced up to see Jeff Carr walking into the office of the P. & S. Though he had been expecting a visit from the investigator he was disturbed at his coming. Unless Carr suspected him, there seemed no reason for waiting so long to make contact.

While he was introducing himself Carr looked the agent over. He saw a plump bulbous-eyed man with a soft pink face. The bone structure had none of the harsh strength that characterized the Jackmans.

"Glad to see you," Roberts said nervously, his fingers shuffling the papers with which he had been working. "I had a letter from headquarters telling me to expect you."

"And naturally you mentioned it to Ranse Jackman since he is your cousin and a law officer," Carr suggested, drawing up a chair.

The agent fitted the waybills into a neat pile before he looked up and answered. "No, I was told to keep it quiet and of course I did."

"Good. Let us start from the beginning. Tell me all you know about the stage robberies."

"We feel sure the Crows' Nest gang are responsible for them."

"Who do you mean by *we*?" Carr asked blandly.

"Why, Sheriff Dunham and Ranse—most everybody in fact."

"How often were the gold shipments made?"

"It varied. Maybe once a month on the average "

"How do you explain the fact that the Sandy Wash stage was never held up except when it carried gold in the box?" Carr inquired.

"I reckon it just happened that way."

Carr had a different opinion and he said so. The robbers must have had inside information. Outside of three or four men nobody knew when the treasure would be shipped. It was not likely that Jim Haley would invite the bandits to come and kill him or that the mine owner would talk. That left Hank Mains, the coach driver, and one other man.

The pink washed out of Roberts' cheeks. "Are you accusing me, Mr. Carr?" he demanded.

"No. I am trying to narrow the field." Carr's gaze held fast to the other man's face. "You bought a house a few weeks ago and paid three thousand cash for it. Where did you get that money?"

"That's my business."

"It is known you were broke when you came here a year ago. You are paid eighty dollars a month."

The agent's palms sweated. His stomach muscles tied into a knot. "If you must know, Ranse lent me the money."

"And took a mortgage on the place?"

"No mortgage. He knows I'm good for it."

Carr smiled incredulously. "Let's get back to the robberies. Begin at the first one. Don't miss anything."

For an hour Roberts talked and Carr asked questions. Twice men came in on business and the interrogation was dropped until they had gone. Beads of sweat stood on the forehead of the agent. After he had told his story the inquisitor pumped queries at him, going over details again and again. His collar wilted under the attack and he began to contradict himself.

He was still explaining when Linc Jackman walked into the room and said arrogantly, "What's going on here?"

The harassed agent passed the buck to his cousin. "He claims I'm in on the stage robberies, Linc."

Carr corrected this statement. "I don't claim anything yet. I'm trying to find out the facts."

"Clam up, Norm," young Jackman told him sharply. "You don't have to tell this fellow a thing."

"Roberts and I are employees of the P. & S. and we are discussing its business," Carr said quietly. "Our talk is private. Unless you are interested in it personally, Mr. Jackman, your interference is out of order."

"This is a public office. I'll stay here long as I like." Linc's voice took on an ugly rasp. "You were seen walking arm in arm with that scalawag Black this morning. What's yore game? Are you lined up with him to whitewash a bunch of bandits?"

He wants to make trouble, Carr thought. *I had better sidestep it if I can.* To Roberts he said, "I'll be back to talk this over with you again," and rose to leave.

Jackman blocked the doorway. The agent said hurriedly, "Don't start anything here, Linc." His cousin paid no attention to him. He was watching Carr with a thin-lipped cruel smile. His fingers shifted closer to the revolver hanging at his hip.

"Fellow, I've had a bellyful of you. It's you or me." The words were spoken low, almost gently, but there was a cold finality to them.

"I'm not armed," Carr said.

Linc glared at him, his urge to kill trapped by the warning. Rage churned up in him. His fingers, now circling the butt of the .45, tightened till the knuckles grew white. The seconds ticked into eternity while the eyes of the two clamped fast, neither yielding a jot.

"For God's sake, Linc," Roberts cried.

The gunman drew in a long deep breath and expelled it violently. He dragged the gun from its holster and flung it on the counter.

"I'll tear him in two with my hands," he promised savagely. "This I'm going to like." A hot devil of malice flamed in his eyes.

"I'm not looking for trouble," Carr said mildly. "This doesn't make sense—unless you were in the holdups."

"By God, you'll be sorry you said that."

Jackman's body swayed slightly like that of a wild animal crouching for the spring. Watching him intently, Carr took in the broad deep shoulders, the hard muscles that packed the frame, the long reach of limb, and the grim steel-trap mouth. *I'm in for it,* he thought, *if this fellow has learned to use all that lithe power to advantage.*

Jackman had no doubt of the issue. He had been in a dozen rough-and-tumble fights and always emerged top man. Carr did not come within twenty pounds of his weight. He would beat the fellow into a bloody pulp. The assurance of triumph was already written on his face.

Jeff anticipated the attack. He feinted with his left for the body and crashed the right into the gambler's cheek. The man's head went back and struck the door jamb hard. While he was still dazed Carr poured in half a dozen jolting blows to the undefended face. Jackman reached out blindly and his arms closed on the body of his foe, driving Carr back against the round-bellied stove. The weight of the men crashing into it drove the stove from its place and several lengths of sooty pipe fell to the floor.

They rolled over in the wreckage, now one on top and now the other. Linc was still dazed and could not put to use his greater strength to pin down his agile foe. As Carr broke from him to regain his feet the heavy boot of Jackman thudded against his thigh and sent a sharp pain through him. The man's hand shot out, caught Jeff by the ankle, and flung him down again. Carr broke the grip and scrambled out of reach. To his surprise Linc was on his feet almost as quickly as he was.

The big man lowered his head and charged, both arms flailing roundhouse blows. Most of them Carr took on his arms and shoulders, but one of them drove into his cheek and sent him spinning to the wall where he hung for an instant helpless. Jackman dived for him and stumbled over a length of stovepipe, his head hitting the counter.

But he was up almost instantly, shaking his head to clear

it. He charged like a mad bull for his foe. Carr fought back, matching his skill against the other's brute strength. Jackman fought to kill, no science back of his great power. The smaller man knew that to weather these savage attacks he must sidestep, dodge, and use his nimble feet. He must not let Jackman's powerful arms clamp around his body and wear him down by sheer force. He fought warily, landing punishing blows when he could, but using his knowledge of boxing to keep him out of infighting. Jeff could see that the man was tiring. His breath was coming in deep gusts. He had stood in front of too many bars to be in perfect condition.

A hard clean blow to the right eye drove Jackman back. As he passed the counter his arm reached for the weapon lying there and just missed. Carr's fingers found the weapon. An instant later the barrel struck Jackman on the side of the head. The man staggered, folded up, and sank unconscious to the floor.

Carr leaned against the counter panting heavily. He knew it had been a near thing and that luck had been with him.

He said to Roberts: "You saw him reach for the forty-five. Don't forget that."

"You better get out of here," Roberts said, his voice quavering.

"Yes. I'll be back. Don't make any mistake about that." Carr looked at the revolver in his hand, emptied the bullets from the barrel, and laid it back on the counter. The bullets he dropped into his pocket.

He walked stiffly out of the building to the sidewalk and stood beside a water barrel, supporting himself by it. He spat blood from his mouth and with his handkerchief wiped away a thin stream of it running from a cut above the left eyebrow.

Already a crowd was gathering. A man looked into the P. & S. office and cried out, "Goddlemightly, Linc Jackman is dead."

"Just knocked out," Carr corrected. "He wouldn't let me get out without a fight."

His eyes, sweeping the group, came to rest on the face of a girl. Margaret Atherton was standing in the doorway of a store beside her brother. She was staring at his battered face in consternation. He would not soon forget that look of horror. Jeff turned away with no sign of recognition. He could not embarrass her by claiming he knew her, not when he had just come out of a fight and looked the sight he did.

To keep from weaving as he moved down the sidewalk he had to pay attention to each step he took. He had taken a beating and a dozen muscles made him aware of it. His head was dizzy from the fight. But it was important that he carry himself like a victor.

A bearded miner with a dinner pail came down the sidewalk. "You run into a buzz saw, fellow?" he asked.

Jeff answered jauntily, "A panther clawed me."

Margaret in amazement watched him moving down the street, unaware that his light strong stride was an effort of the will. She saw a slight rippling of the muscles in the flat straight back that moved her strangely. To find he had such power to stir her emotionally was disturbing. She knew very little about him, yet, more than once when their eyes had met, a wave of excitement had strummed through her. It was as if he touched her with some electric spark that brought her to life. Yet deep in her heart she knew she could not keep step with this turbulent man who seemed to be always in trouble. He lived outside the world in which she was safely sheltered.

Carr went to his room and stripped. He poured water from the ewer into the basin that sat on a small table and bathed his beaten face and body. In having won the fight he found no pleasure. It decided nothing. Each hostile encounter he had led inevitably to another. He was weary and discouraged, and for the moment felt that he would like to drop out of this unequal struggle, yet knowing he would not do so. To go back to ranch life where nobody hated him would be heaven.

As he lay on the bed the words of a cowboy versemaker he had known floated through his mind.

I can see the cattle grazing o'er the hills at early morn,
I can see the camp fires smoking at the breaking of the dawn,

I can hear the broncos neighing, I can hear the cowboys sing.
I'd like to be in Texas when they round up in the spring.

He fell asleep while the words were still jingling in his drowsy thoughts.

XVI

Ranse Jackman was disturbed at the net of evidence beginning to close in on him. He knew there was not yet enough to convict, but even a cloud of suspicion might be fatal to his plans. The road had looked so plain to him. Already he was the most dominant figure in this part of the territory. With money to support his ambition he could go a long distance. The stage robberies had seemed such a simple easy way to get it.

It was this fellow Carr who was wrecking his schemes. With Dunham he could cope easily enough. But ever since the arrival of the man from San Francisco the breaks had been going against him.

The disappearance of Shep Bascom was one cause of worry. The nester had not turned up at Rudabaugh's cabin nor had he later taken the stage. A checkup had shown that he had not returned to his homestead. Bascom had no iron in his blood. If law officers had got hold of him they could break him to a confession. Moreover, Ranse had observed a strange look in the eyes of two or three men when they turned them on him. It was as if there was a question in them. He could see that Carr's audacity and the results of his fights with

Rudabaugh and Linc Jackman had made the man a sort of hero in the public mind. It was a spot that Ranse himself had held until the past few weeks and his vanity suffered at playing second fiddle.

The problem of getting rid of Carr had become more complex. The man was no longer an unknown stranger in whom nobody had any interest. He was known to be a representative of the P. & S. and the whole town was waiting to find out whether he could discover and convict the bandits who had robbed the stages. If he was killed there must be no evidence pointing to the Jackmans.

It irritated him to see the air of casual ease with which Carr sauntered down Fort Street as if he had not a care in the world. Yet he knew the P. & S. investigator was taking no more chances than was necessary. Nobody saw him downtown at night any more. After dark he must be keeping to his room.

Since Ella Gilson no longer suspected that Carr was implicated in the murder of her lover Jim Haley, he had been eating some of his meals at the Gilson House. This both annoyed and worried Ranse. Knowing his brother Linc's fiery temper, sharpened to a fighting edge by his defeat in the office of the transportation company, he was afraid young Jackman might cut loose in a blaze of anger and kill Carr openly. That would be a mistake. A safer way of getting rid of the man could be arranged.

As Ranse came out from breakfast one morning and stopped on the porch to light his customary cigar he saw Carr sitting in a chair tilted back against the wall. He was talking with some of the old-timers who were in their usual seats absorbing the sun. Ranse stiffened. The lips of his dark bony face tightened to a slit.

He nodded to the old men, his keen arrogant eyes passing over Carr without recognition.

Jeff said pleasantly, his smile slightly ironic, "It's a fine day, Mr. Jackman. I envy you Arizonans. You must find it a pleasure to live here."

The gambler's gaze rested on Carr, a bitter-black threat in them. "Sir, I consider you a worthless scoundrel trying to make trouble," he said spacing the words. "You had the impudence to come into the Capitol yesterday. If you ever enter the place again you will be flung out."

He lit the cigar and walked stiff-backed up the street, a fine figure of a man. Carr understood that the threat ran far deeper than the words in which it had been phrased.

The octogenarian Hank Todd looked at Carr out of faded blue eyes. "It ain't supposed to be safe to devil Ranse Jackman." He mentioned in his high-pitched falsetto voice. "If I was an up-and-comin' young fellow like you, with mebbe a lot of good years ahead of him if he wasn't too rambunctious, I would pick another man to act cock-a-doodle-do with."

"Me too, certain," another oldster contributed. "Fact is, you're pressin' yore luck too far. Right doggone now I'd take a run out from here."

Jeff lowered the front legs of the chair and rose. "Obliged for the advice, but I reckon I'll stick around awhile," he said cheerfully. "Tomahawk is an interesting place with so much going on."

"It's been real quiet lately," Hank Todd commented. "Nary a killing in town for six weeks. That ain't natural. Something will bust loose soon." He gazed meditatively at a dog in the road searching its flank for fleas, and when he spoke it was as if he were talking to himself. "By gravy, come to think of it, I know gents in this town with their thumbs on the hammers of their hardware itching to cut loose on a pilgrim who doesn't know enough to pound sand in a rathole, a young smart-aleck sittin' on an open powder keg with a lighted match in his hand."

"Probably he is a fatalist and thinks his time isn't up yet," Carr replied with a grin.

But the grin was a manufactured one. It was no reflection of any mirth within. As Carr walked up the street he thought, *I'm a hell of a bluff whistling to keep my courage up*. But he knew he was not being what Todd called a smart-aleck. He had a feeling that at the first sign of fear in him his enemies would pounce. One comfortable bit of information buoyed him up. He had yesterday received a letter from his uncle that Billy Mawson was on the way to Tomahawk. Mawson had fought Indians, been a ranger, and later a trail-end town marshal. He had a reputation for courage that made him a notable character all over the West. With this famous gunman to side him the Jackmans would think twice before taking the offensive.

When Jeff Carr reached the P. & S. office prior to the arrival of the stage that afternoon he found several others waiting there, among them Clem Jackman. The man's cold hard eyes met those of Carr, but neither of them spoke. Jeff had come to the conclusion that perhaps Hank Todd was right. There were safer amusements than provoking Jackmans. From the inside of the stage, after it drew up a few minutes later, four passengers emerged. Another one descended from the seat beside the driver. He was a small man, coffee-brown, with a pinched-in hat covering iron-gray hair, somewhere in the late forties. Tiny sun-made wrinkles radiated from the corners of the sharp gray eyes that swept the platform to take in those present. Above the thin upper lip of a closely shut mouth there was a drooping mustache. A well-cut suit covered his wiry frame, but the hallmark of the outdoor Westerner was stamped in the custom-made high-heeled boots.

Clem Jackman recognized Billy Mawson at once. He had known him in Kansas at Dodge and later in Trinidad, Colorado. The Jackmans had never liked him. He was incorruptibly straight and bluntly frank. But they had avoided any conflict with him. He was a quiet, dangerous man. An old-timer had once said of him that he was no trouble-hunter but when it came and sat in his lap he sure welcomed it.

For an instant Jackman wondered what Mawson was doing here and while the thought was still in his mind he found out. Carr had stepped forward to shake hands with him. This was a blow to Clem. He was here for the P. & S. to help ferret out the stage bandits.

Carr and Mawson ate supper together at a small corner table in Wun Lung's restaurant. After they had eaten they sat there for an hour while Jeff related the story of his adventures as a sleuth. The tale was told modestly, but it was startling enough to make the experienced frontier officer guess that in this young man there must be an unusually tough and stubborn grit.

Slanting a searching look at his companion he asked, "Since you knew they were out to get you and probably would, why didn't you high-tail it back to San Francisco?"

"I hadn't finished the job," Jeff said.

"Been most young fellows they would have lit out like a streak of cat in front of a bulldog."

"I've been careful—stayed in nights and stuck to Fort Street where there were plenty of people around."

"Hmp!" snorted Mawson. "You can't protect yoreself against a no-good who wants to shoot you in the back. I reckon I didn't drop in too soon."

"Never was so glad to see anybody, Mr. Mawson," the younger man admitted. "Every time I walked down the street I was afraid a bullet would be sent to my address. It gives you a gone feeling."

"Better call me Billy. My friends do." Mawson's smile warmed Jeff. "Keep in mind that only a fool never fears. You carried on. That's the test."

Jeff learned that his uncle Garfield Carr had become alarmed for his safety and had sent the law man to share whatever danger there might be. Mawson took a room at the Gilson House and there the two discussed the case.

It was Billy's opinion that Ranse Jackman was getting worried. Otherwise he and his followers would not have shown such open and active hostility to Carr. There must be weak links in their chain of defense. Shep Bascom was an important one. When the showdown came his testimony would be damning. With enough pressure put on them Foley or Roberts might weaken and turn state's evidence. But before they would do that more outside proof of guilt must be found. Carr had unearthed the fact that Karl Rudabaugh and Linc Jackman had been out of town at the time of the latest stage robbery. They were supposed to have been on a hunting trip in the hills. Their absence from Tomahawk did not of course tie them up with the crime. Half the men in town were big-game hunters.

Mawson and Carr called on Mains, the stage driver, at his

home. He and Mawson talked over old days when the Apaches were raiding the ranches, but when the conversation shifted to the gold thefts Mains became entirely non-committal. If he had any suspicion of who the guilty men were he kept it to himself. His position made him vulnerable. He did not want to be shot down next time masked men stopped the Sandy Wash stage.

The investigators looked up all the residents of the town who had been on any of the robbed stages. Some of these were loudly vocal in complaints of the law's inefficiency but none offered any opinion as to who the road agents had been, except to mention vaguely the Crows' Nest gang.

Carr recalled a suggestion Dunham had made that he talk with Luke Kasford, a cattleman on whose range two of the holdups had taken place. He and Mawson rode out to the man's ranch on Lodgepole Creek.

Kasford was a florid heavily built man in middle life with the reputation of never having branded a calf that was not his own. He was a blunt plain-spoken Westerner who had fought Indians and later rustlers. Strongly individual, he did not like the way the Jackmans ran Tomahawk and was frank to say so. As to the stage robberies he had no information personally, but one of his older cowboys had mentioned seeing four men riding across a hill shoulder an hour after the second holdup. He had chanced to mention this to Kasford the evening of that day, but after hearing of the robbery he had clammed up and said nothing.

At Carr's request the ranchman sent for the range rider. Hod Hooper was a bowlegged old-timer in shiny chaps and run-down-at-the-heel boots. His leathery face was wrinkled as a shrunken winter pippin.

When introduced to Mawson his faded eyes opened wide with interest. "Pleased to meetcha," he said. "I've sure heard tell plenty about you." One glance at Carr was enough for him. His attention centered on the celebrity.

But when he learned what they wanted of him he retreated within himself. Sure, he had seen four men on horseback at a distance but that did not mean a thing. They did not have to be bandits, did they?

Mawson conceded that. The point was that they might be. Were they riding toward Tomahawk or in the other direction? Reluctantly Hod explained that at the top of the ridge the party had split. Three of them turned townward, the other headed for the hills.

"How close were you to them?" Carr asked.

Hod Hooper looked him over with distaste. "Mebbe as far as you might be to get a good shot at a buck." He added doggedly: "I'm not talkin'. Onct I knew a man who lived to be a hundred minding his own business."

Carr decided it would be better to let Mawson handle this character. The ex-marshal went at the questioning more adroitly. He said it was good judgment not to shoot off one's mouth foolishly. In this case there was no risk. Very likely the men were a group of hunters. But an officer had to ask a lot of routine questions that led nowhere. It was just possible one of these hunters might have run into the escaping outlaws. Had Hooper recognized any of them? He could talk freely, since his name would not be divulged as the source of information.

Hod surrendered, not without misgiving. "One of them was a fellow I've seen around town named Foley. I had a good look at him because he stopped to tighten his saddle cinch. The others were in the brush mostly and I wouldn't know who they were."

"Good," Mawson said. "We'll ask Foley if they ran into any fellows that might have been the men we want. By the way, could these hunters have recognized you?"

"No. They never looked my way."

"That's fine. Smart of you not to talk, Hod. Better still keep it under yore hate. We'll do the same."

"I'd be obliged," Hod admitted. "I aim to keep outa trouble when I can."

Jeff thought, as he and his friend turned their backs on the ranch steading, that Hod had put his finger on the reason why men like the Jackmans could dominate a town. Good citizens wanted to keep out of trouble and as a consequence strong scoundrels ruled the roost. He had met some men who were not like that. Mawson was one. He accepted the obli-

gation to fight against evil regardless of the danger into which
it took him. The force of these individuals looked out of their
eyes. Cool eyes, quiet, level, and steady, flinging no flags
of flurry but always sure and dependable. Eyes that could be
hard and steely, or frank and kind, with a promise in them
that their owners, if they are your friends, will ride hard for
you, risk much, take on your trouble as theirs to a fighting
finish. Many riders of the open range must be like that, he
felt.

On the way back to town they looked down from a ridge
on the windmills of the L Lazy C. The home buildings lay
back of a spur and could not be seen. Carr suggested they
make a detour and drop in at the ranch house. A young lady
there had been on the stage at the latest robbery.

He knew she had nothing to tell that had not already been
told. His mind had been made up to stay away from her. This
girl could be no part of his life. Yet he was weakly going
back to the ranch because he felt he must see her again. Her
effect on him was strange. She was the heart of that romantic
country where youth dwells only in dreams. The memory of
her voice was like that of low far church bells in the early
morning. The sound of it was music he could not forget.

They rode into a deserted yard. Evidently all the men were
away at work. From inside the house came the soft notes of
a piano and a young warm voice. Margaret Atherton was
singing to herself that most haunting of tender Scottish songs:

> Will ye no' come back again?
> Will ye no' come back again?
> Better lo'ed ye'll never be,
> Will ye no' come back again?

She must have heard their footsteps on the porch, for she
came to the door to meet them. At sight of Jeff color ran into
her cheeks. Her eyes grew wide with surprise. They were
shy as wild violets.

"My brother is not at home," she said.

Carr introduced Mawson and explained that he was as-
sisting in the stage-robbery cases and would like to talk with

her. She took them into the living room. Already she had regained her composure. The outlines of the small pointed breasts rose and fell evenly. She had withdrawn and built a wall between herself and Jeff. No matter how rebellious her heart might be he was to remain an outsider. She did not pass judgment on him. But he lived a life violent and tumultuous. His code and hers were miles apart. She could not possibly keep step with him. In the darkness of a sleepless night she had come to realize this, and gentle though she was, the girl had the stiff courage of her class and race. No clamorous protest from within would move her.

Jeff shook hands with her when they left. He read her decision in the girl's eyes and he approved it even though his desire resisted. She could never be anything more than a dream to him, yet there would be moments in distant years when his heart would turn back to her. He was surprised at the swiftness of her renunciation, the decisiveness with which she had cut him out of her life. Though there had been no word of love between them, a strong and exciting impulse had drawn them to each other. Because this threatened the quiet and orderly existence in which she was fitted to move she had turned her back on it. Perhaps this was a part of her national and social heritage, to decide her future by common sense rather than by the urge of emotional disturbance. She would marry somebody from her own group, probably Harold Haddon.

XVII

Before Jeff Carr and Billy Mawson reached Tomahawk they had decided to force the hand of the Jackmans by arresting Cad Foley. Ranse would be driven to make a move. He could not remain inactive while they worked on Foley until he perhaps broke under the strain. Uncertain how much evidence they had gathered, Ranse could not be sure the trap was not about to close on him. He would strike swiftly and hard.

Dunham swore the two P. & S. agents in as deputy sheriffs. He offered to make the arrest himself, but Carr thought it would look better not to have him dragged in as a partisan. It would be his job to hold the prisoner after he was in jail.

"If I can." The sheriff followed this by an understatement. "Ranse isn't going to like Foley's arrest."

"No," Carr answered. "He'll be a worried man. My guess is that he'll do something about it."

The morning sun was high in the heavens when Carr and Mawson walked down to the cabin by the *acequia* where Foley lived. Both the men who stayed there were night owls and rose late. Smoke was just beginning to rise from the chimney.

"Looks like we're going to interrupt somebody's breakfast," Mawson said.

At Carr's knock Foley came to the door, a frying pan in his hand. The man's startled gaze slid from one to the other. He tried to slam the door shut but Carr's foot blocked it.

"What you want?" he asked shrilly, backing into the room.

The officers followed. Neither of them had drawn a pistol. Rudabaugh came up from the bed where he had been lying, a roar of anger barking from his throat. On the way up his hand had found a revolver lying under a pillow.

"Easy does it," Mawson advised, his fingers shifting to the holstered weapon at his side. His stern eyes gimleted into those of the huge ruffian. "It's Foley we want. Your turn comes later."

His voice was low and even, but Rudabaugh did not make the mistake of missing the steely threat in it. Mawson's reputation daunted him. It was said that no man in the West had a swifter draw or a more deadly aim than this frontiersman who had survived a score of gun battles. Rudabaugh glared at him angrily. His hand still clutched the butt of the .45 but he did not raise it from his side. The desire to fling a bullet into this little officer was urgent, yet the will was paralyzed. It could not send the message to the arm hanging down at full length. He faced Mawson while the seconds ticked away, and in the end it was *his* eyes that gave way.

"You got no business here," he growled.

"I'll take yore gun," Mawson said quietly. He moved closer and held out his left hand. The right thumb was hitched in his belt close to the butt of the weapon resting there. "Don't make a mistake."

Rudabaugh was tempted to take a chance. With the small man's gun still holstered the advantage lay with him. But the eye too can be a prince of deadly weapons and Mawson's gaze was fixed on him. The ruffian had not the stark nerve to try a showdown. He passed his weapon to the officer, covering his surrender with words to save face. "I ain't lookin' for trouble," he snarled. "Don't get the idea you've bluffed me."

"What you want with me?" Foley wanted to know sulkily. "I ain't done nothing."

"Were arresting you for holding up the Sandy Wash stage," Carr said.

"Nothing to that," Rudabaugh blurted. "He was with me here when it was robbed."

"All three times?" Carr inquired.

"That's right," the big man answered, his voice heavy and bullying.

"With you, but not in the cabin," Carr corrected. "When we first met in the hills you were hell-bent on hanging me then and there. I couldn't understand your eagerness but I do now. You wanted to take the pressure off yourself. If people felt I was guilty they wouldn't look your way."

"That's a lie," Rudabaugh exploded.

"You'll get a chance to prove it at your trial," Carr told him. "It won't be long now. This will be harder on you than the others, since you were the one who killed Jim Haley."

The big ruffian glowered at him. Back of his rage crowded fear. How did Car know he was one of the robbers, let alone the man who had killed Haley? Somebody must have put the finger on him, either one of his partners in crime or a passenger on the stage. Unless Mains had identified him and talked. A wave of alarm washed through him. The others in the affair would get only penitentiary sentences but he would be hanged.

"You've got me wrong," he protested, and turned to Mawson. "This fellow is trying to frame me. He lay in wait and shot me first chance he got after Dunham turned him loose. He's sore at me because I helped arrest him."

"Tell that to the jury when the time comes," the ex-ranger told him scornfully. "We'll be after you soon, but not just yet. Foley today, you tomorrow."

Clem Jackman met the deputies and their prisoner on Fort Street headed for the jail. He held the middle of the sidewalk, to fling a question at Foley. "What does this mean?"

"They're arresting me," Foley cried, his voice high and thin. "Claim I was in the Sandy Wash holdups. Tell 'em there's nothing to that, Clem. Make 'em turn me loose."

"First place, what right you got to arrest anybody?" Clem demanded of Mawson.

Billy pushed back his coat and showed a marshal's star. "Regularly appointed deputies of Sheriff Dunham," he explained.

"What evidence have you against this man?"

"Considerable," Mawson mentioned mildly. "You'll hear it at the proper time."

There was a rawhide toughness about this Jackman. He did not take water for anybody but he was no fighting fool to rush in without considering the consequences. If he started trouble now he would put himself in the wrong. Better consult with Ranse and fix up a plan of attack.

"You can't get away with this," he told Mawson curtly.

"Meaning that we can't arrest him?" the former ranger asked blandly.

"Meaning that this is a frame-up," Jackman retorted. "You are in bad company, Billy. This man Carr, if that is his name, is tied up with the Crows' Nest gang. He is one of the stage bandits, a chum of Alec Black, and he's busting a trace to shift the blame on us. I'm surprised that a man of your reputation would fall for his game. He's just got back from the roost where the scoundrels hang out—came in to town riding the same horse he claimed one of the robbers took from him. That proves he is one of the gang. How else could he have got hold of the horse?"

Carr was surprised at Jackman's knowledge of his movements. The only explanation was that the gamblers had a spy in the Crows' Nest, somebody who within the past few hours had reached town with a report. This meant that the Jackmans knew Shep Bascom was a prisoner of the rustlers and had made a confession. The cards were down on the table now and a showdown was imminent.

"I'm under orders, Clem," Mawson replied quietly. "Better talk this over with Dunham. If you can convince him you are right no doubt he will release Foley. I don't think you can. My opinion is that this man is one of the gold bandits."

"We'll talk nothing over with Dunham. He's up to his neck in this conspiracy." The gambler's words grated harshly. "Get this right, Mawson. Hell is going to break loose in Georgia. We'll not take this lying down. Keep out of it. You'd be backing a bunch of outlaws. No honest man walks in to help the wrong side knowingly."

"I'm already in, on the right side."

"Then throw in yore cards. This isn't yore fight."

Mawson's voice was still low, almost gentle. "You ought to know me better than that, Clem. I never look for a fight, but I don't run away from one forced on me."

"Don't say I didn't warn you." Jackman turned to Foley. "Keep yore mouth shut, Cad. They'll twist everything you say. Talk, and you'll land up framed in the penitentiary. They're out to get you. Don't let them scare you. We'll take care of you all right."

Jackman brushed past them, not stepping from the sidewalk but shouldering Carr out of his way.

"A nice-mannered gent," Carr said.

Mawson nodded, but he did not smile. He knew that nothing could stop bloodshed now. There would be sniping from ambush, the hammering of guns at night, perhaps a mass battle on the street. He did not like the prospect. Since the Jackmans were both desperate and ruthless the advantage would lie with them. The sheriff's forces had to wait until they were attacked and their enemies would surely set the scenes for battle to suit themselves. It was a pattern in which he had become involved several times during his official career and it still amazed him that he was alive.

That Clem Jackman had met them turned out to be unfortunate. Buoyed up by his promise, Foley refused to talk except for repeated assurances of innocence. He had not taken part in any of the stage robberies. If anybody claimed he had been seen on Kasford's range the day of the holdup he was a liar or else mistaken. Nothing Bascom said counted since he was one of the Crows' Nest gang and probably one of those who rode from there to rob the stage. It was an outrage to arrest a decent citizen such as he was and try to shift the guilt to him from a bunch of bandits. They were trying to railroad him to prison.

The grilling went on for an hour before Dunham gave it up. Foley was confident Ranse Jackman would get him out of jail and as long as he was buoyed up by that hope he would confess nothing.

"Arresting me won't get you a thing," Foley boasted. "Soon as Judge Silliman gets back from his hunting trip tonight he'll let me out on bail."

That was probably true. Dunham consulted with his two new deputies and they decided it was better to get Foley out of town. As soon as it was dark Carr and Mawson took him by way of a back alley from the jail. Foley was alarmed. He wanted to know what they were going to do with him.

"We're taking you where you will be safe," Carr told him.

They rode up Lodgepole Creek to a deserted cabin in the hills back of Kasford's ranch. A pack horse carried supplies. Carr stayed with the prisoner. At the end of forty-eight hours he was to be relieved by Mawson or another deputy sheriff. On the way back to town Mawson dropped in to see Kasford. He wanted the ranchman to keep his riders away from the terrain of the hide-out as well as he could. If any of them discovered the cabin was occupied, curiosity would take the man into the hill pocket to see who was there. The ranchman promised not to have that part of the range combed for several days. Hemmed in by the hills, the cattle would not get far from their usual range.

On the road to town Mawson passed Judge Silliman returning from his hunting trip. He rode straight to the jail and found Dunham waiting there.

"We have Foley safe in the hills," he told the sheriff. "Better you shouldn't know just where he's cached."

Dunham agreed to that. At best he was in an awkward position. Since Silliman was a Jackman adherent he would undoubtedly give an order for Foley's release on bond. Any explanation of the prisoner's absence would be unacceptable to the Jackmans.

Ranse and his two brothers reached the jail half an hour after Mawson. They brought with them an order of the judge for freeing Foley.

Dunham read it. "Sorry," he said. "I turned him loose an hour ago. He got a horse and rode out of town. Looked to me like he was scared."

The Jackmans did not accept this story. Why had Dunham turned him loose—if he had? The sheriff explained that the evidence was not very strong.

"Don't believe a word of it," Linc cried. "I'm going to look this jail over from top to bottom."

"All right with me," Dunham agreed.

Ten minutes later they returned to the reception room. No sign of Foley had been seen. The brothers were furious.

"You can't get away with this shenanigan," Ranse said angrily. "You've got Cad hidden somewhere. You're going to tell me where."

"I don't know where he is. All I know is that he started out of town on horseback."

"Alone?"

The sheriff shook his head. "No information on that point."

Clem turned on Mawson, who was sitting on a tilted chair with his feet on the desk. "You're at the bottom of this, Billy. You and that fellow Carr. You know where Foley is."

"My guess is that he has ridden into the hills somewhere. He didn't like the setup here. Afraid we would have enough to put him in the penitentiary."

"That won't wash," Linc broke in. "He would have come straight to us. Come to that, why would you arrest him and then turn him loose?"

"He put up a real good talk claiming he was innocent," Dunham explained. "I figure we had better let him go. If he sticks around here we can pick him up again when we need him."

"It's a damned lie," Linc exploded. "And you both know it. Where's that fellow Carr? I'll tell you where he is—riding herd on Cad."

"That's only an opinion," Mawson said quietly. "I daresay Jeff is in bed sleeping peacefully. No need to get excited about this. Foley will probably pop up one of these days."

Ranse turned on Mawson, a wicked fury burning in his eyes. He chose his words carefully, keeping his voice low and hard. "Billy, I've known you a long time. We've never tangled. Unless you ask for it we don't have to now. But if you side with this damn interfering scoundrel Carr, you've got a fight on your hands. You're tough, and luck has ridden on your shoulder. But a man's luck runs out. Sure as God made little apples we'll send you to hell on a shutter."

"It might be that way," Mawson admitted, a little wearily. "You throw a long shadow, Ranse, but I think your arrogance will destroy you someday. Law is coming to this territory.

You can't stop it. No man can. Anybody who tries it will be swept away. This isn't a fight between you and Carr—or you and me. It's bigger than that. We three are two-spots in a struggle that will go on until this country is a place as free of bandits as Ohio or Connecticut. Your kind can't win."

"You'll never live to find that out," Ranse flung at him.

The Jackmans strode out of the room, a trio of big rangy men being driven against their will to battle and bloodshed as a result of the evil they had themselves set in motion.

They had one ace in the hole they were not discounting. Inside of three days Ranse would be sheriff of the county. He could use not only the Jackman power but his official authority to nullify the evidence against them.

"We ought to have gunned them right there," Linc cried violently. "We do nothing but talk while they drag the net closer around us."

"Keep your shirt on, boy," Clem advised him. "The fireworks will begin soon enough. Don't think because Mawson sat there easy and cool he wasn't watching us every second. If we had started anything probably all five of us would have been shot into rag dolls."

Ranse nodded agreement, and added: "We've got to make this look good, Linc. Until after the election we don't want trouble."

Carr and Mawson too had it in mind that Tuesday was election day. The county was not organized into voting districts and the most important polling place was at Tomahawk. A good many of the cattlemen and their riders did not trouble to come fifteen or twenty miles to vote, with the result that the ballots cast in the town usually decided which ticket was victorious. The killing of Jim Haley, taken with the fact that Dunham had not brought home the crime to anybody, had greatly hurt the chances of the incumbent for re-election. To make public the evidence that implicated the Jackmans in the stage holdups might still save the day.

Six days before the election Carr had written a letter to Alec Black asking him to come down to Tomahawk bringing Shep Bascom with him. The confession had been printed for distribution, but unless Shep was present to acknowledge it

as genuine the charge against the Jackmans would be de-
nounced as a lying campaign trick. Dunham was holding the
circulars to be distributed the day before the voting. They
had not yet heard from Black and were beginning to get
uneasy.

XVIII

Mail for the Crows' Nest was left twice a week at a crossroads' box outside the park, but since the place was a pocket
in the mountains far from the world's activities the letters and
papers were sometimes not picked up for several days.

The afternoon before the election Mollie Kenton collected
from the box enough letters and newspapers for those living
in the Nest to fill both sides of her saddlebags. She was taking
in two deliveries, since nobody had been to the crossroads
to get the earlier one.

When she reached Jugtown she found that Alec Black and
young Nick Sampson had just tied at the store hitch rack.
For Black there was a letter in addition to three newspapers.
He ripped open the letter, read it, and handed it to Mollie.

"Too bad we didn't pick this up Friday," he said.

The letter was from Carr and had been written five days
earlier.

"Maybe it is not too late now," Mollie suggested. "We
could start early tomorrow morning and get to Tomahawk by
noon."

"You inviting yoreself to join the party?" he drawled.

"Yes. I've been meaning to go down for weeks. I want to
buy some dress goods."

"Good," he grinned. "You'll be well chaperoned. Jim will want to go, and several of the other lads. While there, we can give Dunham half a dozen votes."

"I'm in," Nick announced. "Might be some fun. You never can tell."

They left before sunup. One member of the group pleaded in vain to be left at Crows' Nest. Shep Bascom did not want to go to Tomahawk. The Jackmans would be furious at him.

"You got my signed confession. Ain't that enough? They'll get me sure."

Black promised he would be well guarded. At no time would he be without the protection of at least two of them.

The darkness lifted before they got out of the Crows' Nest, but it was noon before they saw the huddled houses of Tomahawk below them. The party dropped down into town, tied at the rack in front of the Gilson House, and ate dinner there. Nick Sampson, before eating, went to the sheriff's office with word of their arrival.

"Afraid you got here too late," Dunham said. "We couldn't wait any longer and yesterday afternoon distributed the printed copies of Bascom's confession. Ranse Jackman had an answer run off on the *Blade* press. He claimed the confession was a fraud and challenged me to produce Bascom to prove it. Last night he called a mass meeting and talked for an hour. Nearly all the town votes have been cast, the majority of them against me. Why didn't Alec get here earlier?"

Nick explained that Carr's letter had been lying in the mailbox uncollected until yesterday afternoon. He left to return to the hotel.

As usual on election day there had been a good deal of drinking. There was excitement in the town, jubilation on the part of the Jackman adherents, a feeling of defeat among those of the opposite faction.

Out of a saloon came Rudabaugh, at his heels two other hard-looking men. He straddled along the sidewalk, stopping when he met Nick. His bad teeth showed in a grin.

"If you came to vote for Dunham it's too late," he jeered.

"Ranse has got him beat two to one. Fork yore broncs and go home."

"We'll go when we get ready," Nick retorted curtly. "Don't get on the prod with me, Karl."

Rudabaugh glared at him, a curly-headed slim young fellow hardly out of his teens. He looked like a safe victim to bully. The big man had been drinking and he felt like throwing his weight around before the two gunmen recently imported by the Jackmans.

"Talk back to me and I'll knock yore head off, you little squirt," Rudabaugh stormed.

Nick Sampson counted himself a full-grown man. He had been in tight places more than once and fought his way out of them. Partly because of his youth he would not give an inch.

"You damned rhinoceros, I'm the same size as you back of a forty-five," he said hardily. "If you're lookin' for trouble you've found it."

The men behind Rudabaugh moved a little to one side. If bullets were going to start drilling they did not want to be in the path of one. This was Karl's fight, not theirs. Neither of them had ever seen this cocky young fellow before.

Light footsteps sounded on the plank walk. Jefferson Carr stood beside Sampson. Coming toward the scene, he had heard enough to guess this quarrel might flare to a killing. Nick's stand, entirely unexpected by the bad man, put the decision squarely up to the fellow. He could see that Rudabaugh, who looked as though he had been drinking a good deal, was taken aback by the challenge.

"Nice to meet you again, Nick," spoke up Jeff genially. "Come to town to see the elephant?"

Nick laughed. "Sure. I've done met one pachyderm." He explained the meaning of the word to Rudabaugh. "There was a picture of one in my school geography. Seems it is a two-ton animal with a thick hide and a hell of a roar."

Jeff tucked an arm under the elbow of Sampson. "If you're heading for dinner at the Gilson I'll trail along with you," he said.

"That's up to Mr. Rudabaugh," Nick replied. "He has first call on my time just now."

The big man had made up his mind. He waved an arm in an angry gesture of dismissal. "Get away from here or I'll send you to hell."

"We'd better go," Carr said. "He doesn't want us around."

They moved down the street as casually as if Rudabaugh did not exist. If it had been night they would have been more careful, but they felt pretty sure that in the light of day he would not dare to shoot them openly in the back."

"How did it start?" Carr asked.

"He began in his bully-puss way to run on me. I don't take that from anybody. But I'm glad you showed up right then."

They walked into the Gilson House dining room. The Crows' Nest party were at one large table. There were two vacant seats. One of them was next to Mollie Kenton. On the other side of her Alec Black sat.

She looked up at Jeff, her dark eyes glowing. She was a woman strong and muscular, one who had ridden fractious horses and roped wild cattle. This had only sharpened and not coarsened her feminine grace. He liked what he saw, a beautiful body slenderly full, a mouth generous, a proud face with lovely planes tanned by Arizona suns. There was in her courage and integrity, and back of her reticence he sensed a nature richly emotional, waiting deeply hidden until the right man stirred it to life. As he sat down he wondered resentfully if that man was Alec Black.

They talked of the ride down, of the election, of trivial things that occurred to them, but both of them thought of that wild moment when they had clung to each other in a long parting kiss. Beneath the tan, warm color ran into her cheeks.

At a smaller table across the room Clem and Linc Jackman sat. There were others present and they watched with strained attention, for it was common knowledge now that the battle lines were drawn between the rustlers of the Crows' Nest and the gamblers who ran the town. Not until the brothers rose to leave did they pay any obvious attention to their enemies. Clem would have passed the large table without stopping but Linc drew up at Black's chair.

"Brought quite an army down with you, Alec," he suggested. "Going to vote for our new sheriff, I reckon."

"We're going to vote for Dunham," Black answered. "No objections I hope."

"Too bad," Linc jeered. "You'll be throwing yore votes away, looks like. But naturally you would vote for a man you can handle."

"We don't support those who spread lies about us, if that's what you mean," Black replied, a touch of hard temper moving in him.

Clem pointed at Shep Bascom, who was sitting unhappily at the foot of the table. "If it's not to tell lies against us, what are you bringing that double-crossing skunk with you for?" he demanded.

Black said, his voice icily low, "I don't like the way you talk. You wouldn't want to make anything of that, would you?"

"Like it or lump it, I don't care which," Clem tossed at him and strode out of the room.

Linc followed reluctantly.

"What Linc says is true," Carr said. "We've lost the election. His brother will win easily."

"Because we didn't get your letter in time," Mollie regretted.

"It might have turned the tide if Bascom had been here earlier," Carr answered. "Then it might not. People are slow to believe that the Jackmans are thieves, even those who don't like them."

"They would rather believe it of us, seeing that we're already dogs with a bad name," Black agreed jauntily.

Mollie's level gaze met his, judgment in her eyes. "Are you proud of that reputation?" she asked quietly.

Alec Black considered that, smiling at her. "Can't say I am. I'll put it this way. If a man amount to a damn there is some hell in him. He'd better get it out of his system while he's young, then settle down with a good wife to grow up with the country."

Mollie did not comment on his reply. Her long look fell

away from his. When she spoke it was to Carr. "Will it matter a great deal if Ranse Jackman is elected?"

"It will give him official standing," Carr explained. "He will represent law. Billy Mawson and I will be made to seem trouble-hunters and criminals. I don't think it will save him in the end."

Black pushed back his chair. He said, light irony in his voice, "If the hungry men are fed we'll go to the polling place and do our duty by voting for good government to stamp out crime."

His followers paid for their dinners and trooped out of the room. Bascom hung back. He did not want to go and face the anger of the Jackmans. The fingers of Jim Kenton closed around his arm.

"You don't want to stop here alone, Shep," he warned. "That would not be safe."

Carr later remembered the haunted eyes of the poor wretch. The terror in them cried louder than words that there was no safety for him anywhere.

Alec Black lingered for a word of advice to Millie. "Stay in the hotel till I get back, then I'll take you shopping. The town is kinda excited today. I wouldn't want you on Fort Street without me to side you."

He followed the others to the hitch rack where they were mounting. It was not more than two hundred and fifty yards to the polling place, but like all riders of the range they made it a habit never to walk anywhere that they could ride.

Mollie watched Black, frowning. She was nettled at his proprietary manner. It took too much for granted. She was an independent self-sufficient girl.

"I'll do my shopping now," she said, more to herself than to Carr.

He walked beside her on the plank walk. Black's advice had been good even if the phrasing of it had been unfortunate. There were a lot of roughs on the street, many of them inflamed by liquor. The bar at the Capitol had been offering free drinks all day.

Not fifty paces in front of them the Crows' Nest group rode slowly along the dusty road, Black and Kenton in front.

They were in pairs, Rufe Crawley in the middle beside Bascom. The couple walking behind them kept pace with the mounted party.

"Will there be trouble today?" Mollie asked.

"Hard to say. Ranse Jackman has imported half a dozen gunmen, but I don't think he will start anything until he has been certified as sheriff. When you have done your shopping I would stay in the hotel if I were you. The Jackman crowd are full of cock-a-doodle-do and you know how hot tempered Alec is."

"He's the most reckless man alive, but he promised me to stay out of a fight if he could."

Carr glanced at her troubled face. He thought it was a tragic thing that the happiness of so fine a girl should be tied up with the fat of a scamp like Alec Black. It was borne in on him that her splendid physique reflected her unhampered love of living. Her long trim legs moved with the smooth animal vigor of one who had grown up among the hilltops in the wind and the sun.

The sound of a shot rocketing up the street startled them. One of the Crows' Nest riders collapsed in the saddle. His body fell forward and for a moment his hands clung to the horn, then his grip loosened and he began to slide down. He plowed head first into the dust of the road and lay there motionless.

"It's Shep Bascom," Jeff cried. "They've got him."

He expected a volley to follow the first shot but none came. The riders swung from their saddles and backed to the other side of the street, the mounts in a half-circle in front of them. A window in the Palace Saloon crashed. One of the dismounted horsemen had fired at the spot from which Bascom had been ambushed. With Black leading them the rustlers charged across the road into the Palace.

Carr turned to the girl. "Get back to the hotel—quick. I've got work to do."

The girl said, "Bascom?"

"He's dead. We can't do anything for him. Please go." His eyes were urgent.

Inside the Palace guns hammered. Mollie had a foolish

wish to run to the scene and order men to stop firing but she did not give way to it She nodded at Carr and without a word started back to the hotel

Jeff raced up the street, stopped a moment to make sure Bascom was dead, and glanced through the window at the Palace Bullets had shattered bottles and looking glass back of the bar, but there was no evidence of any casualties The Crows' Nest men were pouring out of the back door

Except for the horses of the rustlers the street was empty Bystanders had run into stores and offices or shelter. Jeff pushed through the swing doors of the Capitol.

He was putting himself in the place of the killer. Since there had been one shot only and no follow-up his guess was that a drunken ruffian had ambushed Bascom without orders from the Jackmans. The fellow would probably run to the Capitol for protection. If so, he must still be here. It was not likely that the killer was one of the Jackmans' imported warriors. He was one of the home group who had a personal reason for wanting Bascom dead, perhaps a man afraid that the trapped bandit's testimony would put a rope around his neck. The name Karl Rudabaugh jumped to Carr's mind.

XIX

A young man, Emmett Jelks, ran through the Capitol to the office of Ranse with news.

"Karl Rudabaugh just shot Bascom from the window of the Palace while the rustlers were riding up the street," he burst out excitedly.

Jackman ripped out an oath. "The dumb fool! He's been

drinking all day. I should have got rid of him long ago." His mind faced the possibilities. "This may be it, Emmett. Get the Toledo Kid and Texas Jim. Tell them to gather our men and meet here. If you see Linc or Clem, notify them."

Rudabaugh shuffled into the building by the back door. He hurried to the office. His face was a map of fear. All the Dutch courage drink had given him was gone.

"You gotta hide me, Ranse," he bleated. "I got Shep Bascom. They're after me."

"You blundering idiot, you spoil everything," Ranse stormed. "I've a good mind to turn you over to Alec Black." The thought had occurred to him but he had rejected it. He would have sacrificed Rudabaugh without a moment's regret but he could not do it and keep his men in line. The outlaw code would not let him give up one of the gang.

Jackman pushed his desk aside and swept back an Indian rug. His fingers found an iron ring in the floor and he pulled up a trap door. "Get down there and keep still," he ordered.

Rudabaugh stumbled down the steps. Ranse lowered the door and dragged the Navajo rug over it. Before he and Jelks had lifted the desk back into place Jeff Carr opened the office door. He had a .45 in his hand.

"Where is he?" Jeff demanded.

"Who d'you mean? I told you never to come here again."

"You know who. The murderer, Karl Rudabaugh."

"I don't know what you are talking about. Get out."

Carr's eyes swept the room. The desk was out of its usual position and the hands of the two men were on it, just starting to replace it. The rug was rumpled. Emmett Jelks' swift glance at it was a give away.

"Keep your hands where they are," Carr ordered. With his foot he brushed the rug aside, revealing the trap door.

Ranse Jackman was unarmed. There was a revolver in the drawer of the desk, but at the present moment it might as well have been in Chicago. Carr was standing in front of the desk, grim and watchful. Before he could possibly reach the weapon he would be shot down.

Jeff with his left hand drew open the drawer of the desk and saw the .45. He left it there, locked the drawer, and put the key in his pocket, the weapon in his hand still covering the two men.

"You'll be dead before the day is out," Jackman threatened, his voice thick with fury.

That Carr ignored. He spoke to the younger man. "Jelks, lift your left hand from the desk slowly, reach across and draw your pistol from its holster, then pass it across the desk to me butt first. Don't let your finger touch the trigger. I'll gun you certain if you do."

He watched Jelks draw the gun out and push it as directed across the top of the desk, but every instant of the time he watched Jackman even more closely.

"Now get Jackman's gun, Jelks. Stand behind him and not in front."

Jelks said after patting the body of his chief, "No pistol."

"Draw back his coat."

He did so. Ranse was not wearing a shoulder holster.

The newly elected sheriff ground his teeth with rage. He was a man who could not take even a temporary reverse without a sense of humiliation. "If I had a cutter on me you would have a bullet in your belly before this," he snarled.

"You're doing fine, Jelks," Carr said with ironical praise. "Now pull up the trap door and I'll have a talk with Mr. Rudabaugh."

Jackman's body swayed. His gaze was fixed on the revolver lying on the desk. In another moment he would have leaped for it.

"Don't move," Carr warned. He picked up Jelks' weapon and sent it crashing through a window into the alley. "All right, Jelks. Get going."

"Tell him to go to hell, Emmett," Jackman ordered harshly. "He acts like Mr. Big behind that pistol, but he's a bluff. The fellow hasn't the nerve to cut loose on you."

Carr said, coolly and without any emotion in his voice, "I won't kill you, Jelks—just pump bullets into your legs."

Jelks flung a panicky look at his master, another at Carr, and made up his mind. "I got to do like he says, Ranse." He stooped and raised the cellar door.

Evidently there was a window in the cellar, for the pit

below was not entirely dark. Carr faced a dilemma. If he went down the steps before his eyes had become accustomed to the dim light he would be at the mercy of the killer below. If he survived this peril the two men in the room would have a chance to get revolvers somewhere and would shoot him down when he came up from the cellar. He postponed a decision.

"I've got you, Rudabaugh," he called down. "Come up with your hands in the air."

"Stay where you're at, Karl, or come up with your gun smoking," Ranse shouted. "It's Carr wants you. He has no authority. You're my prisoner."

Outside the office there was a noise of tramping feet. Mawson and Dunham came into the room. Jeff's heart lifted. The arrivals might have been reinforcements for the gambler. He explained the situation.

"Rudabaugh is the man who shot Bascom. He is in the cellar. Cover these men and I'll bring up the killer."

"Just a minute. He's armed." Mawson considered possibilities. "I'll go with you."

"You'll neither of you go," Jackman told them. "This man is accused of robbing the mail. I'm a United States marshal. He's my prisoner under arrest by me. Nobody else has any standing in this case."

"I'm sheriff of this county and he has just committed a murder," Dunham said. "The place for him is in our jail."

"The place for him is wherever I want him," Jackman answered arrogantly. "With the town full of your outlaw friends he is safer where he is."

"Are you backing his play in shooting down Bascom without warning, Ranse?" Mawson asked.

"I don't know that he did shoot him," the gambler retorted stiffly. "Maybe one of the Crows' Nest gang did it."

"Counting the bartender there were three men in the Palace when the shot was fired," Dunham mentioned. "All of them agree Rudabaugh did it."

Jackman's black eyes challenged Dunham. "That will have to be proved by me. I believe nothing you say unless it is

backed by competent evidence. You are too thick with thiev
and bandits."

Carr interrupted the hot retort on Dunham's lips. "I a
not going to leave this room until I have seen Rudabau
brought up and disarmed. Take your choice, Jackman C
him up here or I will."

The gambler shrugged his broad shoulders, a crafty sm
on his thin lips. "There are three of you to one, and I a
unarmed. If you want to go down after this man I can't preve
you. However, I warn you that it is a lawless business a
you go at your own risk."

Jeff pushed back Mawson, who had taken a step towa
the stairs. He called to the man below. "I'm coming to g
you, Rudabaugh, dead or alive. Billy Mawson is with m
and Sheriff Dunham. Surrender and we will try to get ye
to jail. If you use a pistol you will be shot down where ye
are."

"Knowing how fond of him you are, he'll probably believ
you and give up like a lamb being led to the slaughter
Jackman jeered, his voice loud enough to carry to the bas
ment.

Mawson said to Carr, "Better let me bring him up, son

"No," Jeff answered. "I've made the play. I'll go throug
with it."

"All right. If you feel you must." The ex-ranger steppe
to the edge of the trap door. "Rudabaugh, listen. This is Bill
Mawson talking. If you make a gunplay you'll be dead insic
of two minutes. Fix that in yore mind first. I advise you t
holster yore hardware and come to the foot of the stairs wit
yore hands up."

There came no answer from below. Mawson waited for
few seconds. "We're going to take you to jail alive, unles
you force us to kill. Which is it to be?"

A shaky voice replied. "I didn't go for to kill Bascom.
slipped and the gun went off."

"Tell that to the jury." In Mawson's quiet voice was th
sting of whiplash. "Three seconds to make up yore mind
Rudabaugh. Do you want us to come and get you?"

The man below whined, "You come and get me, Ranse.

Jackman said: "Stay there where I've put you. If you come up I wash my hands of you."

"I'm coming for you now," Carr said. "Don't forget that if you go to shooting, either Mawson or I will get you."

As he took the treads to the foot of the steps he felt a chill run up and down his spine. The reaction of the fellow in the cellar was unpredictable. If he fired it would be because he was stampeded by terror, for he must know that out in the street were outraged men ready to exact vengeance on him.

In the dim light Carr could see the big hulk of a figure crouched back of a barrel, a revolver pointed at him.

"Stay where you're at," Rudabaugh ordered, panic in the voice.

"Don't be foolish," Carr told him, moving forward slowly. "You hear that shouting outside. If a pistol sounds a dozen men will bust in to shoot you down. Your one chance is to go with us quick as you can to jail." The deputy kept the sound of his words casual and easy. Only his hard will forced his feet to take the last steps toward the frightened man. There was a chance that at any moment a slug would tear into his body.

"Keep back there," the killer shouted. "Don't you hear me?"

On impulse Carr pushed his revolver back into its holster. He held out his left hand for the pistol of the cornered bad man.

"Better give me that forty-five," he suggested quietly. "You'll be safer without it."

"No. You can't have it." Rudabaugh glared at Carr who stood close enough to touch him with his hand still outstretched.

For seconds the eyes of the men clashed, then the arm of the big man moved slowly forward and Carr took the weapon.

"Smart of you," Jeff said. "We'll go upstairs."

At sight of them Mawson drew a long breath of relief. "I wanted to come down there, Jeff, but I was afraid that might start the shooting," he said.

Ranse Jackman's gaze rested on the cowering killer. "So you prefer being hanged," he told him contemptuously.

"You'll fix it for me, won't you, Ranse?" the man pleaded.

Jackman knew he was in a tight spot. If this man went to jail and told what he knew, it would mean ruin for him and his brothers. He would have liked to cut loose from Rudabaugh but he dared not.

"You're my prisoner, Karl," he said. "Don't forget that for a moment. By six o'clock tonight I'll be sheriff. These fellows have got it in for you and for all of us. They will try to get you to tell a lot of stuff that will help them play their game. Keep yore mouth clamped and say nothing. Do that, and I'll see you get justice."

Dunham and his deputies took their prisoner out of the back door of the Capitol, a dozen men in the gambling house watching them. Before they had gone fifty yards a group was growling at their heels like a wolf pack.

"Hang him! Hang him!" somebody shouted.

There was a yell of approval.

Carr glanced back. The alley was filling with men. Some were in front of the officers, hampering their progress. Rufe Crawley was one.

"We're going to have trouble," Dunham said. "Keep close together."

He and Mawson locked arms with the prisoner. Carr moved in front of him. The pressure increased as the crowd grew. The law men and the killer were tossed to and fro, the heart of a howling mob fighting to get its victim. Fists hammered at him and reaching fingers ripped off his clothes. The guards were battered almost as badly as Rudabaugh. Mawson stumbled and went down, but Carr hauled him to his feet. Crawley's knuckles lashed at Jeff's cheek and for a few moments made him groggy.

"We'll never make the jail," Jeff heard Dunham cry.

Twice Rudabaugh, glassy-eyed with terror, was almost dragged from his protectors. Fighting desperately, they just managed to hold on to him.

Six men debouched from the rear of a dry-goods store and plowed into the crowd, clawing and pushing a way to the center of it. They were Jackman warriors, Linc at their head, for the moment on the side of their enemies.

"You can't reach the jail," young Jackman shouted, making his voice heard above the roar of the mob. "We'll cut into Frost's saddle shop."

With the help of the reinforcements the officers reached the back door of the small store and bolted it behind them.

Rudabaugh's coat and shirt had been torn from his back. His body was a mass of bloody bruises. The officers too looked as if they had been through a war. All of them were completely exhausted.

XX

Fists beat on the door and harsh voices demanded admittance. Sheriff Dunham cooled the ardor of those outside with a blunt statement.

"There are nine armed men in this room. If we have to shoot we will. I intend to put Rudabaugh behind bars. You can't have him."

The fierce lust of a mob intent on a kill is as savage as the instinct of a pouncing wild beast but the ebb and flow of its emotions are swift. No group of lynchers will face a small body of determined armed men. It was so now. After threats and curses it disintegrated, a few on the outskirts dropping away first and then the others almost in a panic to get away before any shots might be fired.

Alec Black and Jim Kenton walked into the shop by the front door. Neither of them had been in the mob from which the prisoner had just escaped. Linc Jackman and two Texan gunslingers imported by his brothers moved forward to meet them. Carr and Mawson joined them.

Black said curtly, "We've come to get Rudabaugh."

The laugh of young Jackman mocked him. "He's come to get Karl, boys. Ain't that something?"

The chisel-hard eyes of the rustler swept the group and rested on Carr. "So you've thrown in with this bunch of miscreants after all yore fine talk," he jeered.

"Billy and I are deputies of Sheriff Dunham," Carr replied. "It's our job to get this killer to jail. We can't lie down on it, Alec."

"So you're going to take him to jail, and before night Dunham will hand the keys to that upright character Ranse Jackman. What do you reckon Ranse will do?"

"Probably turn the man loose. We can't help that. We have to play out the hand the way it has been dealt to us," Carr said.

"That's double-crossing talk," Black retorted. "It's the same as siding with the dirty ambusher. He murdered Shep Bascom to get rid of the witness that would have hanged him."

"That's how it looks to me," Carr admitted.

"And on a technicality you're helping the bastard to escape."

Mawson interrupted quietly. "We're not helping him to escape, Alec. Within two hours we won't be deputy sheriffs any longer and we'll start to keep a watch on the jail."

"It's a hell of a deal," Black sneered. "I was nursing this Bascom so that you and Carr would have evidence these Jackmans are the double-crossing crooks we know them to be. Bascom wasn't my man. We didn't owe him a thing. But I tell you straight that if he had been I wouldn't have left this room until I had pumped lead into Rudabaugh. You may all go to hell for me."

Kenton had a word to add. "I never did like this Carr. He's too damned mealymouthed. I wouldn't trust him farther than I could throw a yearling by the tail."

The bearded man followed his chief from the store.

Linc Jackman's eyes blazed with rage. "For a plugged quarter I would have drilled him," he cried. "If it hadn't been—"

He cut his sentence short. The reason that had restrained

him from gunsmoke was a warning Ranse had given him, not to let his anger take him precipitately into action. If they played it carefully they had the winning cards in their hands now. They could move under cover of law to protect themselves, to destroy their enemies.

The town buzzed with excitement. A killing on the street was no uncommon event. It was the implications back of this homicide that aroused interest. The rumor of what had taken place in the Capitol; the sight of Jackman adherents aiding Dunham and his deputies to take Rudabaugh to jail; the presence of the angry rustlers in the town. All of these pointed to a situation dangerously explosive. Before night it grew worse. Rufe Crawley, after drinking heavily, had gone into the Capitol and raised a disturbance, swaggering around and challenging any Jackman alive to fight him. Clem walked up to him and knocked the man unconscious with the barrel of his revolver, after which he removed the fellow's pistol and had him flung into the street.

Clem said, the rasp of sandpaper in his voice, "Beginning at six o'clock tonight this town will no longer be a resort for outlaws and swaggering scoundrels." His frosty eyes swept the room. "A strong and honest man has been elected sheriff. All of you who are good citizens will be protected."

Shortly after the polls had closed, a count of the votes showed that Ranse Jackman had been elected by a considerable majority. The faction that had backed him celebrated the victory by a jamboree of heavy drinking and noisy roistering. Saloons and gambling houses were crowded with patrons.

The Crows' Nest contingent did not go home but put up at the Gilson House for the night. Mollie was distressed at this. She urged Alec Black to start at once for home and camp in the hills. If they stayed, there would be trouble, she feared. Black flatly declined to go.

"We're not running away like a whipped cur with its tail between its legs," he boasted. "After breakfast tomorrow we'll pull out—maybe."

"You're asking for trouble, Alec," she insisted. "With all

this drinking somebody will start a shooting. It's none of our business. Let the people of Tomahawk settle it themselves."

"Keep out of this, sis," Jim Kenton told her harshly. "No need of you buttin' in. I told you not to come down with us." To Black he said, changing the subject: "Ranse Jackman is in a tight spot about Rudabaugh. The town won't stand for any shenanigans. If he stands back of him Ranse will lose a lot of support. What is he going to do?"

"Probably try some kind of a straddle." Black's hard gaze rested on two men who had come into the hotel lobby, Carr and Mawson, and were moving across the room to join them. "Oughtn't you to be down at the Capitol celebrating with yore new friends the Jackmans?" he asked scornfully.

"They are not our friends, Alec," Carr answered quietly. "Before we are through we hope to see them in the penitentiary. Billy and I arrested Rudabaugh. As officers we had to get him to the jail."

"So Ranse Jackman could turn him loose."

"He may at that, after dark tonight, and claim it is a jail break, laying the blame on the jailer Stubby Harper who was appointed by Dunham. We're on our way now to watch the jail doors."

"That's what you say," Kenton cut in dourly.

"Don't be silly, Jim," his sister flashed. "You and Alec act like children. Do you expect deputy sheriffs to throw down on their job and turn a prisoner over to a mob? You ought to respect them for putting up so good a fight and taking so hard a beating while doing their duty."

Indignation rang in her voice. She was, Jeff thought, a strange product to come out of a region such as the Crows' Nest, to have been close to evil and lawlessness for years and remain clean and strong with beauty tempered like a fine blade.

Black knew she was right and he gave way grudingly. "All right. Give them a medal if you wish. I just don't like law men. But we'll forget it. I'll say this, if they expect to pull down Ranse Jackman now he is sheriff and riding high they've got a hell of a job before them."

"He's riding a narrow crooked trail along a high ledge and

he's liable to take a fall," Mawson said. "Time we were
getting to our post, Jeff."

"Yes." Carr looked at Black but his words were for Mollie.
"I hated to have you think we had double-crossed you."

The younger outlaw offered to join them in watching the
jail but Jeff declined the help. Two of them were enough, he
said. If there were more it would attract attention.

XXI

One of Ranse Jackman's imported Texans, who had been
set to watch Carr and Mawson, reported to his chief that the
two men were loitering in the shadows across the street from
the jail. "Two-three of us could take care of them for you,"
the gunslinger suggested.

"Not now, Landers," the sheriff demurred. "Maybe later."

Within a few minutes a second bulletin was brought to
him by Wolf Landers. The men had separated. Carr was
checking on the front door of the jail, the other at the back.

Jackman's mind worked as Carr had guessed it would.
Rudabaugh was a white elephant on his hands and he had to
get rid of him. If he ever came to trial he would certainly
betray the men who had been his confederates in crime. The
gambler was both crafty and bold. He must move swiftly
while Stubby Harper was still jailer. He needed somebody to
take the blame.

Radabaugh was eating the supper Harper had brought him
when he looked up to see the new sheriff unlocking the door
of his cell and entering. Ranse sat down on the cot and began
at once to pump fear into the mind of the prisoner.

"This is a bad break for you, Karl," he said, shaking his head ruefully. "I don't believe I'm going to be able to stand off this crazy mob that wants to get at you."

The killer stopped eating to stare at the officer, terror jumping to his eyes. "Goddlemightly, Ranse, you ain't going to—to give me up to them, are you?"

"If you are here when they come, they will break in. No doubt of that."

"Then lemme out." Rudabaugh pushed the food aside and rose, panic sweeping through him. He pleaded abjectly, reminding the other of all he had done for him.

The sheriff nodded, apparently yielding to the big man's urgency. "I'm going to turn you loose, Karl," he said. "Maybe I ought not to, but I will. Here is your pistol. Harper is a tough man. You will probably have to protect yourself. He'll fight if he gets a chance. The time for you to make your move is when he comes for the dishes. Listen carefully. I'll leave the key in the front door. After you get outside don't let anybody stop you. I'll have a horse tied in the cottonwoods across the street. Light a shuck out of town and keep going till you are across the line. By the way, you had better take Stubby's forty-five too. You might need it. It's up to you, Karl."

The gambler rose and shook hands, a cruel smile on his lips. He might be condemning the man to death. The odds were that either he or the man waiting across the street would be dead within fifteen minutes. He hoped it would be Carr, but even if Rudabaugh was the victim it would be all to the good. The big man was dangerous, far better dead. An arrant coward, under pressure he would tell all he knew. That he was probably also sacrificing honest Stubby Harper did not disturb Jackman. When one had his back to the wall he had to look out only for himself.

Jackman stopped for a word with the jailer before he left. "Better get the dishes in about ten minutes and lock Karl up for the night, Stubby. I'll be drifting now but I'll be back early tomorrow. If you and I can hit it off you will keep your job."

Ranse went out the back door and walked down the alley

to the Capitol. One could not be sure how even a well-laid plan would turn out, but he had done the best he had been able to improvise.

The house was doing a good business. The faro, roulette, and bird cage games had all the customers they could handle. Ranse noticed that his brother Clem was playing billiards, a game at which he was an expert, and he stopped to drop a word in his ear. When he had finished playing he would like to see him at the office.

Clem nodded, then made a difficult cushion shot. He chalked his cue and started to walk around the table to size up the lie of the balls. Before he had taken three steps a gun crashed. Jackman swayed on his feet, took a step forward, and clutched at the edge of the table. The cue dropped from his hand. He teetered on the balls of his feet, made a feeble gesture toward the .44 at his hip, then pitched forward with arms outstretched on the green cloth. Somebody had stood on a dry-goods box on the opposite side of the street and shot him through the window. The pounding hoofs of a galloping horse grew fainter with distance.

His brother helped lift Clem to the billiard table. There was anguished shock in the face of Ranse. The tie that bound the Jackmans together was a close one.

"I'm—going—west," Clem murmured.

They were the last words he ever spoke.

XXII

Stubby Harper was a small man in the mid-forties. He walked a little lame from a wound he had received in the Apache war against Geronimo. Since Rudabaugh was a giant with great physical strength he made the prisoner bring the tray of dishes forward and lay it close to the door and then back away to the other end of the cell, after which he unlocked the door.

Harper picked up the tray and started out of the cell, still facing the killer.

"How about some chewing tobacco?" Rudabaugh asked.

"I'll bring you a plug," the jailer promised.

The bad man showed his teeth in a cruel rancorous smile. "I reckon I'll go get it myself," he said, almost in a murmur. His revolver had flashed out and was covering the officer.

In Stubby's stomach the muscles tightened to an icy ball. There was a dreadful crawling up and down his spine. In a moment a flash of yellow fire would signal his death. But the little man had in him an indomitable fighting spirit. He flung the loaded tray at Rudabaugh and reached for his weapon.

He never got it from the holster. Rudabaugh's first bullet caught him in the stomach. He staggered back against the grating and as his body hung there the second slug tore into his throat. His torso slid sideways to the ground.

The murderer straddled toward the door and stood gloating over his victim. "You would have it," he jeered.

From the jailer's holster he drew the revolver, closed the door, and walked down the stairs on tiptoe to the dark hall.

Terror rose and choked his throat. The sound of the shots must have been heard. He must get away fast on the horse waiting in the cottonwoods. It did not occur to him that there was no horse there. He groped along the passage to the front door, found a key in the lock, and turned it. Cautiously he opened the door a few inches and peered out. Except a man sauntering up the walk fifty yards away he saw nobody. The dull roar of the night life beat along Fort Street to him. Soon he would be astride a horse heading for Mexico. It struck him that he had been a fool not to have got from Ranse Jackman what money he had on him. But a man in a jam could not think of everything.

He crossed the road, still carrying both guns in his hands. His mind was comparatively at ease now. Life in Sonora would be pleasant. The dark-eyed senoritas had plenty of jingle. There would be a place for him in one of the outlaw bands that raided the border. Considering everything that had happened today, he was lucky to be alive. He thought of Stubby Harper lying dead on the floor of the cell and a sense of triumph flooded him. When people got in his way he rubbed them out. Pity he hadn't bumped off that fellow Carr. But the luck had been against him there.

At the edge of the cottonwood grove he stopped, his eyes searching for the horse. It must be deeper in the grove.

From behind a tree a man stepped. Through Rudabaugh swept a chill wind. Fear tightened his stomach muscles, but a comforting reflection came to him. This must be Ranse, here to make sure he got away. He peered through the dim light of the shadowed grove.

His whisper, dry as the rustle of leaves, croaked, "That you, Ranse?"

"Wrong guess," a voice answered. "It's Jeff Carr."

Rudabaugh's eyes were getting accustomed to the darkness. He could see the poised wariness of his enemy's stance and his heart sank with a premonition of death. But he could not let himself be captured. This was his last chance.

Flashes from both of his revolvers stabbed the darkness. The crash of Carr's .45 flung back an answer. The hammering of the guns whipped through the night. The murderer caught at his stomach. One of the pistols dropped from his hand. His legs bent at the hinges and his huge body sank slowly to the ground. As it went down a forefinger twitched and the sound of the explosion racketed into the trees. While one could have counted ten he lay there motionless, a huddled heap. Then an arm slid from the breast and fell into the sand lax and still.

Jeff's mind was tensely concentrated on that slack figure, though he was vaguely aware of the slap of running feet. Rudabaugh was dead, he decided. A sickness ran through him. He had killed a man, in self-defense, and a worthless ruffian at that, but the horror of it shocked him. To put an end to a human life is so dreadfully final.

He started to move forward and saw that three men were already on the scene. One of them was Billy Mawson, another the stage driver Hank Mains.

Mawson asked swiftly, "Are you hurt?"

Carr shook his head. "No. A miracle I'm not. He slammed away with both guns as fast as he could trigger them. Couldn't wait to take aim."

Billy Mawson looked at the two revolvers, one in the dead man's hand, the other on the ground beside him. From one of them a thin trickle of smoke still rose. "Why two pistols?" he asked.

"Why any?" the old stage driver wanted to know. "How come he isn't still in jail?"

"Our new sheriff will have to explain that," Mawson said bleakly. "Examine the pistols, Hank. Find out how many shots have been fired."

By this time two other men had arrived. More could be seen heading toward the grove.

The stage driver reported. "This pearl-handled pistol belonged to Rudabaugh. It had the notches on it for the men he has killed. Four shots fired from it. Three from the other."

Carr said bitterly, "If he had lived he could have put two more notches on it, for the two men he killed today."

Mains was surprised. "Did you say two?"

"Two, I am afraid," Carr replied. "Two shots were fired in the jail just before Rudabaugh came out of it. Unless I am mistaken we'll find Stubby Harper in there dead or badly wounded. The second pistol must be his."

A bystander spoke up. "Funny Rudabaugh had his pearl-handled six-shooter. Wasn't he searched before they put him in the cell?"

"I took the forty-five from him myself when we arrested him at the Capitol," answered Carr. "I gave it to Sheriff Dunham. Later I saw him turn it over to the new sheriff. Better ask Ranse Jackman how his man Rudabaugh got hold of it. He'll have a nice explanation for you."

From across the street a voice called, "The jail door isn't locked, boys."

Men crowded in and pounded up the stairs. Somebody brought a lamp from the lower floor. The door of the cell in which Rudabaugh had been was also unlocked. Dishes and remnants of food were scattered over the floor. Near the entrance lay the bullet-torn body of Harper.

While they were still in the jail word reached Carr and Mawson that Clem Jackman had been shot from ambush. As yet nobody had come forward to name the killer, but Rufe Crawley had been seen to fork his horse and jump it to a gallop, evidently in a hurry to get out of town.

Carr was shocked at the news. He knew the Jackmans too well not to feel sure they would never rest until they had revenge for the murder of their brother. Unless the Crows' Nest men left Tomahawk at once there might be a pitched battle on Fort Street.

He could see how dangerously explosive the excitement was. Four men had been shot down in one day and trigger-hungry gunmen were walking the streets. A challenging word might start a dozen guns smoking.

To Mawson he said, "I'd better get to the hotel and try to persuade Black to leave at once."

Mawson nodded. "Go the back way. I'll take charge here and see the evidence isn't juggled."

XXIII

Through unlit alleys and across vacant lots Jeff Carr made his way to the Gilson House. He found Mollie Kenton in a little parlor opening from the lobby. She was much distressed. Her brother and the other Crows' Nest men were out on the street somewhere. She had tried in vain to get them to stay in the hotel. He agreed with her entirely.

"They ought to leave Tomahawk at once. I came here to tell them so, though they already know it." He slanted a quick look at her. "Have you heard about Clem Jackman getting killed?"

"Yes. They say Rufe Crawley did it."

"I think so. He left town on the jump immediately afterward."

"They will blame all our boys for it, and none of them had anything to do with it. You know Rufe is a murderous ruffian. Clem Jackman beat him up today. This was his revenge."

"I know, but trouble is in the air. I must find Alec and get him to leave. The Jackmans have half a dozen imported gunfighters. It is madness for him to stay here."

The girl's troubled eyes fastened on him. "For him, but not for you I suppose. Isn't it true that you just killed one of their men, this Rudabaugh?"

"Yes, in self-defense. He had escaped from jail after killing a deputy sheriff. When he saw me he began firing. I had to stop him."

"Will that make any difference to the Jackmans? You know

it won't." Storm waves swept the girl's face. She spoke with passionate feminine ferocity. "You'll be shot down just as Clem Jackman and Shep Bascom were. If you keep hounding them they dare not let you stay alive. Why don't you go away too, tonight while there is still time?"

"I can't," he answered quietly. "I'm like an enlisted soldier. Billy Mawson and I are here to help bring law into the country. Somebody has to do it. Bad men get control of affairs and things go from bad to worse until law steps in and the riffraff are swept away. Then peace comes to the land."

"Peace!" she echoed with a despairing scorn. "What's the matter with this country? Listen and you can hear the tramp of feet on the sidewalks, the feet of men who are like wild beasts thinking of nothing but how they can destroy one another. They trample down all kindness and decency. There are women and children in this town who want a better life than this. Isn't there any way for them to get it except through hate ending in death? You are an outsider, but you come here and are forced to kill a man. One killing leads to another. Go away, Jeff Carr. Go now."

She was a girl who lived within herself, but now words poured out in a flood. A heat was flaming in her bosom and it choked her throat. For years she had stayed with her brother trying to keep him from the lawlessness that infested those about him. It was a losing battle. She had lately come to realize that. He had chosen his way, as Alec Black had, and both of them were treading a crooked trail that could lead them only to destruction. The influence of her presence would save neither of them.

"The history of all our wild trail-end towns is the same," Carr explained. "The people get tired of those preying on them, and the cleanup brings law and order."

Mollie had been pacing the floor. She stopped in front of Carr, emotion welling over. "Oh, Jeff—Jeff, do you have to stay?" she cried.

"I have to stay," he told her gently. "For a little time. Not long, I hope."

"A little time! It takes only the fraction of a second for the crook of a finger to kill."

Jeff stared at the girl breathlessly. A sudden drum beat wildly inside him. He had made a discovery, amazing and wonderful.

"It takes only a fraction of a second for a man to learn he is in love," he cried, and swept her into his arms.

As he held her close in that sweet intimate clinging of body to body he saw in her face the light that shines in a woman's eyes for not more than one man in a lifetime. For a few brief moments they forgot everything except that they had found each other.

She was the first to remember the outer world of turmoil in which they were living, to escape from that inner one into which a tide of ecstasy had swept them. The warmth went out of her eyes as the flame goes from a blown candle. The nearness of impending tragedy shadowed her.

"What are we going to do, Jeff?" she cried.

He came back to the clear-edged picture of the present. "First, I am going out to find Alec and your brother. You and I will talk sense into them and they will go back with you to the Crows' Nest. When I am through with this job I will come and get you. Don't worry about me, dear." He gave her a whimsical white-toothed smile that lit his lean tanned face. "As from this hour I am wearing invisible armor and nothing can hurt me."

She wondered what it was that set the spark of love shining in a woman. It could not be only the turn of a man's head, the look in his eyes, the lithe graceful build of him, but something deep and vital inside of him that found expression in all he did and said.

Mollie said, so low the words were almost a whisper, "You will be careful, Jeff?"

Pride walked in his tread as he swung out of the hotel. He had found his woman and the superb insolence of youth quickened his blood. No evil could harm him tonight.

XXIV

Anger ran deep in Ranse Jackman at the cowardly murder of his brother, the tide of it so strong that he did not allow it to be wasted in a heat of passion. He gave strict orders to his followers to avoid immediate trouble if they could. Rumors sifted to him of a fierce resentment building in the town. The general opinion was that he had given Rudabaugh back his pistol and allowed him to escape. The swift retribution that had befallen the man after his callous shooting of Stubby Harper was meeting vigorous approval.

To offset this adverse talk he sent his followers out to explain the escape of Rudabaugh. Stubby Harper must have been careless and allowed the big ruffian to snatch his pistol from him and later Karl had found his own weapon in the desk downstairs. Ranse from the musicians' stand in the Capitol spoke to a full house deploring the violence in Tomahawk and urging all good citizens to support the law and help him re-establish order which was so greatly threatened by the outlaws and trouble makers who had descended upon the place. He offered a two-thousand-dollar reward for the arrest dead or alive of Rufe Crawley, the murderer of his brother.

Seeing Billy Mawson in the crowd, Ranse called him to the stand and asked him to say a few words. The old ranger advised his hearers to go home and sleep. By morning the intense excitement would have subsided and the facts could be judged without passion. He agreed with Ranse that the shooting of Clem Jackman had been coldblooded murder and the killer should be punished.

Mawson met Carr on the street and the two of them found the Crows' Nest men in the Palace saloon. Black was holding them in a compact body in order to meet any attack that might be made on the hillmen. He was coming to the opinion that it would be wise for them to be on their way. When Mawson told him that Ranse Jackman had given his men instructions to keep the peace the young rustler leader could see no sense in staying out of stubborn defiance. It would be interpreted as support of Crawley's ambush of Clem Jackman.

The rustlers left Tomahawk shortly after midnight. Carr rode with them for a few miles. He and Mollie brought up the rear of the small cavalcade. Alec Black gave no sign of disapproval. He had known for some time that he and Mollie were drifting apart. His ways were not her ways. Fond of her though he was, he knew he could not tolerate a wife who sat in judgment on him. If he married at all—and at present he was not ready for domestic life—his wife must be one who took him as he was and did not want to make him over.

Mollie did not want to make Jeff Carr over. In her love for him there was a deep content. She realized that the past few weeks had made a change in her. There had been growing in her a sense of futility in life, a sullen resentment at conditions she could not change. She had stood aloof, no part of them, but her loyalties had been at war, on the one side her brother and on the other the wildness of this no man's land. Now she felt a wind-swept cleanness, for she had come to a decision. She was going to leave the Crows' Nest forever.

They drew up on a knoll above the little ranch of Jack Adams to say good-bye. Since Alec Black had fallen back to join them they parted with a handshake. Mollie's throat ached at leaving Jeff, a lump born of loneliness in it. This new wonder in her life had been with her for so short a time. If anything happened to him the memory of it would be all she had to carry on with.

On the road back to town Jeff's mind tried to look at himself objectively. He was not a fickle man. Always he had held fast to his friends. Yet in the space almost of days he had met two women who had stirred him more than any he had met in all the years. Margaret Atherton had seemed to

him an embodiment of unreachable loveliness To him she
had been only a dream, though no doubt to Harold Haddon
she was a warm and close reality.

But Mollie—Some lines of Wordsworth jumped to his
mind.

> *A creature not too bright or good*
> *For human nature's daily food;*
> *For transient sorrows, simple wiles,*
> *Praise, blame, love, kisses, tears, and smiles.*

Mollie would do to walk with through the years. She would
understand him and he would understand her. Brave, stead-
fast, loyal. She was all woman, quivering with life. Tonight
she had been beautiful for him as never before. Love had
warmed her, sent color flooding into her cheeks. Beauty, he
thought, must be partly at least in the heart of him who
sees it. Mollie had become for him suddenly a changed woman.
Her eyes, lips, the lift of her head quickened the rash and
eager youth in him.

XXV

Skirting the boundaries of the Kasford ranch, Carr rode
up Lodgepole Creek and turned off into a narrow gulch that
ran into a wooded pocket where a cabin huddled close to a
rocky bluff. There were two men in the hut, one of them
cooking dinner in a Dutch oven and on an open fire, the other
lying on a bed with one foot chained to one of its posts.

Carr said to the cook, "How is it going, Johnny May?"

May put down the frypan in his hand and rose. "Fine and dandy," he replied. "Did you bring any smoking?"

Jeff tossed to him three sacks of smoking tobacco. "And a gunny sack of grub. How's your guest?" He turned to the man on the bed. "I bought you a copy of the Tomahawk *Blade*. You'll find some interesting news in it."

"You got no right to keep me here," Foley snarled. "I've told you that a dozen times. It's kidnapping. You can go to the pen for this."

"I wouldn't think so," Carr differed mildly. "I was a deputy sheriff obeying orders. You're a lot safer here than in town. If you don't think so, take a look at the front page of the *Blade*."

The prisoner's sullen eyes dropped to the paper. Presently he let out a yelp. "Goddlemighty! Clem Jackman killed— and Karl Rudabaugh."

"Keep on reading," Carr advised.

Foley's shifting gaze raced over the page. "And Shep Bascom, the dirty rat."

"One more," Carr suggested. "Stubby Harper."

Johnny May's face was a map of startled surprise. "Is this true, Jeff?"

"It is, I'm sorry to say."

"You killed Rudabaugh, the paper says," Foley flung out.

May snatched the paper from the man on the bed. "Lemme see."

"I'll bring in the sack with the grub," Carr said. "I brought some airtights—tomatoes and peaches."

When he returned carrying the sack, both men demanded a personal account of the trouble. Carr told the story, touching lightly on his own part in the tragic events. He could see that Foley was greatly shaken by the news, particularly by the killing of Clem Jackman. His trust in the power of Ranse was breaking. Why had not Jackman found and released him?

Carr did not press the weakening man but let the facts sink into him. Foley was avid for information. How come Clem had been killed, seeing nobody even claimed he was one of the stage robbers? Jeff explained that Clem had pistol-whipped the drunken bully while he was in the Capitol making trouble and the fellow had shot him in revenge. Foley was impressed by Carr's victory in the duel with Rudabaugh, a notorious bad man and killer. It was seeping into him that he had better try to make his peace with the law.

He began by saying he reckoned there wouldn't be any complaints about the bumping off of Rudabaugh. He never had liked the fellow. Karl had always been looking for trouble. He was better dead. If the fellow hadn't been a born killer he certainly would not have murdered good old Stubby Harper. Or for that matter Jim Haley.

"Yes, you fellows made a mistake in taking a fellow as mean and violent as Rudabaugh with you when you robbed the stages," Carr said.

"I didn't say I was along with those who held them up," Foley cut in quickly.

"You don't need to say it. We have the evidence."

"If I was to give you some information maybe you would go easy on me."

"It would make a difference," Carr admitted.

"Shep didn't get anywhere by ratting."

"It was a mistake taking him to town. We would leave you safely here."

After a good deal of hesitation and several false starts Foley wrote out a confession implicating Linc Jackman, his brother Ranse, and Norman Roberts. Ranse had done the planning but had taken no part in the actual robberies. Roberts had given information as to when the gold shipments were going out. The prisoner in the written statement insisted that he had not wanted to join them in the holdups but had been bullied into doing so by Karl Rudabaugh and Ranse Jackman. The shooting of Jim Haley had been entirely unnecessary and to three of the bandits totally unexpected. They had been greatly shocked by the killing.

Carr and May put their names as witnesses on the signed confession.

Foley was a badly worried man. Maybe he had made a mistake. If Ranse was still at large when he discovered that his partner in crime had betrayed him he would not hesitate an instant to destroy Foley.

"You have my signed story and now you can let me go," the man on the bed pleaded. "You got no business holding me anyhow now that Ranse is sheriff."

"I can turn you over to him," Carr said. "Is that what you want?"

"Hell's bells, no! I wouldn't be safe an hour when he hears about that paper you've got. I want to get outa the country sudden."

Carr shook his head. "I can't let you go. You'll have to stay here. It won't be for long."

"It ain't safe. One of Kasford's riders saw our smoke yesterday and rode up to the cabin. He'll talk certain."

"That's true?" Carr asked May.

The guard admitted it was. "He didn't see Foley since I walked out to meet him before he reached the door, but he sure will wonder what in hell I am doing here."

"We'll have to move," Carr said. "But where?" His fingers drummed on the table while he thought of the possibilities. "What kind of a man is the marshal at Sarasota? Is he a friend of the Jackmans?"

"Tom Bell is a good guy, honest and square. He doesn't cotton to the Jackman crowd much."

"Can he keep his mouth shut?"

"You mean not give it out that Foley is his prisoner?"

"Yes. If he even whispered it the news might reach Jackman."

"Tom wouldn't talk, but someone might see Foley."

"We'll have to risk that," Carr decided. "Soon as it is dark we'll pull out for Sarasota."

To Johnny May this whole country was familiar from boyhood. He had ridden for two outfits whose stock ran in the hills and he had many times hunted the rugged country above the ranches. He led them in and out of gulches and across a pass that took them to the other side of the divide. Foley rode between them, his feet tied by a rope that stretched from stirrup to stirrup beneath the belly of the horse. In the upper reaches the night was cool, as Arizona nights are likely to be. At times a harsh wind hit them as it screamed down from the mountains. May and Carr were tough, hard outdoor men who had ridden out blizzards and took weather as it came, but Foley had lived a soft existence in town and complained bitterly.

"Fellow, quit yore whinin'," May told him roughly. "We ain't making this night ride for pleasure but to get yore worthless skin to Sarasota safe without anybody seeing you."

Light sifted into the sky to announce the coming of day just before they dropped down from the hills into town. May swung off the main street to a house that sat by itself in a cultivated two-acre patch. After two or three knocks on the door a man's sleepy voice came from a window above. It asked what they wanted.

"Got a prisoner for you, Tom," Dunham's ex-deputy answered. "This is Johnny May."

The marshal came down grumbling. He had put a pair of trousers on but the braces were hanging down.

"Doggone it, do you have to wake a man out of his sleep?" he asked.

Johnny introduced Carr and explained the situation. The marshal, a middle-aged Westerner whose bowed legs certified that in his youth he had ridden the range for years, looked Carr over with interest and liked what he saw. There had been a lot of talk about this young fellow who had dropped into Tomahawk and within a few weeks had shaken the Jackman domination of the county. A hard, game man himself, Bell recognized tough strength when he met it. The light close-knit figure with the packed shoulder muscles, the cool blue eyes level and direct in the tanned face, advertised one with no bounce or swagger but with an intrepid determination. It was his opinion that Carr would do to take along.

"Sure, I'll keep the prisoner safe for you," he promised.

Foley protested against being held on the ground that these men were no longer deputy sheriffs.

Bell said with a grin, "If he wants to make this so damned legal you had better turn him over to Ranse Jackman."

"Perhaps you are right," Carr agreed. "I am sure Ranse will be glad to take care of him."

Hurriedly Foley made his choice If he had to stay in jail he preferred Sarasota.

The marshal finished dressing and they took Foley across an unfenced stretch of mesquite to the back door of the jail. Smoke was beginning to come from two or three chimneys in the town but as yet nobody was in sight. They got the prisoner inside unseen.

The two men from Tomahawk accepted an invitation from Bell to eat breakfast with him. His wife, the marshal boasted, made the best flapjacks in Arizona. She was a comely smiling woman, ten years younger than her husband, and she justified his bragging. Her guests, hungry after the long night ride, devoured stacks of her delicious hot cakes, cleared off a large platter of eggs sunny side up, and washed down the food with the best coffee they had tasted for some time.

Breakfast finished, they took the cutoff trail for Tomahawk. When they were deep in the hills they unsaddled, picketed their mounts, and made up five hours' arrears of sleep. They reached Tomahawk at dusk.

XXVI

The news that Ranse Jackman had offered a reward of two thousand dollars for the capture of Rufe Crawley dead or alive stirred in a good many men a longing to collect it. Most of them had no intention of doing anything about it, since Crawley was a notorious gunman and in any case was either across the line in Mexico or cached far up in some of the defiles in the Crows' Nest country. But there were nesters in the rustlers' paradise around Jugtown who weighed the matter more deliberately.

Crawley had been a murderer wanted by the law even before the killing of Clem Jackman. He had fled to the Crows' Nest to find a hiding place because he knew that the posses of sheriffs seldom visited there. The residents of the district resented his coming. Though a few of them had killed in self-defense or in the heat of passion, they drew a line at cold-blooded murder. They did not even regard themselves as thieves. The ownership of cattle was a unique business. The stock that ranged the hills were a temptation to all light-fingered men. They knew that many a stockman had branded all the mavericks that strayed his way and it seemed fair enough to lift some of their ill-gotten gains.

To harbor a man like Crawley was dangerous. It gave a region already in bad odor a worse name. They had not invited him to come. He was not one of them but had imposed himself upon them for the reason that this was a no man's land outside the law.

All of the rustler group were poor men. Two thousand dollars seemed to them a fortune. It was within the reach of anybody with nerve enough to risk his life for it.

Crawley sensed this tenseness in the atmosphere. When he went into the store at Jugtown he felt eyes watching him. He stood at the end of the bar where nobody could get back of him. His jumpy eyes swept the room trying to read what thoughts lurked in the minds of those present. He judged them by himself, knowing that he would have killed his best friend—if he had had one—for half of two thousand dollars. Twice since his return a bullet from the brush had whistled past him. An obsession filled him that he was under sentence of death. It was a terrifying dread always with him, the fear that a slug might crash into him at any time, from any direction, from the gun of almost anybody in the neighborhood. To escape his thoughts he drank heavily and started unnecessary quarrels. At night he woke from sleep to see eyes in the darkness of the room fastened on him from every side, to hear voices whispering to him, "Murderer!"

Alec Black said to Kenton one day, "Rufe is nervous as

a wet cat, so goosy that he is liable out of sheer panic to kill somebody."

"If somebody doesn't rub him out first," Kenton murmured, his slitted gaze fixed on his companion.

"I'm going to order him to leave," Black decided. "He can make a break for Mexico."

"Where he can keep on killing men if he reaches there."

Black looked quickly at the man in front of the bar beside him. "Meaning anything particular, Jim?"

"Let's step outside to the corral, Alec."

With their arms on the top bar of the fence they watched Nick Sampson trying to rope a bay horse from a group of a dozen racing around the corral, the bay staying deep inside the group. It took three casts before Nick dropped the loop over the head of the skittish animal.

"About Crawley," Alec reminded Kenton.

"I've been thinking about him quite some," his friend answered in a low voice. "If he stays here or if we help him escape we're all tarred with the brand of murderers. It would give us a lift among the good people down below to turn him over to the law. And two thousand is a nice reward to divide between us."

"Ranse Jackman would see he was lynched inside of twenty-four hours."

"Maybe so. Isn't that what he deserves?"

"I reckon." Black looked for a long time at the hills rising above a ridge in the distance. Before he spoke he knew he could not go along with Kenton on this proposition. Perhaps he was too finicky, but something in him rebelled at taking blood money. "I can't do it, Jim. He came here hunting a refuge. Rightly or wrongly we let him stay. He's a bad lot. I grant you that. But I can't break faith and turn him over to Jackman knowing what would be done to him, and then take pay for it."

"Use your head, Alec. We didn't ask him to come here. He wasn't welcome, and he knew it. Then he goes down to Tomahawk and in cold blood kills another man, getting us in bad again. We have to protect ourselves."

"I'll drive him out of here I doubt if he reaches the line, but that is his lookout."

Kenton shook his head. "It won't be that way, Alec. You are not thorough enough If you don't want to side me in this I'll get somebody else. I need that dough "

That Jim Kenton was a stubborn man Alec knew. He could not be argued out of what he had in mind. It was a perilous undertaking, one in which he might be killed. Alec was his friend, and he had Mollie to consider. After all, Crawley ought to be turned over to justice. He could not let Jim try to get this fellow without his help. Kenton might get himself killed.

"I'll take a hand, Jim," he agreed. "On two conditions. The first is that we take Crawley down alive; the second that I won't accept any of the reward."

"The bigger fool you. But suit yourself. There will be more for me."

"I don't like it," Black said sharply. "I don't care how bad a man is, he still ought to have a chance for his white alley. Ranse will rub him out certain."

"What chance did Crawley give Clem Jackman?" Kenton asked dryly. "He is the same kind of killer Rudabaugh was, and if I remember right you walked into Frost's saddle shop to shoot that wolf down *pronto*."

Black grinned wryly. Kenton had him there. Yet it hadn't been quite the same, he felt. "We were all het up because of Bascom's murder," he explained. "And there were half a dozen armed men there to protect him."

It would be easy enough to shoot Crawley from ambush, though two attempts had been made without success, but it would be difficult to capture him alive. Asleep or awake, there would be no moment day or night when a pistol was not within his reach. They had noticed that even when drinking at the Jugtown saloon he had lifted the glass with his left hand, the right thumb hitched in his belt close to the .44 holstered on his hip. Unless he was taken completely by surprise the man would go down in smoke rather than surrender.

The men sat on the top rail of the corral fence for an hour

discussing possibilities They discarded one plan after another

"We have to catch him when both of his hands are busy, but jumpy the way he is now he won't let us get near him except when his right hand is free " Kenton rolled a cigarette and put a match to it

"If he knows we are there," Black amended His eyes lit An idea had crossed his mind. "When he is saddling a horse It takes two hands to do that."

"You mean wait in the stable for him?"

"That's right. He always gets up around nine and fixes his breakfast Then he saddles to ride to Jugtown or to be sure he's fixed for a quick getaway. We'll be Johnny-on-the-spot."

"Could be done. The right time would be when he was lifting the saddle to the back of the horse. We would have him dead to rights."

"Unless he spotted we were there before he picked up the saddle."

"We'll have to take that chance."

Alec dropped around to the Kenton place in time to eat one of Mollie's breakfasts. Jim had explained casually to her that they were going out to the Kasford ranch to look at a bull offered for sale and he might not be back until late. It was possible they might stay all night.

Mollie put a blunt question to Black. "Is this a night riding trip to raid somebody's stock, Alec?"

He shook his head, smiling at her. "Nothing like that, Mollie. I'm a reformed character."

With some apprehension she watched them ride away. They might be going on legitimate business, but some instinct warned her they were not. Though she had decided that she could not continue to live here with this bearded older brother, she was still torn by a maternal feeling that she ought to stay and be a check on his activities. To a certain extent she had a sense of responsibility toward Alec Black also. He was a man she had come near to loving and still liked very much.

On the way to the cove where Crawley lived in a deserted cabin Black stressed again that if they were unable to surprise Rufe there was to be no shooting. They would pass as hunters of stray stock, or offer any other explanation of their presence that seemed reasonable.

Near the entrance to the small park there was a clump of cottonwoods and here they tied their mounts. The buildings lay just to the right of a canyon running deeper into the hills. Crawley had chosen the place because it offered a chance of escape by way of the canyon in case of attack.

No smoke rose from the chimney of the house. They edged along the rim of the saucer and dropped down a rough brushy slope that brought them to the rear of the decrepit stable. The only possible hiding places inside the log building were behind the sagging rear door and back of an oat bin upon which was piled some old saddle blankets.

"Take yore choice, Jim." Black said.

Kenton chose the position back of the open door.

Through a crevice between the logs Black watched the cabin. The leaden minutes dragged. It was a nerve-racking task to wait for the coming of the desperate killer in the house. The idea of catching him off guard did not look so feasible now. It was quite possible he would catch sight of one of them when he entered the stable. Alec had a premonition of disaster. He would have liked even now to drop the business, but he had not the courage. His companion would take it as a sign of weakness.

"Smoke rising from the chimney," Black mentioned after what seemed an endless wait. "He'll fix himself some breakfast."

With a nervous laugh Kenton reversed the slang phrase current on the frontier. "From breakfast to hell," he jeered.

"No, Jim," Black answered sharply. "There will be no gunplay unless he starts it."

"Sure—sure. But he's a crack shot. Don't let him get the jump on us."

"He'll probably rope his horse in the corral before he comes here."

Black's guess was correct. Crawley opened the cabin door a few inches and scanned the terrain carefully. When he came out there was a revolver in his hand. As he walked down to the corral his glance jumped from one side to the other. His

.44 he thrust into its holster while he roped the cow pony but after the animal was caught he drew the weapon again. On the way to the stable he kept on the far side of the horse. The thought of that two-thousand-dollars reward was always in his mind. Anybody hunting him did not have to take a chance, since the poster read dead or alive. If somebody got him it would probably be from behind cover.

Inside the stable he stopped behind the horse, his eyes stabbing right and left. Nothing he saw alarmed him. He turned to get the bridle on a wooden peg that had been driven between the logs.

A sound, the faint creak of a hinge on the back door, jerked him around. He stood crouched, the pistol held close against his side. A bullet from the .44 crashed through the door. Kenton, badly wounded, came out firing. The roar of guns, flame leaping from the barrels. Lanes of death pumped from crooking fingers. Oaths, groans, smoke, and presently silence more terrible than the hammering of the guns. Two men lay lax and still.

Alec Black moved forward, a thin vapor still rising from the blue barrel of his weapon, and after a glance to make sure Crawley was dead knelt down beside his friend. There was no life in his body.

The young outlaw rose and leaned against the door jamb. He was sick in mind and body. The crooked trails he had started to ride with such a light heart years ago had brought him to this. He faced squarely for the first time a future violent and lawless.

He thought of Mollie, of her face when he broke the news of her brother's death. That he must change the story to protect his memory he knew. What he must stress was that Jim had acted from a sense of duty to arrest a murderer, that both of them had rejected any thought of accepting the reward. He must make that very clear to her.

XXVII

The first word Jeff Carr had of the tragedy in the Crows' Nest came to him in a letter, the only one he had ever received from Mollie Kenton. He stood in the post office reading it, for Billy Mawson was to meet him there prior to a talk they were going to have with Norman Roberts.

"*Dearest Friend*," the letter began. The written words struck in him a vibrant response. It was as if she were present and he could hear her deep voice and feel the life throbbing in her.

You may have heard the bad news of my brother's death. Alec was with him at the time. I will tell you how it happened. Jim and Alec decided they ought to arrest Rufe Crawley and take him down to the sheriff. They were afraid that in fear of capture the man would kill somebody else. They had agreed, Alec tells me, to refuse any reward, and I believe him. If I did not I would be even more unhappy than I am. When they attempted to take Crawley he began firing. He and Jim were both killed almost instantly.

We buried Jim today on that knoll high above our house where he and I had often watched the sunset behind the mountains. There he will rest in peace.

I am leaving here for good either tomorrow or the next day and will meet you at the Gilson House as soon as I arrive. Alec will ride down with me. He has been most kind and has offered to sell our holdings in the Crows' Nest and send or bring the money to me.

Dearest, the thought of you is a very great comfort to me. The Bible somewhere says of a man that he shall be like rivers of water in a dry place and the shadow of a great rock in a weary land. That is what you mean to me. Oh, my lover, be careful. Jim's death has quickened my fear for you. I dream of a day when you and I will be far from all this violence.

The letter was signed simply "Mollie."

When he had finished reading the letter he glanced over the room. Billy Mawson had not yet arrived. Nobody was in the office except himself and the postmaster back of the boxes. He started to read again what Mollie had written.

Footsteps sounded outside. Somebody came in by the side entrance. Carr looked up, expecting to see Mawson. Linc Jackman was standing beside him, the barrel of a revolver pressed against his ribs. Through the front doorway walked another man, a Texan known as "Sure Shot" Webb, one of Ranse Jackman's imported killers. He ranged himself on the other side of Carr.

Jeff said, and his voice sounded almost indifferent, "Looks like I've been careless."

"We're going to take a walk," Jackman said.

"Are we?" Carr asked politely. "That will be nice." He was trapped. If he took that walk with them he would probably not return. All he could do was play for time. "Billy Mawson will be here in a minute. Maybe he would like to join us in that stroll."

"Mawson has been detained," Jackman answered, an edge of triumph in his tone. "He won't be here."

A chill wind blew through Jeff. Was he being told that Mawson had been killed? It might be that way. With both Mawson and him dead the gamblers would be safe, at least for a time. When he spoke his voice was cold and his eyes steel-hard.

"Are you sure? Billy is one man who keeps his appointments."

"Quite sure." The gambler's smile was cruel. "This is one he won't keep."

"What are we waiting for?" Webb asked.

He too, like the others, spoke low. They might have been discussing the weather. The excitement and significance of what they were saying lay below the surface.

"I haven't quite made up my mind to accept your invitation," Carr said.

"As you please. It's your choice." Jackman's lips still held the set smile that did not reach his eyes. "Maybe you would rather have it here." He pushed the end of the revolver deeper into Carr's ribs.

"You are so pressing I think I had better go with you." Jeff raised his voice to reach the postmaster working back of the letter boxes. "Mr. Hatch, will you tell Billy Mawson when he comes in that I have gone for a walk with two friends, Linc Jackman and Sure Shot Webb?"

"Y'betcha," Hatch answered, and was so surprised at the conjunction of this particular three in amity that he came from his seclusion to verify it with his eyes. He could not see the drawn revolver. Two men stood between him and it. But he had a feeling there was something not right about this situation. That Linc hated Carr for whipping him was well known.

"All right, Hatch, get back to yore job," Jackman said gruffly.

He was annoyed that the postmaster had been dragged in as a witness. Carr had of course done it on purpose to leave evidence that he had been last seen with him and Webb. In desperate peril though he was, the young fellow's derisive grin told him that. He had scored one minor point at least.

The men walked out of the side door and turned toward the Mexican quarter, Carr in the middle between the other two. Night was beginning to fall and soon the lights of Fort Street would be glimmering. They cut into an alley which led to the *acequia* and crossed the ditch on a foot bridge. Here they stopped. Webb had drawn his .44 as soon as they struck the alley.

Carr thought, *It will be here.* Both covered him. There was no chance to run, none to fight. His heart was racing wildly, but he said, coolly to his surprise; "Nails in your coffin, Linc. Up till now you had only a prison sentence coming."

"That's what you think, wise guy, but you'll never live to see it."

Jackman's arm lifted swiftly. The long barrel of the revolver crashed down on his victim's head. A hundred tiny lights sparked in a dark night. A bolt of lightning struck him. Jeff was falling—falling from a great height. Then everything went black.

XXVIII

Carr came back from unconsciousness to a world that had no weight or substance, one that weaved to and fro dizzily. Disembodied voices drifted to him, sounds that floated in the air like those at a seance he had once attended. He gave them little thought. A hammer was pounding in his head. Somebody had got into it and seemed to be sawing off the top of his skull.

The voices continued. One said: "You didn't kill him, Linc. He's waking up." The cadence of it was oddly familiar.

Who was waking up? Carr wondered. He concentrated on that and vaguely became aware that this had some reference to him. He must be the one waking up. If the workman with the hammer would stop hitting his head he could think better.

Slowly his eyes opened. He closed them, for he must be seeing something that did not exist. What he had appeared to see was a strange room, if it could be called a room. The walls were dirt, unplastered. So was the floor. The ceiling was of rough planking. There had been the figures of men. Presently he looked again and picked up details. There were kitchen chairs and an old battered table. No stove. No bed.

He lay on half a dozen gunny sacks. On the table was a cheap lighted lamp, the wick untrimmed and the chimney black with smoke.

His vision was clearer now. Not counting himself, three men were in the room—the two Jackmans and "Sure Shot" Webb. Jeff was puzzled. He ought not to be here. He ought not to be alive at all. It would have been so easy for them to pump bullets into his body and bury him in the desert sand. He did not make the mistake of thinking that they were going to let him live. All three of them were ruthless and implacable. For some reason as yet unknown to him they had merely postponed his death.

Ranse was reading aloud snatches of the letter from Mollie Kenton that Carr had received that evening. He punctuated the sentences with comment.

"So, we get the breaks at last. Crawley is killed with no trouble or expense to us. It seems Alec Black is too noble to take a reward. Where was I? Oh, yes! The last I read was what a great comfort our guest is to the lady. She quotes the Bible. He is the shadow of a great rock in a weary land and he is to be very careful until they meet again. I wonder when that will be." He turned to Carr, his voice heavy with jeering mockery. "Have you an opinion as to the time? We would not want to interfere with any appointment you may have with a lady."

Carr said, "If you want an opinion from me, take this one, that you are lost to all decency."

Webb sat in a chair tilted against the wall, his feet hitched in the lower rung, a cigarette drooping from his mouth. He was a small man with eyes cold as those of a dead cod set in a face wrinkled and weathered by years of a Texas sun. He let the legs of the chair drop to the floor and rose lazily. As he sauntered forward he picked a quirt from the table.

"I'd better work him over a bit, sheriff, don't you reckon?" he drawled.

"Not just yet," Ranse said. "I'll have a little talk with him first. I don't want him passing out again now."

This was not going to be good, Carr knew, but he steeled his will to take what he must.

"I found out where you were keeping Foley but not until you had moved him. Where did you take him?" Ranse demanded.

In Carr's mind the missing block fell into the pattern of the picture. This was why they had not yet killed him. As long as Foley was a captive he was a danger to the Jackmans. A confession from him, added to the one made by Bascom, would be a heavy blow to any hope Ranse had of political advancement. It might be enough to put Linc into the penitentiary. The gamblers had to force from their prisoner information as to where Foley was being held.

Carr had something to buoy him up but not much. Unless he told them they could torture but not kill him. His life depended on refusing to tell. If he gave way he would be dead within the hour.

"No information about that," he said, his level eyes fixed on the gloating face that looked down at him. "Ask me something easier."

Ranse glared malignantly at this slim long-backed man whose eyes flung no flag of fear. He noticed the prisoner's jaw muscles were set and stood out like steel ropes.

"I'm not asking you," the older Jackman told him brutally. "I'm telling you. You're going to talk. Maybe you think you are tough. I've softened harder men than you, my friend."

Thoughts flashed through Jeff's mind. If he shouted, could anybody hear him? Was there any chance that Mawson, granting that he was alive, could find this place?

The sheriff guessed at his mental searchings. "For your information, we are miles out on the desert. If you scream, nobody can hear you. But we won't take a chance. "Sure Shot" will at once drive a bullet through your brain. Talk, fellow."

"On any subject but one." A shutter had dropped over Carr's eyes leaving them opaque and blank. "You choose the theme—the dry spell, law in Tomahawk, how it will feel to be hanged."

A red-hot devil of malice looked out of Linc's face. "He thinks he's God Almighty. Lemme settle his hash right now. He's asking for it."

His brother brushed aside the hand with the revolver. "Not yet, Linc. He's throwing a bluff. Scared and is trying to save face before he comes through. I'm not bargaining with him. Before I'm finished with him he'll beg for a chance to talk."

Ranse flung himself on their victim to pin down his arms. Jeff struggled to throw him off. The other two joined in the melee. By sheer force they overcame the prisoner, tore away his coat and shirt, and gagged him. He was pulled to his feet and tied to an iron ring fastened in a post running down from the ceiling and set in the dirt floor.

The mouth of Ranse Jackman was a thin tight slit. He opened it slightly to say. "Take over, Webb, and let's see how he likes to have his back tickled."

How Carr underwent the ordeal without yielding he did not know. His body writhed at the fall of the lash but no sound came from between his clenched teeth. The quirt was like a rope of fire, the pain increasing with each stroke. The punishment seemed to him interminable. His head fell and his torso relaxed. He had fainted.

When he came back to life the light that filtered through the grating at one corner of the ceiling showed a faraway star. It must still be night. He discovered that he was tied to the post. A sick man and in pain, an involuntary groan escaped from him.

From the table where he had been laboriously spelling out the words of a newspaper by the light of the blackened lamp a gross man, unshaven and unclean, shuffled across the floor to look at him. A day or two before he had been pointed out to Carr as one of the Jackman's imported gunmen. He was passing under the name of Ben Dubbs.

Jeff shifted the weight of his body to ease the lacerated back. "Where are the others?" he asked.

"Sleeping, I reckon." Dubbs added bluntly: "You in a hurry to see them again?"

"No hurry. How about a drink of water?"

"Against orders," the guard growled.

"I get it," Carr said. "Part of the plan to break me down. A nice outfit, the Jackmans."

The big man gazed at him dourly. He did not like any part

of this. It was one thing to end a life with a clean bullet, another to torture a prisoner before destroying him. He was a gun for hire, but he had never before helped a hell brew like this.

"To hell with the orders," he snarled, and walked to the table where there sat a pail of water. He brought back a `·` perful.

Carr drank it to the last drop. "If you can spare me another I'd like to slosh my hot face with it," he said. A fever burned in him.

The guard grunted but did as he had been asked. He was thinking that whatever else the prisoner might be, he was a man hardy and resolute. "Why the hell didn't they kill you right off?" he blurted out.

"They mean to do that after they have got some information. Of course they will be hanged. Probably you too, Mr. Dubbs."

"I don't scare," the man retorted roughly.

"I'll say a word for you at the trial. You've done me a good turn."

"If there is a trial you won't be there," Dubbs said plainly. "It won't do any good to soft-soap me."

"A pity," Carr murmured, as if to himself. "He's a cut above the other scoundrels, but when he walks up the gallow's steps with them nobody will know that. He'll be strangled just the same as they are."

"Cut out the gab," Dubbs ordered, and went back to the newspaper.

Carr presently fell into troubled sleep and dreamed that he had been caught by Apaches and was going to be staked out on an anthill. He awoke, to see Dubbs still spelling out the words of the newspaper. The man gave him another drink. The guard knew that this was between them and would never be mentioned to the Jackmans. After a little Carr dropped into a doze.

The heavy-footed Dubbs tiptoed over to stare at him. He was troubled in mind about this. Ranse Jackman had decided they could not get Carr to talk by physical violence. The captured man would let them kill him before he would talk.

But long days and nights of hunger and thirst might break his will so that he would tell where Foley was and let them make an end of him. Dubb's gorge rose at the prospect. What kind of a devil was Ranse Jackman? And why had he let himself get involved in a business so damnable? Like Carr, he too was caught in a trap.

A faint gleam of coming day showed in the grating when Jeff awakened. Dubbs had given up his reading. An elbow rested on the table and the man's shaggy head lay heavily on his open hand. But he was not asleep, though close to it.

The pain in Carr's back was less sharp. The fact that the night was nearly over brought him no comfort. The Jackmans would be back soon.

"Your shift must be about over," he said.

"Yeah!" The sleepy guard glared at him. He was sorry for Carr and also annoyed at him. Sulkily he told the prisoner for whatever comfort it might bring him that Ranse Jackman had shifted to the starvation plan of breaking him down "Unless he changes his mind again."

Carr nodded thanks. "Why are you trailing with this pack of wolves?" he asked. "When the law catches up with the Jackmans they will try to slide out and slip the noose over to your throat. You know that. Get word to Billy Mawson or Dunham of the jam I'm in and then cut your stick for Mexico. I promise you we'll never try to bring you back."

"I'm taking Jackman's money," Dubbs answered harshly. "I'll not throw him down."

But what Carr had said nagged at his mind. He had no illusions about the Jackmans. They would work this out for themselves, sacrificing any of their hired help if it became necessary. Their gunslinger Rudabaugh had shot down their own ally Bascom when he had grown to be a danger to them. Ranse was a wily schemer not to be trusted. Maybe he had better cut loose from them in time.

"If I tried to get away you would shoot me," Carr suggested.

"That's right," the gunman answered harshly.

"Perhaps before the others come you would get me another dipper of water. I'll have a long dry day ahead of me."

Dubbs brought the water and his prisoner drank.

"You are an interesting instance of a tenderhearted murderer," Carr jeered amiably. "I daresay you don't read the poets. There is a line in Tennyson that might have been written for you.

> *'His honor rooted in dishonor stood,*
> *And faith unfaithful kept him falsely true.'*

It means that you owe your own decency a lot more than you do that villain Ranse Jackman."

"You talk too damn much," Dubbs told him grimly.

But the hired killer was troubled. There was something about this young fellow doomed to death that carried him back to his own youth, to the days before he had chosen the wrong path—some spark of intrepid strength that could not be put out as long as there was life in him. In the killer's distorted code two qualities stood out as supreme. One was courage and the other faithfulness to the side upon which he had enlisted. Now the two were at war. He felt an urgent reluctant admiration for this beaten unconquered foe, but he was a Jackman man bought and paid for until the end of the war.

XXIX

Alec Black drove Mollie to Tomahawk in a light wagon, bringing with them her trunk and two telescope valises. Nick Sampson rode behind them leading the horse that was Mollie's personal mount. He had volunteered for the journey and Black had been glad to have him along. There would probably be no trouble, but if there was any Nick would be a good man to side him.

Before they had been in town fifteen minutes Billy Mawson told Mollie a shocking piece of news. Jeff Carr had disappeared. Though Billy did not say so, she knew he feared his friend had been killed. The two were to have met at the post office. As Mawson passed an alley on the way there somebody had stepped from its shadow and knocked him on the head with a club. Half an hour later he reached the post office, still groggy from the blow. He was too late. The postmaster, Jim Hatch, had given him a message from Jeff, that he was taking a walk with Linc Jackman and the Texas gunman Webb.

Mawson had not needed any explanation to understand the message. It was notification to him that Carr had been captured by the enemy and was going with them as a prisoner. The only additional information Hatch had was that the three had started toward the Mexican quarter of the town.

The ex-ranger had wasted no time. He found Dunham at his house and told him what had occurred.

"I am going to see Ranse Jackman," he explained. "I don't think there will be another attack on me, but I am telling you

160

where I am going so that if I disappear too you will understand the Jackmans are responsible."

"Wouldn't it be better for me to go with you?" Dunham said. "They could not get rid of both of us without raising an awful row."

"No. It's up to you to carry on if I don't show up. I'm going alone." Mawson spoke decisively.

Dunham knew he had made up his mind.

Billy Mawson pushed through the swing doors of the Capitol and walked through the gambling house to the office. Two men were in it, Ranse Jackman and one of his gunmen, Ben Dubbs.

Ranse looked up from the desk where he was going over ɪe accounts. His eyes flashed a warning to Dubbs before he spoke. It was not necessary. The man's fingers had already shifted to the butt of the .44 resting on his hip.

"Nice to have you drop in, Billy," Ranse said.

"What have you done with Carr?" Mawson demanded, a chill threat in his low voice.

"With Carr? Nothing—nothing at all. What do you mean?" A sudden fierce excitement had leaped to the gambler's face and been instantly wiped out. The words of the ex-ranger told him that Carr had been caught in the trap set for him.

Mawson said, without shifting his gaze from Jackman: "Take yore hand from that pistol, Dubbs. I'm not going to kill this scoundrel yet."

"Since you've got Mr. Mawson scared, Ben," Jackman retorted scornfully, "I'll explain that we aren't assassins."

"I didn't come here to listen to lies, Ranse," Mawson replied, still in a quiet manner more deadly than blustering anger. "Yore brother Linc and Webb took Carr with them into the Mexican quarter not twenty minutes ago. If he is still alive I want him freed at once. If he is dead I serve notice that I will kill you on sight."

"You are a fool to come here and threaten me, Mawson. I tell you I don't know anything about where Carr is." Ranse rose from the chair, a big rawboned man, strong and fearless. "Now get out of my house while you still have a chance."

"Think it over, Ranse." The little man's eyes were cold as the wind sweeping over a glacier. "If Carr is alive, see he stays that way. I keep my promises. If you have killed him— or kill him later—I'll rub you out certain."

Mawson turned and walked out of the room and the building. Almost before he had reached the front door Jackman left by the rear entrance. A saddled horse was tied to a rack. He swung into the hull and put the horse to a canter. His destination was a deserted ranch house that now held tenants. One of them, held unwillingly, he wanted very much to see.

Mollie listened tensely to the story of the P. & S. stage company agent, her heart sick with fear.

"Is that all you know? Do you think—?" The girl left the second question unfinished. She could not put into words the despair sweeping through her.

"I know a little more," Mawson said. "There is reason to believe that Jeff may be alive. A dozen good men are working with me, citizens who have had more than they can stand of the Jackman rule. We have combed the town as well as we can. If Jeff is being held captive I don't think he is in Tomahawk. Some good Mexican friends feel sure they would have learned of it if he had been kept in that quarter of the town."

"What ground have you for feeling Carr may still be living?" Alec Black asked.

"I have been tipped off that Ranse Jackman rode out of town just after I talked with him. His brother Linc was seen here next morning, then he disappeared again. Some of their gunmen were missing and later showed up. We have checked the corrals and the livery stables. Webb rented a horse at the Maverick corral and has not yet returned it."

"Why didn't you have these men followed?" Black wanted to know.

"We have tried that, but they slip away in the dark. Johnny May followed Linc last night, but there was no moon and he lost him in the hills. We are trying to keep them covered, but with no luck so far." Mawson drew a folded placard from his pocket and handed it to Mollie. "I had these printed yesterday and tacked up all over town."

Mollie read the paper.

$2000

Reward will be paid for information leading to the finding of

JEFFERSON CARR

who was *kidnapped* about 7 P.M. at the post office, Monday, June 22. He was last seen in the company of *Lincoln Jackman* and *"Sure Shot" Webb.* If said *Carr* has been killed the same amount will be paid for information resulting in the arrest and conviction of the murderers.

William Mawson
Acting for and by the authority of
James Whitman, President of the Pacific & Southern Stage Company

"Any results?" Mollie asked.

"Not yet," Mawson admitted. "Some guesses by men trying to edge in on the reward. But the poster has drawn a lot of attention and put the whole town on the alert."

It occurred to Black, though he did not say so before Mollie, that the offer of so large a sum might increase the danger to Carr if he was still alive. The Jackmans might get panicky and decide it was safer to get rid of him. But Alec did not believe Jeff was among the living. His opinion was that the gamblers had wiped him out at once and buried the body somewhere in the desert or the hills.

"Give me one good reason why they would run the risk of letting him stay alive this long," he challenged after they had left Mollie.

"Give me a reason why they are dodging in and out of town unless it is because they are guarding Jeff," countered Mawson. "Maybe I'm banking on a thin chance but it is all we have."

"Where do we go from here?" Black inquired.

"We keep trying to get a check on where those fellows go

when they leave town and we comb the hills trying to run across any camp they may have hidden in them."

"Fat chance of finding their hideout in this rough country of gulches and pockets," the rustler grumbled.

"I know. I know." Mawson lifted his hand in a gesture of exasperated discouragement. "But what else can we do?"

"Play tit for tat with them. Grab Linc Jackman and hide him out. Serve notice on Ranse that if he doesn't produce Jeff his brother is a gone goose."

Mawson was struck by the audacity of this counter-move. It was realistic, and it might get results. Ranse had lost one brother. He would go far to save the life of the other. If Carr was still alive he would not dare kill him, not while Linc was in the hands of his enemies. To capture Linc would be a touchy business, since it was not likely he would appear alone even on crowded Fort Street. But Billy Mawson had done several impossible things in a danger-crowded lifetime. Perhaps with the help of this young daredevil he could pull off another.

The two went into a committee of ways and means. After long discussion they hit on a plan that might succeed. They submitted it to Mollie, because it was necessary for her to find out how matters stood between young Jackman and Ella Gilson. If he was no longer interested in her the plan would have to be discarded.

Mollie and Ella were the only two young women at the hotel and they had struck up a friendship. It was easy for Mollie to get Ella to talk about Linc Jackman. He was still ardently pursuing her and she had been holding him off. What he had been urging was that she meet him in the garden behind the hotel after her day's work was done. He could get nowhere with her when he never saw her except in a roomful of diners, he complained. She was not giving herself a chance to find out what he was really like.

Ella could see how unhappy Mollie was about Jeff Carr but she shrank from letting herself be used as a bait to trap Linc Jackman. She did not want to become involved with him in any way. He had been one of the gang who had killed her lover.

"And now he is one of those who are going to kill my

man," Mollie said unhappily. "This is our one hope of saving Jeff."

Ella let herself be persuaded. While she was serving dinner to the Jackmans she slipped a note into the hand of the younger brother. Linc pocketed it without reading the message. This was something he wanted to keep from Ranse. When he opened it later he read five words. "In the garden at nine."

This was just like a woman, he reflected, elated at his victory, to fight the desire that drew her to him and to give way impulsively in the end. His feeling of triumph was greater because she believed he had been one of the outlaws present when Jim Haley was killed and yet had not been able to resist his advances.

XXX

Lincoln Jackman slipped out of the back door of the Capitol, glancing over his shoulder to make sure he was not observed. He had not much more than an hour of free time, for at ten o'clock he was to leave town to be night guard over Carr. He hurried down the alley, staying as close to the buildings as he could. At Santa Rita Street he stopped, his eyes shuttling to right and left to check on anybody who might be in sight. He knew the friends of Carr were watching those of his faction and he did not intend to be caught unaware. After crossing Santa Rita he ducked between two stores and reached an open space fenced for a pasture. This brought him to the vacant ground behind the Gilson House garden.

In the shadow of some cottonwoods he tarried to make sure the vista was free of enemies. His vigilance was probably unnecessary, he thought, since only he and Ella Gilson knew of the rendezvous, but there was an off chance somebody on the other side might be around and take a shot at him He had learned that Alec Black and Nick Sampson were in town They were not now active enemies Probably they were in Tomahawk to collect the reward money Ranse had offered for Crawley. But they were an undependable pair, certainly not friendly to him.

Carefully he came out from cover of the cottonwoods to the back gate. On each side of it was a small frame building, one a root house, the other a tool shed. He passed through the gate and stood close to the root house where he would be less likely to be noticed.

Ella had not come out yet. He peered down at the dim face of his watch and saw that it was five minutes to nine. That checkup of time was a mistake, for in the fraction of a second while he had been making it events had happened swiftly.

The loop of a rope dropped over his head and tightened to pinion his arms to the body. One hundred and sixty pounds of hard bone and muscle plowed into him and flung him from his feet. He opened his mouth to shout for help and a gag was rammed into it stifling the cry.

Pinned down though he was, his lithe strong body tossed and writhed. One of his outflung legs caught a man in the stomach and hurled his back momentarily. His imprisoned arm clutched at the weapon in his belt but iron fingers closed on his wrist. Trying to spit out the gag, he found that a cord attached to it had been slipped over the back of his head. A fist driven into his jaw like the kick of a mule stunned him. Before he recovered, a rope had been wound around his legs and drawn tight. He was completely helpless.

During the struggle it had seemed to him that there must be half a dozen of his enemies but now he saw there were only three—Billy Mawson, Alec Black, and Nick Sampson. The attack had been timed with perfect co-ordination, each covering his assigned job, with the result that there had been only a minimum noise of scuffling feet.

He was picked up and carried through the gate to the

cottonwoods. Here Mawson and Black guarded him while Sampson went to bring the light wagon Alec had driven to town. To it the team had already been hitched and left tied to a tree in the mesquite.

The rustlers drove out of town. Their destination was the seldom visited and now deserted cabin of Shep Bascom. Mawson remained in town. He paid another visit to the Capitol, this time taking Dunham with him.

They found Ranse Jackman both annoyed and nervous. His brother Linc could not be located to take his turn as guard of the prisoner. He was pacing the floor, occasionally barking harsh comments at "Sure Shot" Webb who was lounging indolently against the wall. Though it expressed itself in anger, he had a strong presentiment that Linc was in trouble.

At the entrance of Mawson and Dunham the Texan turned his hooded eyes on them. His right hand shifted an inch or two but otherwise there was no movement of his negligent attitude. His gaze did not lift from the visitors.

"I told you to stay away from here," Ranse told Mawson.

"That's right," agreed Mawson. "But the *Blade* does not come out until tomorrow, so I thought I would drift around and keep you up on the news. Yore brother Linc has gone into retirement for a while."

Ranse absorbed the shock with startled eyes. "What have you done with him?" he demanded.

Mawson smiled. "I recall asking you that question about Jeff Carr. I did not get a satisfactory answer."

"If you've hurt him—" Ranse began, and was interrupted by the ex-ranger.

"The very point I made with you about Jeff," he said, almost in a murmur.

"Would you like me to take over, Mr. Jackman?" the Texan asked gently. "Mawson claims to have quite a rep. He and I could settle this in two seconds."

The little officer looked at him, level-eyed and cool. "What would that settle, Webb? You or I would be dead, perhaps both of us. The point at issue is whether Linc Jackman and Jeff Carr have got to die."

Ranse slammed a fist on the desk. "You can't do this to

me. I'm sheriff of this county. If I arrested Carr I had a right to do so. He killed a man in this town a few days ago."

"An escaped murderer released by you."

"You dare say that to my face?" Jackman cried.

"Why not, Ranse?" Mawson replied mildly. "I say what all this town thinks. Better get yore mind on the immediate problem. Do we or don't we do business?"

Webb said casually: "He doesn't like my proposition, Mr. Jackman. How do you like it?"

The sheriff brushed his hired gunman aside impatiently. "Not now, Webb. If this scoundrel has kidnapped Linc I have to think of the boy's life."

"That would seem wise," Dunham said. "There has been too much killing already. Let's have no more."

"What kind of talk is that from you, Dunham? You can't lay any killing at my door. These spies came nosing around claiming I am a criminal. Did I lift a hand against them, even after they killed my brother?" With an effort Ranse had swallowed any sign of his anger. He had to talk softly for the present.

"You used other men's hands and pistols," Mawson told him coldly. "This is a time for plain talking. Yore gunfighter Rudabaugh killed Jim Haley, Shep Bascom, and Stubby Harper. He did his best to kill Jeff Carr. Not one soul in this town believes yore hands are clean of these crimes. The shooting of Clem was a cowardly murder and Crawley has paid for it with his life. All that is beside the point." Mawson's hard gaze held fast to Jackman's face. "If you have killed Carr you are in trouble you will never escape."

"So far as I know he is alive."

"I hope you are telling the truth. You'd better be if you want ever to see Linc again."

"If you have kidnapped Linc it is a dastardly crime," the gambler cried. "If I'm holding Carr it is lawfully as sheriff of this county. You'll go to the penitentiary for this."

"Then I'll probably meet you there and we'll break rocks together," Mawson countered.

"You haven't proved to me that you have taken Linc prisoner. I don't believe you have."

Billy Mawson laid on the desk a revolver and a pocket knife. "Recognize them?" he asked.

The gambler nodded. He had always been arrogant and high-handed but he realized temporary defeat. "I understand you are offering a trade. Bring Linc here to me safe and sound and I'll see Carr is freed, but I tell you it is a damned outrage."

Mawson shook his head. "You have the cart before the horse, Ranse. Carr must first be delivered to us. We are not sure he is alive."

"Never in this world," Jackman exploded, his face hot with anger. "I'm holding Carr lawfully, if he is my prisoner at all. What I have said stands. I won't go an inch farther than I have said."

His rage was partly fictitious. He felt sure Mawson would keep faith, but what stuck in his mind and made the situation awkward was that when the friends of Carr found he had been mistreated they might deal out punishment to Linc.

Mawson lifted his shoulders in a shrug. "Up to you, Ranse. This trade will be my way or not at all. Do you think we are soft-headed fools? We have to be convinced Carr is alive before we free yore brother."

"Tough, isn't he?" Webb sneered. "Maybe you like his talk. Don't believe I would if I were you. I'd tell him where to get off at. Certain and sudden." The words seemed to drip from the man's mouth with drawling deadlines.

There was a smile on Mawson's lips when he answered, but none in his eyes. "Why be in such a hurry, Webb? You aren't going to live forever anyhow, and you'll be a long time dead." To Jackman he said, "I'll be at the hotel if you change yore mind and want me."

With which suggestion he turned and walked beside Dunham out of the room. The next move was up to Ranse Jackman.

XXXI

Jeff Carr looked up at the small grating which let air and light into the cellar. "Night coming on," he said. "You'll be relieved in a couple of hours and you can get back to that poker game you love. I'll miss you."

Ben Dubbs' leather face scowled down at his prisoner. "Yeah, I'm a chuckle-headed fool. I give you water and I slip you bread and cheese every day, knowing that if Ranse Jackman finds out he'll send me straight to hell. Will you tell me why I do it?"

"Because though you are a cross-grained old ruffian you have in that tough ill-shaped carcass of yours some kind of a conscience. It may save you yet."

The guard knitted heavy brows that thatched his red eyes. At one moment he resented his prisoner and the next gave him reluctant admiration. "It won't save you," he growled. "I give you water and food, but I won't free you."

"You have told me that half a dozen times. Why keep saying it if it's not in your mind? That afore-named conscience is nagging you."

"Man, I have killed not once but four times," Dubbs flung back at him impatiently. "Killer Dubbs they called me at San Antone. A man with his soul sold to the devil. Are five black marks any worse than four?"

"Yet I would give odds you never shot a man in the back," Carr said.

"And you would be right. But this is a black business I am in now. I grant you that. Yet I'm in and I stay."

170

Jeff grinned at the uncouth awkward Texan caught in a dilemma from which he saw no way out that would leave him satisfied.

"Too bad you are on the side that is both the wrong and losing one," Carr sympathized. "If it is necessary I'll get my tail out of this crack without any help from you. But for your own sake you had better arrange it. Man, the penitentiary gates are just yawning for you."

"How?" demanded Dubbs. "How will you get away?"

Carr wished he could answer that question. On the evidence available it did not seem likely to him that he would, yet there was a buoyant and persistent hope in him that would not be killed.

"Now is it reasonable that I would tell you my plan, Ben," the prisoner said lightly. "Fond as I am of you I can't share all my secrets."

Dubbs lit a lamp and spent the next hours reading an old paper.

From outside came the sound of horses' hoofs followed by the tread of feet on the floor above the cellar. A trap door was opened and Ranse Jackman came down, "Sure Shot" Webb at his heels.

"Everything all right?" Jackman snarled.

Carr could see the man was in a vile humor and guessed that he would be in for a bad time. His fear was not fulfilled. As soon as Dubbs had ridden away, Ranse had Webb make coffee and prepare food upstairs. When this was offered to Jeff he was completely surprised. He was also warily suspicious.

He lifted an eyebrow at Jackman. "Greeks bearing gifts?" he asked.

"I find I can't starve a man to death," the gambler answered harshly. "Eat, and then we'll talk."

Eggs, bacon, flapjacks, and coffee had never tasted so good to Carr before. When he had finished Ranse asked him if he had had enough.

"Best meal I ever ate," Carr said.

Jackman tossed him a sack of tobacco, a book of cigarette papers, and a match.

Jeff rolled and lit his cigarette and leaned back contentedly against the wall. "The life of Riley," he commented.

"Fact of the matter is that I am fed up with all this trouble we have been having," the sheriff began. "Let us have a pow-wow and agree on a compromise."

There was something false about this, Carr thought. He had a feeling that anger was running strong in the man despite his talk, that he was putting on himself a rigid restraint.

"Nothing would suit me better," Carr replied promptly. "I probably needed to diet to take off a few pounds, but one can have too much of a good thing."

"I'm prepared to free you on two conditions," Jackman continued. "One is that you tell me where my friend Foley is, the other is that you promise to leave Tomahawk tomorrow taking Mawson with you and that both of you stay out of this territory."

Carr reflected that he was beginning to understand this change of tactics. The man assumed he had been softened up enough to give the information wanted and that he would jump at the chance to be free on any terms. It did not occur to Jeff that a new vital factor had changed the equation. His opinion was that if he told where Foley was he would be signing the man's death warrant as well as his own.

"Sorry," he said. "That isn't a compromise. It leaves us just where we were before."

"I've been patient with you," Jackman said, "but there comes an end to patience."

The imprisoned man nodded agreement. His heart was beating wildly, but he spoke coolly enough, concealing the icy chill that knotted his stomach muscles. "So there is nothing left for you to do but beat me again or kill me."

Jackman paced the floor, struggling with his hate and rage. He knew his hands were tied. He had no weapon but persuasion left to deal with this unconquerable fool.

"For God's sake, have some sense," he broke out. "I want to rescue my friend from your illegal kidnapping. Is that asking too much? I want you to give up this persistent persecution of us. You are in no position to bargain. Use your brains. You are in my power. If Webb crooks a finger you are dead."

Webb said, showing his teeth in a grin, "My finger is itching."

It began to reach the prisoner that some outside event had taken place which was disturbing Jackman. He was acting almost as if he no longer held the whip hand. His arrogance seemed to be tempered by some fear. In his voice and manner was an unexplained urgency suggesting a lack of assurance. Carr put out a feeler.

"If what you say is true, why bargain with me?" he asked.

The sheriff slammed a fist down on the table so hard that the lamp jumped. "Can't you see that I am trying to save your life? It's no pleasure to me to kill. I won't do it unless I'm driven by necessity. You are dooming yourself by your own obstinacy."

Carr did not believe him. The man had sent Stubby Harper to his death ruthlessly, for no reason except that the harmless old jailer stood in his way. Jackman had a far greater motive for destroying him. He was still alive only because Ranse had to find out where Foley was being held.

"I'm willing to compromise," Carr said. "As soon as you have freed me I'll tell you where Foley is."

"And have him moved before I can reach him. No. I'll turn you loose six hours after you have told me. That's a promise."

"One I don't trust."

Jackman strode to the corner of the cellar and back again. A furious hatred of this man churned in him. Only the thought of his brother a captive of Billy Mawson restrained him from giving Webb the word to fire. He glared down at Carr.

"Think it over, you fool," he said hoarsely. "You have till morning. If you still defy me you'll be shot down and buried in this cellar. That's another promise."

He tramped up the steps and slammed the trap door. Carr heard the sound of a galloping horse growing fainter and fainter. he said pleasantly, "Nice friendly gent you work for, Webb."

XXXII

The night clerk at the Gilson House was reading a dime novel by the light of a wall lamp when a barefoot boy walked into the lobby with a sealed note addressed to Billy Mawson.

"He's not in, but I'll see he gets it," the clerk said.

The boy held on to the envelope. "The man said I was not to give it to anybody but him. It's important, he told me. I got a dollar for bringing it."

Mollie walked into the lobby from the small parlor adjoining. "Who was the man that sent it?" she asked.

"I dunno. A kinda rough-lookin' fellow. He was saddlin' a horse down at the corral when he stopped to write it."

"I'm a friend of Mr. Mawson," Mollie explained. "He told me to take any message that came for him." She opened her purse, took out a shining silver dollar, and shut it up in the youngster's dirty hand.

He handed Mollie the note a little reluctantly, but he trusted her smile. Moreover, this second dollar added to the first made him rich beyond the dreams of avarice. A quarter had been the top sum he had ever owned before.

Mollie ripped open the envelope and read the enclosure. The writing had been done with a blunt pencil by an uneducated man. The scrawl ran:

Car is in the selar of the old Rout house. Be quik if you aim to save him. Im liting out for Mexico.

The note was unsigned.

Excitement hammered in the veins of the girl. She must find Mawson at once, but she did not know where to look for him. He was out somewhere trying to check on the movements of the Jackman men.

Johnny May walked into the lobby. She knew he had been a deputy under Dunham and that Carr trusted him.

"Can you tell me where the Routt house is?" she asked.

He shook his head. "Nobody of that name in town far as I know." Then his eyes lit. "Used to be an old homesteader up in the hills named Routt. He has been dead five years and the place is deserted."

"That must be it," she said, and showed him the letter.

He was inclined to think the writer was some busybody who knew nothing about the matter.

"It's a chance," Mollie insisted. "The man who wrote it was saddling to get away. Do you know where Mr. Mawson is?"

"I don't right now. He'll show up later."

"We can't wait. I'm going to ride to the Routt place. Do you know where it is?"

"Sure. Up in the hills. Nobody hardly ever goes there." He added a protest. "You mustn't go, Miss Mollie. It might be dangerous."

She brushed aside his remonstrance. "My horse is at the Maverick corral. Saddle it please, and get a mount for yourself. And hurry."

"Now looky here, Miss Mollie," he protested. "I'll hunt up Mawson, and we'll get some of the boys. Inside of a couple of hours we'll be on the road."

"That might be too late. Don't argue please. I'll leave word for Mr. Mawson to follow us as soon as he can."

Johnny started to remonstrate but gave up the idea. The girl's eyes were bright with purpose. If he did not go with her he would find somebody else to take her. He guessed she was in love with Carr. Since she was a woman passionately alive she could not sit still and let the hours tick away without trying to save him.

"I'll be back in ten minutes," he said.

Mollie penciled a note and put it in an envelope along with the one the boy had brought. She wrote on the envelope beneath Mawson's name the word Urgent!!! and left it with the clerk. A cowboy was lounging in a chair reading a two-weeks-old newspaper. He was a frank-faced boyish range rider and Mollie easily persuaded him to find Mawson and urge him to return to the hotel at once. "Tell him I said it's maybe life or death."

"Sure, lady," he promised. "I'll bring him here if I have to hogtie him first."

Mollie ran upstairs to her room, flung off her dress, and got into levis, boots, and leather vest. When Johnny reported, bringing two saddled horses with him, she was waiting at the door. She noticed that he had found a revolver somewhere and had it strapped to his side.

They rode down Santa Rita Street through the dwindling outskirts of the town. Already the house lights were beginning to go out. A gun-barrel road took them into the desert, but after they had traveled a mile they left to take an arroyo leading to a canyon. The ground rose sharply as they drew deeper into the hills. They crossed steep shoulders which dipped into gulches, with exits in a tangled terrain of huddled boulders or slopes strewn with ocotillo. Never once did May seem to be in doubt. The way was as crooked as the pieces of a picture puzzle and there were no trails to guide them, but her companion led Mollie with complete assurance. He took her up a ledge which brought them to a pass from which they looked down into a dark gulf below them. A faint light gleamed out of the gloom.

"Somebody roostin' there," May said. "It's either a camp-fire or lamps burnin' in the Routt cabin. Looks like you got a straight tip."

They let their mounts pick their own footing down the precipitous rocky decline. May broke a long silence.

"The lights are in the cabin," he announced.

In a thick spread of mesquite they stopped and he dismounted.

"What do we do now?" Mollie asked.

"You wait here till I come back. I won't be long. I'm going down to see how this stacks up."

Mollie assented reluctantly. She wanted to go with him but realized it was better for him to go alone. "You'll be awf'ly careful not to let them see you," she said anxiously.

"You can bet on that," he told her dryly. "I don't want anybody to put holes in Johnny May's hide."

Before he started, the lights in the house went out. "They must be going to bed," Mollie guessed.

"I reckon, but someone is still up. There's a dim light there somewhere. Look. There is another one moving. Must be a lantern. I'll mosey down. Be back soon."

He slipped into the darkness and vanished. Mollie watched the light of the lantern. Sometimes it moved. Then it would be still. After a time it went out. Not many minutes later she heard the sound of a horse's hoof striking a stone. Somebody had been using the lantern to see while he saddled a mount.

The rider passed not thirty yards below where she crouched. His horse stumbled and he exclaimed roughly, "Damn it, keep your feet."

He must be, Mollie thought, on his way back to town. She lost him soon in the darkness. Her anxiety increased. The minutes while she waited for May became to her hours. Once she almost decided to go find what was delaying him.

Almost silently he reappeared. When he spoke his voice was jubilant. "Jeff is in the cellar. That's where the light comes from. He is fastened to a chair and he is playing pitch with the fellow guarding him. It's that Texan "Sure Shot" Webb. A fellow just rode away. I don't believe there is anybody else there watching Jeff."

"Is Jeff—all right?"

May chuckled. "You can't get that guy down. I could see through a small grating. He raked in a pot while I was there. He is devilin' Webb. Says he expects to be at his hanging. Webb is fit to be tied. What we had better do is beat it back to town where I can get Mawson and some of the boys."

"You do that," Mollie said. "I'm going to let this Webb know I'm here. He may have orders to kill Jeff tonight. With me as a witness he couldn't do it."

May stared at her in astonishment. "Hell's bells! You can't do that. This Webb is a notorious killer. No knowing what he would do to you."

"He wouldn't shoot a woman, Johnny. He wouldn't dare. And now we have found Jeff I can't go away and leave him. You see that."

"I don't see it," May denied vehemently. "Knowing the hide-out is discovered he would likely kill you both and light out."

His objection got nowhere with the girl and finally he surrendered. "You're the doggonedest obstinate girl I ever did meet. But have it yore way. You will anyhow no matter what I say. Only I'm staying too. I figure Webb is alone. But we'll play this my way. Understand?"

Having won her point, Mollie was willing to discuss details and let him take the lead. She was to stay close to him, May decided. Through the grating she could if it seemed necessary call to Jeff and tell him she was there with friends. If Webb came ramping out of the house May would meet him as he reached the porch. If he flung up his hands and surrendered he would probably obey the order to release Jeff. It was impossible to know in advance what the man would do.

Mollie was frightened. "Suppose he starts shooting?" she asked.

"Then there will be two of us shooting," May said. "Let's hope he won't."

His private opinion was that a man would be dead in the space of minutes, perhaps two men or three. This was a crazy business, but at least it was better than to let Mollie walk in on the fellow.

"If he thinks we have the house surrounded he'll give up, won't he?" she wanted to know, seeking reassurance.

"Like I said, that's one thing I can't tell you," he replied. "Webb is a desperado, a sure-enough hard case. He may figure he'd rather go out in smoke. If he does I'd look for him to kill Jeff first."

Mollie reversed her decision. "Maybe we had better just sit at the grating and watch until Mr. Mawson comes."

"Now you're talking sense. He'll be along with a posse in two-three hours."

They moved down the hillside very quietly and trod softly across the grass-grown yard. As they passed the corral Mollie noticed with relief that there was only one horse in it. On tip-toe they soft-footed along the side of the house to the cellar grating. The girl peered through it into the room below. The cards lay scattered on the table. Evidently the men had finished their game. Webb had dragged the chair in which his prisoner sat to the post and was fastening him to it.

"Do I spend the night in the chair?" Carr inquired.

Webb was in a sullen angry mood. The prospect of long hours in a damp cellar with only sacks to sleep on frayed his always trigger-quick temper. "If I had my druthers you'd go to sleep quick in smoke. Ranse is a lunkhead for letting you stay alive this long. Maybe I'd better finish the job right damn now." He drew his .44 from the holster and pointed it at Carr with a jeering grin. "How about it? Will you have it now?"

Carr knew this was cat-and-mouse tactics. The fellow enjoyed trying to throw fear into him.

But Mollie did not know it. She gave a cry of terror.

Webb looked up at the grating and saw a woman's face snatched away and a man's replacing it.

"We've got the house surrounded," May called out. "Reach for the ceiling, Webb." The barrel of his pistol was pushed through the wires.

The guard turned swiftly to fling a shot at the bound man. Carr tilted the chair over and went down with it. A bullet roared past his head and imbedded itself in the wall. Webb swung the barrel up toward the grating and fired. The bullet struck the iron web of the grill and was deflected. At almost the same instant May's revolver sounded. Webb staggered and clutched at his stomach. His body swayed, but his feet held fast as if rooted to the ground. He sent a slug wildly into the dirt wall. The crash of May's .45 filled the night with noises as he emptied it into the wavering figure of the outlaw. The knees of Webb buckled and slowly he sagged to the floor, already a dead man.

Mollie looked into the smoke-filled cellar. "Jeff—Jeff!" she cried. "Are you all right?"

"Right as can be, Mollie," he answered. "What miracle brought you here?"

She did not wait to answer but ran into the house to join him. May lit matches, found the cellar door, and opened it. They went down and with his pocket knife Johnny cut the ropes that bound Carr.

Mollie put an arm around the released man to steady him. "Are you sure you aren't hurt?" she repeated.

He said, a glad smile in his eyes at this unexpected happy ending to his perilous adventure, "I think maybe I bumped my head when I went over with the chair, but I am not sure. Oh, Mollie girl, what golden luck you have brought me."

She broke down in his arms and began to weep.

Johnny May thought they did not need him there just now. He said he would saddle Webb's horse and they could start for town.

Before they left, Carr penciled on a corner of a newspaper a note for Mawson and put it on the table. On the way back to Tomahawk they would probably miss him, and Jeff wanted his friend to know at once the good news.

As Carr put his foot on the lowest step to leave the cellar his eyes fell on the dead desperado. He thought, *If it had not been for Mollie I would probably have been the one lying there.*

XXXIII

The news that Jeff Carr had escaped and that "Sure Shot" Webb had been found dead on the floor of the cellar was a jolting blow to Ranse Jackman. The only explanation he could figure out was that Webb had grown careless and let the prisoner get hold of his gun. A letter mailed at Nogales set him right. Ben Dubbs had two-timed him. The message said:

I hired my gun to yu but not for torchur. Yure two much of a wulf for me. Keep the pay. I dont want it.

Ben

Within hours after he read the note Wolf Landers brought him the story, already racing all over town, that Mollie Kenton and Johnny May had maneuvered the rescue. Even when his brother Lincoln walked into the Capitol and told him he had been freed by Mawson, the sheriff found little comfort in the fact. It irked him to feel that his enemies felt they could afford to release the hostage. The next issue of the *Blade* carried the signed confession of Foley with the information that he had been taken to the Tucson jail for safekeeping by the United States marshal for the territory of Arizona.

Ranse paced the floor in a passion of wild resentment. He had had the devil's own luck. Evidence was piling up against him. The control of the town that he had held in the hollow of his hand was lost to him. When he walked down Fort Street he held his head high with scornful arrogance, but he knew this was futile gesture. In the eyes of men watching

181

him he read the thought that he was done, would soon be under arrest and in the penitentiary. There was no longer a place for him in the territory. It was time to leave for parts unnamed.

But before he left he had one score to settle. He meant to leave Carr dead. It became a consuming resolve with him. Because of this man all his hopes had been wiped out, his ambitions wrecked. His hatred was a torment that rode him day and night. One other fixed idea was in his head. Carr thought he had him in a net that would land him in prison. The smart-aleck was wrong about that. If it came to a show-down he would go out in smoke and take his enemies with him. But it had not come to that yet. He meant to strike and make a safe getaway.

Business went on as usual at the Capitol. Customers crowded the hall to play the games. Patrons of the wheel backed the numbers they favored. The rattle of chips sounded from the poker tables. But beneath the surface activity was a tensity, a sense of impending trouble. Ranse moved in and out of the throng with an impassive face. It betrayed none of the turbulent desperation that was burning him up.

Meanwhile he was secretly gathering together all the cash he could. He dropped in one morning at the house of Collins, the proprietor of the Arcade, a rival gambling resort. The man was surprised at the call. He had been doing very well but he knew his place was small potatoes compared with the Capitol. The Jackmans had been barely civil with him.

"How would you like to buy the Capitol lock, stock, and barrel, Charley?" Ranse asked him bluntly.

Collins had the hard, gray face of a professional gambler. On that wooden visage Jackman could read no evidence of the man's reaction. He lit a cigar slowly and carefully before he answered.

"I haven't that kind of money, Ranse."

"I'm offering you a bargain because I'm tired of this town and am moving to Montana. Since Clem was killed I hate this place."

The owner of the Arcade had long nursed a grudge against the Jackmans. He was jealous of their success and angry a being ignored. He thought jubilantly, *The fellow is whipped and is running out*.

"How much?" he asked casually.

Ranse named a price less than one half of what Collins had expected. By borrowing a few thousand at the bank he could manage the buy easily enough. After a perfunctory protest he accepted the offer. Jackman made two stipulations. He was to be paid the full amount at once in cash and the deal was to be kept a secret until after he had left town.

"When do you expect to go?" Collins inquired.

Jackman looked at him bleakly. "Soon," he answered curtly.

With his brother Lincoln he ate supper as usual at the Gilson House. They sat across the room from a group of their enemies. Carr, Mawson, Black, and Mollie Kenton had a table in another corner. No interchange of greetings took place. All of them knew that events were marching to a tragic culmination. The pattern for it was almost complete. Only a few small pieces had to be fitted into place.

"When are you going back to the Crows' Nest?" Mawson asked Black.

The young rustler grinned. "Don't push on the reins, Billy," he replied. "The boys up there are doing fine without me. I came down to see the elephant. So far I've missed the circus, but I aim to have a ringside seat at the next performance. Can you tell me when it starts?"

Mawson glanced at Carr, who nodded. "It's up to Jim Keeley, the United States marshal at Phoenix. I had a letter from him today. He has been right busy but he reckons he can make it here by Friday. That ought to bring the show-down."

Alec Black glanced at the Jackmans, two fierce strong men who must realize that they had their backs to the wall. "Betcha five bucks against a dollar Mex that it will be a smoky one."

None of the others commented.

"Why don't they light out while there is time?" Black continued. "I hear they are settling their business affairs. Me, I would move fast if I was in Ranse's shoes, heading for a point where it would take about five stamps on a letter to

reach me. Course I know they are stubborn as government
mules, but still—"

He let the conclusion ride.

Carr made a suggestion. "You've said it, Alec. They still
have unfinished business. It won't be long now. I look to see
them move fast as chain lightning—to finish it."

Mollie looked at him from a troubled face. She guessed,
as all of them did, what that unfinished business was. There
was nothing she could do about it. When she had asked him
to go away and let other men complete this task he had told
her smilingly that he had set his hand to the plow and could
not leave it till the end of the furrow. And deep in her heart
she knew that if he walked out she would have been disappointed in him. It was that indomitable quality of his, together
with the gaiety that covered it, which set him apart for her
from other men. When she married him if he lived to join
hands with her, he would always make his own decisions on
vital matters and she would have to accept them. It was so
unfair, she felt. Life for them was meant to be a splendid
adventure, but he must jeopardize their chances by waiting
for those two men across the room to strike at him again
because an officer in Phoenix was detained by some routine
matter.

His eyes met hers and held them. There was good cheer
in that look. It told her that no outside peril could touch their
future, and it told her too that he thought her beautiful.

Billy Mawson was of opinion that the crisis would be
reached before Friday. Since he and Carr had no authority to
make arrests they could do nothing but wait for the arrival
of Keeley. Long experience had given him a sixth sense that
smelled out imminent danger. He impressed on his friends
that they must keep close contact with one another and maintain a wary vigilance. Any hour might be the one.

"I'm not so doggoned sure they won't make a break to
get away either tonight or tomorrow night," Alec Black said.
"They know they are in a tight spot and every day brings the
showdown closer. When they had only you two and Dunham
against them, they figured they could handle the situation

but not now, seeing the government has moved in on account of their robbing the mail."

"It's a question of timing," Mawson explained. "The cashier of the bank, Rivers, told me this afternoon that Charley Collins who runs the Arcade was in to borrow five thousand dollars giving as security a mortgage note on the Capitol gambling house which he has just bought from Ranse Jackman. Collins impressed it on Rivers that this was an absolute secret but after he had mulled it over the cashier thought he ought to tell me."

"Did Mr. Rivers make the loan?" Mollie asked.

"He agreed to make it, but it will take a day or two to get the papers ready. Collins has nearly twenty thousand in the bank and is going to draw it out to complete the payment to Ranse."

"So Ranse is waiting to collect that dough before he hits the breeze," Black commented. "Can't say I blame him—if he doesn't wait too long. Yet I dunno. There are times when a guy can't afford to be greedy."

"Ranse is figuring it closely. No doubt he will get word by wire from Phoenix when Marshal Keeley leaves there. Don't underestimate him. He's both shrewd and game. He has at least five tough fighting men he can count on." Mawson ticked off on his fingers the names. "First there are Ranse and Linc. Young Emmett Jelks will go with them to a fare-you-well. And there are his three imported gunmen, Longely, Landers, and Hardiman. They can't count on Norman Roberts. He isn't a fighter, But the Jackmans realize we aren't likely to attack a bunch like that."

"I reckon too they have in mind how the Earps rode openly out of Tombstone five years ago when the town got too hot for them," Carr said. "And we might remember it too. On their way out they took time off to kill three of their enemies."

"They caught them one at a time," Mawson added. "That's why I keep pounding it home that if one of us strays far from the herd he is likely to be cut off."

"Let me get this straight," Black put in. "If these birds sitting over there and their gang wanted to saddle up and pull their freight this aft we would look on and let them go. Is that right?"

"Right." Mawson smiled. "But inside of two weeks the ones we want would be dragged back here for trial."

Mollie wished fervently the outlaws would decide to go.

XXXIV

It was the intention of Ranse Jackman to cash in all his assets before he killed Jefferson Carr. He wanted to get out of Tomahawk immediately after he had rubbed out his enemy. Unless forced to it he did not want a pitched battle between his men and those crowding him. His idea was, as sheriff, to arrange it so that Carr would be killed while resisting arrest. But he knew that with his opponents alert and watchful it might be difficult to set the scene in the way he would like. To regret the past was of no use, but it nagged at the gambler that he had played his cards badly. If it had not been for his love of easy money he would never have planned the stage robberies. That was his first mistake. The second was not having Carr shot down by one of his hired warriors. That would have been easy to arrange if he had not tried to move so safely.

From where he sat he watched covertly the party of diners across the room. Carr sat next to Mollie Kenton. That they were in love was plain. Ranse let his mind hover over the thought of using the girl to get Carr alone but he saw no way to bring that about. Since Mawson had used Ella Gilson as bait he and his friends would be wary of any similar trap.

Linc had not seen Ella Gilson during the past two days,

he had stayed out of the dining room and let the other
vaitress take care of the customers. But today the press of
usiness forced her hand. Caught by an influx of diners, Ella
ad come in to help. On her way back to the kitchen Linc
fted a hand and stopped her as she passed his table.

"So you threw me down," he said in a low voice. "You
etrayed my friendship for you to sell me out."

"I—couldn't help it," the girl murmured. "Mollie was so
nhappy about Mr. Carr."

"You'll be sorry about this," Linc told her. "It's not safe
) play tricks with me."

Ranse spoke suavely. "Don't misunderstand my brother.
le does not mean to harm you. We Jackmans do not war
ith women nor do we use them to help us in foul schemes.
ou have made a mistake, but I think you are a good girl. I
m sure you are sorry. Possibly you may have a chance to
rove that later." It was in his mind that perhaps he might
e able to use her as a messenger to arrange a meeting with
arr on the pretext of patching up a truce.

In any case he did not want to make more foes than they
lready had.

Ella hurried out of the room on the verge of tears. She
as a girl easily put in the wrong, and though Linc Jackman
ad been present when her lover was killed she did not believe
e had taken any part in it. Later she went to Mollie, who
omforted her. No harm had come of what she had done, and
erhaps great good. The captors of Jeff Carr had intended to
ill him and it was possible the few hours gained might have
ived his life.

Despite the warning of Mawson it was not feasible for
eir party to remain in a pack all the time, but at least they
ould travel in couples. Usually Black and Carr stayed to-
ether. They were both lighthearted youths and Alec had
tirely got over his desire to marry Mollie. As they strolled
own Fort Street, Linc Jackman and Wolf Landers pushed
rough the swing doors of the Capitol and almost brushed
gainst the other two.

Linc blocked the way. "You hired out as a nursemaid,
lec?" he jeered.

"Why, no. I'm still free," Black retorted. "You lookin' for one, Linc?" His eyes grew bright with anticipation. If there was any challenge back of the remark made by Jackman he would be Johnny-on-the spot.

"Why don't you go home?"

"Another guy asked me that today," the young rustler replied. "Home for me is under my hat. Looks like there might be some fun here in Tomahawk. Figured I'd stick around—if you don't mind." Black let the last four words drip from his mouth in a slow derisive drawl.

Wolf Landers made a comment. "Thought you were a cattleman and not a snoop, Black."

The rustler laughed, but with no mirth in his watchful eyes. This might be the hour and the minute. "Another county heard from," he said to his companion. "It can't be that I'm not popular around here, can it?"

"A man who minds his own business lives longer," the hired gunman growled. "You're a right limber young fellow, Black. If I was you I'd drift."

"I appreciate yore interest certain, Mr. Landers," Alec told the man grimly. "But every chucklehead has to make his own mistakes. I'm kinda set in my ways."

Carr had kept a tight-lipped silence. He knew he was the real target of the Jackman men's hostility and he had been weighing the situation. He did not think this meeting had been arranged. It had come about by chance. Yet the lift of a hand, a sudden move, might set guns blazing. Standing close as they were, within touching distance, the issue of a battle would very likely leave them all dead or dying. Linc Jackman's impulsive anger had brought about this impasse, but in his black eyes Carr thought he saw a doubt flicker. The gambler was game enough, but he did not want to be one of the victims of a massacre. Tough though he was, he did not have the cold, iron hardness that had marked his brother Clem. As for Landers, he was a gun for hire. Fifty dollars a month did not call for this kind of fighting. He would take his cue from Linc.

Jeff resolved to ramrod it through. He said, his voice low

and hard, "Make your choice, Jackman. Get out of our way
or come a-shooting."

The eye is a prince of deadly weapons. The gaze of the
challenger fastened on his foe's face with unblinking stead-
iness. In a heavy racking silence the seconds ticked away.
Linc's nerve broke, though his feet clung to the pavement
and he tried to hold out against this bleak and flameless will.

To Carr he made no answer. "Another time," he barked
hoarsely to Landers, and wheeled back through the swing
doors into the Capitol. Landers followed at his heels.

Black looked at Carr with a wry grin. "Mister, you sure
burned the hide off'n that guy plenty. He hated like hell to
throw in his hand. How come you knew he would?"

"I wasn't sure, but I had to take a chance. Look who is
coming our way."

The rustler slewed his head around to see. The two Jackman gunmen Longley and Hardiman were moving toward
them fifty yards farther up the street.

"Holy smoke! We would have had them on our necks too,"
Black exclaimed. "Let's beat it. I got to see a man."

At the office of the Pacific & Southern they found Mawson
and Johnny May. The old-timer had news for them. He had
just received a wire from the United States marshal Keeley
saying that he and two deputies were leaving Phoenix at once
for Tomahawk.

"Time is running out for the Jackmans," Johnny May said.

"The agent told me Ranse got a wire too," Mawson mentioned. "From one of his spies at Phoenix. He knows how
thin a margin of hours he has left. Rivers tells me that Collins
pays up today for the Capitol. After that, Ranse will make
his choice, to light out—or fight first and then run."

"He would be a fool to fight," Black said. "They'll head
for Mexico certain. If we lay for them back of Juan Martinez's
adobe wall we can hold them up, or if they are rambunctious
knock 'em out of their saddles."

Mawson shook his head. "We have no authority to stop
them, Alec."

"Three-four Winchesters and some six-guns would be a
hell of a lot of authority," Black grumbled.

"We have to stay inside the law," Carr reminded him. "That is our great advantage and we can't throw it away."

"Hmp! Were you inside the law when you told Linc Jackman ten minutes ago to get the blazes outa yore way or get a slug in his guts?" Black asked.

Jeff grinned. "I was too scared to think about the law."

Though the Jackman group were not advertising their departure it was impossible to keep secret the fact that they meant to travel. Three of their trunks had gone out on the stage the day before. Norman Roberts had sold his house at a loss. The Capitol had been bought by Collins and the money for it had been paid Ranse whose other holdings had also been disposed of at a considerable loss. Two of the gunmen had been seen carrying bedrolls to the Capitol.

In Tomahawk there was a stir of excitement. Never in the history of the town had there been such a flitting. The whisper was that the Jackmans were decamping to avoid arrest, driven out by the evidence Carr and Mawson had collected. What made the interest feverish was the likelihood that this tough bunch would not go without a fight. The betting was against a quiet departure since the Jackmans were arrogant, headstrong, and vindictive.

Only a few weeks earlier the Jackmans had been riding high. They dominated the place, its politics and its policies. Largely because they wanted an open town, Tomahawk had been turbulent and wild. But they had made the mistake of thinking they were invincible and could be law to themselves. All along the frontier from Canada to Mexico, a line irregular as that of a broken rocky coast, ruffians had made that same error, had come into districts where law was not yet established and had ruled for a short time by fear and violence. They had failed to realize that in the end the wish of plain honest people who outnumbered them ten to one would be enforced by strong peace officers, and that when the day of judgment came, the evildoers would be driven out, imprisoned, or if necessary killed. In a thousand Western towns, valleys, and ranches the pattern had repeated itself. The bad man was rubbed out.

Tomahawk was making its cleanup. Guns were going out and little red schoolhouses coming in.

XXXV

Nick Sampson tied in front of the Gilson House and walked with jingling spurs and tiptilled hat into the office. He had just ridden in from the Crows' Nest and was feeling higher than a spitting cat's back. After washing off the dust of travel he meant to try his luck at faro.

He interrupted "Old Man" Gilson, who was laboriously writing a letter with the help of a mouth that spelled out each word, to sign for a room and buy a five-cent cigar.

His cigar lit, he asked, "Where's everybody?"

Gilson looked up with furrowed brow. He had just written, "Your resent communication" and had it in his mind that he had tackled a word too long for him. "How do you spell communication?" he inquired.

"Hell, I don't spell it," Nick said. "Where's Alec Black?"

"He went out a while ago." Gilson added severely, "Didn't you ever go to school, young man?"

"Sure I went to school. That's where I got my education. Ask me who was the first President and I'll tell you. Did he go out alone?"

"Washington?"

"No, doggone it, Alec Black."

"Carr was with him."

"Anything doing in this town since I left the other day?"

Since Gilson had customers in both camps he was careful to take no side. He mentioned news that had no dynamite in it. "Mrs. Harnshaw had twins yesterday."

"Shucks!" Nick put on an exhibition of chagrin. "I could of saved my nickel and got a free cigar from Steve Harnshaw. After I've got a pound or two of Arizona off my face and clothes I reckon I'll go collect anyhow."

As he strolled down Fort Street he noticed few signs of life. He dropped into the Palace for a beer. The bartender had not seen Black for several hours.

"What's the matter with this town today?" Nick complained. "It's deader than a skinned rabbit. Looks like Rip Van Winkle might live here."

"Maybe it's an off day," the bartender commented. He had an uneasy feeling of tenseness in the atmosphere, a doubt whether the quiet would last till night. But like Gilson he was not saying anything that could later be quoted against him.

Nick sauntered toward the Capitol. Two women went into a store. An ore wagon rumbled past. Except for himself and two men standing in front of the Capitol the sidewalks were empty. "Filled with absentees," the visitor murmured. "Now whyfor?"

The two men seemed to be guarding a lot of bedrolls lying on the sidewalk. One of them, Wolf Landers, was carrying a saddle gun.

"Scared these war sacks are gonna stampede?" Sampson asked with amiable sarcasm.

Wolf snapped, "Take the other side of the street."

The eyes of the young rustler opened innocently. "Sure, if you've took an option on this side. Why don't you put up a 'No Trespass' sign?"

"Sheriff's orders," Landers grunted curtly.

"Now I ask you," Nick said cheerfully, "how in Mexico can Ranse make money if he won't let a guy in to take a whirl at the wheel?"

"Cut the cackle, smart guy," Landers snapped.

Nick had the last word as he started across the road. "Ranse got out a no-talk order too?" he wanted to know.

On the sidewalk a drunk lay sleeping in the shade of an adobe wall. A boy passed, stopping every few yards to spin a top. A flop-eared hound sunning itself in front of a shoemaker's shop was busily intent on digging into its loin for fleas. Tomahawk looked peaceful as a New England Sunday but Sampson had a prickly sense of impending trouble.

The two women came out of Frisbee's dry-goods store and one of them hailed him. She was Mollie Kenton and her companion was Ella Gilson.

"Glad to find somebody alive in this graveyard," he said, grinning. "Is today Sunday in Tomahawk?"

Mollie did not smile. "I think there may be more trouble. The United States marshal is on his way from Phoenix to arrest the Jackmans."

"Do they know it?"

"Yes. Ranse Jackman has sold out everything he has here. They must be going to leave on the horses hitched in front of the Capitol."

"Does that spell trouble? I'd call it good riddance."

"Jeff thinks there will be a fight before they go."

"Then you girls had better beat it back to the hotel. Where are Jeff and Alec?"

"Scouting around somewhere. Trying to keep an eye on the Jackman crowd. Nobody knows what those ruffians will try to do." Mollie was plainly worried. "If you find our boys, urge them to come back to the hotel, Nick."

Sampson had always been half in love with Mollie. To him she was beautiful as only youth can be, with life flowing through her veins abundantly. He liked the grace of her strong body and the spirit that animated it. But he knew, as he phrased it, that he was only a two-bit bronco peeler, and she was not for him.

"Sure, I'll tell them what you said. And what good will it do? Don't you worry about them. They're tough ranikins and can look after themselves. But *you* got no business downtown if there's trouble in the offing. I'll walk back with you to the hotel."

"We're perfectly safe," Mollie answered. "Nobody would

hurt us. I'm worried about our friends. They should have waited all together at the Gilson House."

"Maybe we had better go home," Ella suggested.

"All right," Mollie agreed. "We'll go. You go find the boys, Nick, and bring them back with you if you can."

The sound of a shot racketed down the street canyon. Before the echo of it had died there came another and a third.

Sampson's fingers closed around an arm of each of the young women. "Get a wiggle on you," he cried. "Hell's bells are ringing. You gotta get out of here quick." He hurried them along the sidewalk toward the hotel. After he got them there safely he meant to take a hand in the fight.

A six-shooter roared and a man came out from the alley above the Capitol, the still smoking gun in his hand. He ran across the street and disappeared in a saloon. Nick had swung his head around at the explosion.

"That was Ranse's gunslinger Longley," he said. "This thing has just begun. I'll leave you girls here, seeing you are out of the fighting zone. Keep humping right along."

He turned into Frisbee's store heading for the alley back of it.

XXXVI

When Johnny May brought word to Carr that he had seen two of the Jackman hired warriors carrying their bedrolls to the Capitol, the law-and-order party held a consultation. Counting Roberts there would be seven riders. They would need several more mounts and it was the opinion of Carr that they would not buy these but would go to the stable of the

Pacific & Southern and seize as many of the stage horses as they required. The company horses would be better, they would cost nothing, and to take them would be a gesture of defiance characteristic of Ranse.

Mawson thought that likely. It occurred to him too that the outlaw gang might decide to rob the company safe where several thousand dollars' worth of gold dust was awaiting shipment. Roberts knew it was there and he had the key. The treasure might already have been taken.

They decided to split their force. Carr and Black would defend the stable and the other three the office. The buildings were not more than two hundred yards apart and if one was attacked those in the second post could come to the aid. To separate involved the risk of having to face double their number but they were not men to count the cost too closely. Mawson carried the scars of old-time battles and had toughened with the years. Recklessness pounded in the veins of both Carr and Black. The scent of peril in their nostrils did not paralyze either of them. As law officers, Dunham and May had stood up to bad men and arrested them.

By way of the *acequia* they made a half-circle to reach the Pacific & Southern buildings from the rear. The party divided behind the stable.

Alec Black waved a hand at Mawson. "Give 'em hell, old-timer," he shouted.

"Not unless they crowd us," Mawson answered. "Keep in mind, Alec, that our job is to protect the company property and not to collect scalps."

"Sure—sure. I'm a peace officer, ain't I?" Alec grinned at Carr. "When I'm not chousin' another guy's cattle over the hills to the Crows' Nest in a hurry." He added, halfway in earnest: "Seems like there's a moral in this business somewhere. One thing leads to another. The Jackmans pull of two-three stage robberies to get some easy money and pretty soon half a dozen men are dead and they are riding hell-for-leather to Mexico two jumps ahead of the law. A fellow would almost think it paid to be honest."

The stable was a long one, open at both ends with stalls along the sides. In the stalls were half a dozen horses. A long-legged boy in levis and a checked cotton shirt was pitch-forking hay down from the loft.

"Anything you want, Mr. Carr?" he asked.

"Beat it out of here," Jeff told him. "There may be some trouble. If there is, I don't want you around."

"What kind of trouble?" the boy wanted to know.

"Don't ask questions. Light a shuck *pronto*."

The boy was leaving by the back door when a man walked into the other end of the stable. At sight of them he dragged a forty-four from its holster. The new arrival was the scowling leather-faced gunman Sim Longley.

"What in blazes you doing here?" he demanded.

"I'll ask you that," Carr answered quietly.

Longley had them covered, but Black was standing at the entrance to one of the stalls and his friend fifteen feet away at the foot of the ladder. "Git yore hands up and move over beside Black," the Texan ordered.

"I'll explain this to you, Longley," Carr said, his voice cool and easy. "If you start smoking, our guns will be out in two-fifths of a second. If you were lucky you would get one of us, but you wouldn't find time to enjoy that because the other one would be pumping a hole into your belly. You wouldn't like that."

Black laughed. "Kind of a dilemma, ain't it, Sim. Fact is, I doubt if you would get either of us. You would have just one crack before the roof fell on you. Better put up that forty-four and behave yoreself."

Longley was a cold-blooded, careful man who liked the odds in his favor. If these had been ordinary men he might have taken the risk, but he knew that both had the reputation of being lightning-quick and accurate shots. Even if by good luck he got them it very likely would not save him, since there is often an instant after the bullet has torn into the body before the nerves are paralyzed, a flash of time during which a man fatally wounded can fling death at his foe.

"That kind of talk don't get anywhere with me," Longley said. "I've got the drop on you and you know it. But mebbe I'm softhearted. Get the hell out of here. Ranse can kill his own snakes."

"No." Carr spoke firmly with no uncertainty in his voice. "Go back and tell Ranse he'll have to get his horses somewhere else. He can't have these. And put that hogleg back in its holster before you make a mistake. It's not worth getting killed for fifty bucks a month."

An urgent impulse carried a message to Longley's twitching finger. It told him to rub out these men fast. Carr could read it on the fellow's heavily jowled unshaven face. But the rule that guided him as a gunman, to take no unnecessary chances, was nagging at him too. Moreover, the wary watchfulness of their steady eyes disconcerted him. He shrugged his shoulders and said, "To hell with it." Slowly he backed out of the stable. This was the fault of Ranse. Instead of sending him to start saddling the horses, he ought to have put two or three men on the job in place of arranging to have the others come later. He used that excuse to bolster his ego and save face. A gun for hire wasn't expected to play a lone hand.

Black leaned with exaggerated limpness against the edge of the stall. "I 'most died of heart failure while Longley was making up his mind. If it had been Ranse our bluff wouldn't of worked."

"It will be Ranse inside of five minutes, with four or five of his scalawags back of him," Carr said. "Let's get these broncs out of here before he busts in."

They freed the horses and drove them out of the rear entrance. With the ropes that had tied two of the animals they stung the rumps of the leaders and sent them galloping down the alley, the rest of the group at their heels. To get rid of the mounts had taken several minutes and when the men turned to head for the stage office it was too late. A bullet whistled past their heads. A man was running up the alley toward them, a smoking revolver in his hand. Three others poured out of the back door of the Capitol. One of them carried a rifle.

"Ranse in person," Alec exclaimed. "Time for us to light out."

Cut off from their allies, they dived into the stable, the blast of the guns roaring up the alley. They ran into the street, crossed it, and went into a lumber yard where piles of stacked planks offered some protection. Behind one of these they took their stand, one covering each end of the pile.

The attackers did not rush them at once. Armed men under cover were dangerous. Faint whispers of sound told the defenders that the party had divided and that the men were spreading to search the yard cautiously. Their aim was to kill without being killed.

A soft footstep reached Black. Somebody was tiptoeing toward him. A head peered around the corner. Alec slashed down at it with the barrel of his revolver and the man went down like the trunk of a chopped tree. His startled shout had been cut off abruptly.

"Mr. Linc Jackman gone to sleep," Black announced.

"We'd better move to another pile," Carr suggested. "Somebody must have heard him."

They slipped to a lumber stack adjoining and from it to a third. A slug whipped the hat from Carr's head.

They had reached a place from which retreat was no longer possible. A high fence blocked the way.

An excited voice shouted, "Cripes, here's Linc lying dead."

The men who were crouched behind the lumber heard the slap of running feet moving in the direction of the cry.

"I'm all right," Linc said. "Got knocked out."

"They must be back of those two-by-fours," Longley said.

Alec knew their reprieve was for only a few moments. "We'd better make a run for the office where we can hold them off," he suggested.

Carr was doubtful about that. They would have to cross an open stretch. There was risk whether they went or stayed. "All right," he agreed. "Let's go."

Before they had taken five strides a slug smashed into the lumber behind them. Hardiman yelled, "Cut 'em off, Ranse."

From the right a pistol smoked. Nick Sampson was astride the fence taking a hand in the battle. He dropped to the ground and fired again.

Ranse Jackman emerged from an alley. He was directly in the path of the runners. The roar of his .45 beat across the yard.

Black and Sampson pulled up, to face Landers and Hardiman. Carr slackened his pace and moved to meet Jackman. He knew beyond the shadow of a doubt that this was the hour of decision. Every move they had made since they had first set eyes on each other had led to this. The body of one of them would be carried lifeless from the enclosure.

"Come on, boys," Hardiman yelped. "We've got 'em."

Linc Jackman joined him, still groggy from Black's blow. The crashing of the guns was fast as the popping of a bunch of firecrackers.

Hardiman cried, "Damn it, I'm hit."

Carr paid no attention to the firing behind him. He was moving slowly toward the older Jackman, intent gaze fixed on him. Ranse was pumping shots at him fast. The hammer of Carr's weapon fell twice. Both bullets whistled past the gambler. A slug tore into Jeff's shoulder. It did not stop his deliberate advance. The men were now not fifteen yards apart. Carr's third shot was a hit. It staggered Jackman. He clutched at his chest, wavered, steadied himself, and continued shooting at his foe. But the shock had shaken his control and the bullets were flying wildly. Two more of Carr's slugs hit him, one in the stomach and the other just below the heart.

Though Jackman swayed like a drunken man, his feet still clung to the earth. His finger pulled the trigger of a gun empty of cartridges. His body sagged, knees bent, and he went to the ground in a huddled heap. One hand lifted an inch or two and dropped. The last flicker of life had gone out of him.

The sight of Ranse Jackman lying lax on the ground chilled the attackers. Hardiman had been hit and Linc Jackman was still dazed and unsteady. It was time to save themselves by getting out of town. They had better join Wolf Landers and Emmett Jelks at the Capitol, pick up a pair of saddled horses in front of some saloon, and start the long ride to the border.

Longley cried, "I'm pulling out," and disappeared behind a lumber pile. The others followed at his heels.

Nick Sampson said, "We'd better find cover in case the others come."

Black shook his head. "They won't be back. They've had

a bellyful. Me, I've got a punctured leg I want Doc Lindsay to fix up. It's bleeding like a stuck pig."

Carr agreed. He too carried souvenir of the battle in his shoulder.

"Some gents heading this way," Nick announced, suddenly alerted.

Mawson, Dunham, and May were hurrying down the street. The retreating outlaws would in a few moments meet them head on. Carr watched the two groups tensely. Would there be another gunfight?

The outlaws pulled up, seemed to hesitate an instant, then backed through the swing doors of the Palace. Mawson's party did not follow them but kept coming and turned in to the lumber yard.

Mawson said, "Thank God you're all alive." His gaze fell on the dead man. "You got Ranse."

"Jeff did," Black answered. "Nick and I were busy with the other guys. I knocked out Linc and Nick nicked Hardiman, though I noticed both of them were able to light out plumb lively. We need Doc Lindsay, Billy, Jeff and me both. We're toting slugs sent compliments of these wolves."

Mawson would not hear of letting them walk to the office of the doctor. He sent May to bring Lindsay and after the doctor had treated them saw that they were taken to the Gilson House in a surrey and put to bed. Doctor Lindsay promised that barring complications both of them would be good as new in a couple of weeks.

Mollie came into the bedroom and looked down at Jeff, the eyes of the girl misted with tears.

"Honey, you don't need to worry any more," Jeff told her. "You've heard about Ranse Jackman. The rest of his crowd will hit the road soon as they can."

"I'm not worrying," she said. "They've already gone. I guess I was just thinking for a moment how near it came to ending differently."

"I told you it would be all right," he replied, and grinned happily at her.

"I know. The doctor says you are going to do fine. I'm to

e your nurse." An imp of mischief danced in her eyes.
Unless you would rather have Margaret Atherton. Maybe
ve could get her."

"Who told you about Margaret Atherton?" he demanded.

"You did."

"I told you I had met a young lady of that name and that
he testified for me."

"You did not tell me you had saved her life. Somebody
lse told me that. And you did not mention that she is the
oveliest girl in the territory."

"Almost the prettiest," he corrected. "Don't try to squirm
ut of it. Come here and fix my pillow. I want my head
aised, nurse."

"My, you're a cross patient," Mollie said, and put a second
illow under the first. "You must have decided to make the
est of me or you wouldn't boss me around so."

His fingers closed on her wrist. "I always kiss my nurses
o start them on a friendly basis."

"Oh, do you? How many nurses have you had?"

"You're the first. I'm making the rule as from now."

"In that case I'll see that for the rest of your life you have
nly one nurse."

Mollie knelt beside the bed and put her arms around him.
he kissed him as a girl does the man she loves.

"I like this," he mentioned. "I'm going to take a long time
o get well."

"Only one a day until you are much better," she said with
nock severity. "I'm not the kind of nurse who raises the
emperature of her patients."

"Then I'll be up and around in a day or two. By the way,
vho is going to nurse poor Alec Black?"

"Oh, he draws Mrs. Gilson," Mollie answered airily.

They were keeping their words light because neither of
hem was used to the easy expression of love. A lean vo-
abulary of affection was a part of the frontier heritage. Hu-
nor often covers deep emotion. So it was now. A strong tide

of feeling was sweeping them together, but they had no pa
phrases to voice their gladness that out of the nettle dange
they had plucked not only the flower safety, but a passionat
affection that was to endure throughout their lives.

Renegade by Ramsay Thorne

___#1		*(C30-827, $2.25)*
___#2	BLOOD RUNNER	*(C30-780, $2.25)*
___#3	FEAR MERCHANT	*(C30-774, $2.25)*
___#4	DEATH HUNTER	*(C90-902, $1.95)*
___#5	MUCUMBA KILLER	*(C30-775, $2.25)*
___#6	PANAMA GUNNER	*(C30-829, $2.25)*
___#8	OVER THE ANDES TO HELL	*(C30-781, $2.25)*
___#9	HELL RAIDER	*(C30-777, $2.25)*
___#10	THE GREAT GAME	*(C30-830, $2.25)*
___#11	CITADEL OF DEATH	*(C30-778, $2.25)*
___#12	THE BADLANDS BRIGADE	*(C30-779, $2.25)*
___#13	THE MAHOGANY PIRATES	*(C30-123, $1.95)*
___#14	HARVEST OF DEATH	*(C30-124, $1.95)*
___#16	MEXICAN MARAUDER	*(C32-253, $2.50)*
___#17	SLAUGHTER IN SINALOA	*(C30-257, $2.25)*
___#18	CAVERN OF DOOM	*(C30-258, $2.25)*
___#19	HELLFIRE IN HONDURAS	*(C30-630, $2.25, U.S.A.)*
		(C30-818, $2.95, CAN.)
___#20	SHOTS AT SUNRISE	*(C30-631, $2.25, U.S.A.)*
		(C30-878, $2.95, CAN.)
___#21	RIVER OF REVENGE	*(C30-632, $2.50, U.S.A.)*
		(C30-963, $3.25, CAN.)
___#22	PAYOFF IN PANAMA	*(C30-984, $2.50, U.S.A.)*
		(C30-985, $3.25, CAN.)
___#23	VOLCANO OF VIOLENCE	*(C30-986, $2.50, U.S.A.)*
		(C30-987, $3.25, CAN.)
___#24	GUATEMALA GUNMAN	*(C30-988, $2.50, U.S.A.)*
		(C30-989, $3.25, CAN.)
___#25	HIGH SEA SHOWDOWN	*(C30-990, $2.50, U.S.A.)*
		(C30-991, $3.25, CAN.)
___#26	BLOOD ON THE BORDER	*(C30-992, $2.50, U.S.A.)*
		(C30-993, $3.25, CAN.)
___#27	SAVAGE SAFARI	*(C30-995, $2.50, U.S.A.)*
		(C30-994, $3.25, CAN.)

WARNER BOOKS
P.O. Box 690
New York, N.Y. 10019

Please send me the books I have checked. I enclose a check or money order (not cash), plus 50¢ per order and 50¢ per copy to cover postage and handling.*
(Allow 4 weeks for delivery.)

_____ Please send me your free mail order catalog. (If ordering only the catalog, include a large self-addressed, stamped envelope.)

Name _____

Address _____

City _____

State _____ Zip _____

*N.Y. State and California residents add applicable sales tax.   11